# Popcorn, Parasites, Precious & Pearls

*(companion pieces to The Wilderness Diary*

*– from the curb)*

KEITH BRAZIL

KEITH BRAZIL

Books by Keith Brazil

The Anthology of Joy:

The Land of Bliss (a fairy story)
An Alchemist's Wedding
In Consideration Of Cats
The Chameleon's Last Dance


The Yin-Yang Experiment:

The Wilderness Diary
Popcorn, Parasites, Precious and Pearls.

KEITH BRAZIL

# DEDICATION

To Bacchus and Buddha
*(hic)*
The best of friends (?)


To Michael for Endurance and Love
and oh so much fun!


To all those with addictive personalities


To the Wizard Recovery-of-Self Team – who are you?


To all the Psychonauts
and 'altered states' explorers out there –


from the World with love

POPCORN, PARASITES, PRECIOUS & PEARLS

# DESPERADOS – WANTED!

# DEAD OR ALIVE

## Temperance

**the Teacher of Truth, Enthusiasm, Tolerance and Beauty**

"I come not to bring peace, but to bring a sword"

(Jesus – Gospel of Matthew 10:34)

"If the fool would persist in his folly he would become wise."

"Enough! Or too much…"

"The Road of Excess leads to the Palace of Wisdom."

"One law for the lion and ox is oppression."

(William Blake – Proverbs of Hell)

*

"We are all in the gutter, but some of us are looking at the stars."

"I can resist everything except Temptation."

(Oscar Wilde – Lord Darlington, Lady Windermere's Fan)

*

"Oho!" said the pot to the kettle;
"You are dirty and ugly and black!
Sure no one would think you were metal,
Except when you're given a crack."

"Not so! Not so!" kettle said to the pot;
"'Tis your own dirty image you see;
For I am so clean – without blemish or blot –
That your blackness is mirrored in me."

(Poem - Maxwell's Elementary Grammar)

# CONTENTS

# QUOTES/ACKNOWLEDGMENTS

Meher Baba, John Betjeman, The Big Bang Theory - guys and gals, William Blake, Blondie, Robert Burns, Kate Bush, John Carder Bush, Cabaret, Jonathan Cainer, Julian Clary, Patrick Collinson, Nikka Costa, Oracle of Delphi, Joan Didion, Walt Disney - Mary Poppins & Pinocchio, Fyodor Dostoyevsky, John Dryden, T. S. Eliot, Ian Fleming, Foundation for the Law of Time, Hergé, Aingeal & James Hillard, The King & I, Laurel & Hardy, Marvel Comics, A.A.Milne, Joni Mitchell, The Monkeys, Raj Patel, Periander, Plato, Beatrix Potter, Monty Python, Fionn Regan, Teal Scott, William Shakespeare, South Park, Alexander Pope, Stevie Smith, Speedy Gonzales, Star Trek, Star Wars, Stephen Sondheim, Talking Heads, James Taylor, The Wiccan Rede, Tom Welton, Oscar Wilde, & Virginia Woolf – and with apologies to anyone I might have missed out.

Cover Design: Adam Wiltshire
Editor: Kitty Malone
Poster illustration: Colin Francolino-Scott

Special thanks to: my family, Michael, Kitty, Jason, Adam, Colin, Stephen Pucci, Rachel, Aingeal & Randy, Mark & Jim, Tom & Mike, Matt, Rolf, Roger & Craig, to all those at 'Play To Win' & 'Las Vegas' – for all their support, hard work, insights and inspiration.

# 1. Pure Madness

*(for amusement only)*

This is madness. Pure madness. Yet what manner of madness is this? What particular matter of agitation and art-mania, magnetism or manna am I experiencing? I am in an eddying spin. Am I in an amusement arcade, or is this a revelation of Arcadia-within? This growing transcendent grab-flash-art? What manner of spark? Is it divine love – the flowering genesis of revelation – or mental sickness that descends? Many have died for 'it', and there have been so many past causes, formations and reformations. So what shall it be for me? What profit this lunacy to the different parts of my purse and soul and cosmic identity? What purpose if not for fun!

I am on a tumble run momentarily whisked-up on the turntables of Time. Those fruit drupes are reeling me in, painted faces upon the spinning wheels of a slot machine, as a carousel rounds in an edifying gain, going up and down, round and round, to dizzying nowhere. Within my whirling spin, within Eternity's infinite twirling, there are translucent love-forms everywhere. Now I am on my side again like cartwheels on an old, horse-drawn, hay wain, like a child head-over-heels rolling downhill in endless circles. So bounty's reels race and roll. Paradise or fool? In this madness am I brave enough to become plenty's hunter? Those fruity faces – are they cheering for me or jeering at me? They chase and lock in endless combinations of win and lose, giving me the chance to choose again. Any matching of fruits in a line is applauded with a prize from the Banana Bank on the money-vine. Highest wins pay left to right on consecutive reels. It is a curious monkey-puzzle.

Those swirling, fearless fruit all lick their kiss-smacking lips at me: Awesome Apples, Cheery Cherries, Perfect Pears, Plump Plums, Grateful Grapes, Lucky Lemons, Succulent Strawberries and rapture's elusive jackpot – Heaven's Sevens and ding-dong Bells. Playing their game can be sweet or sour. Playing their game can take several hours! Some mysterious monkeys beat their Congo drums to the bonanza bonus of the big-bunched Banana Game, whilst small wins furiously whiplash their meanness and generosity. The monkeys can stop the rot whilst chasing a loss, but they simultaneously wipe clean the jungle-vine-climb. An eager elephant trumpets its alarm on erroneous holds, nudges and mistaken cancellations. Out on the circumference edge of reason it is a veritable jungle! It is the mad soul's hunting season.

So let us go then, you and I; let us climb together the leafy ladder into the yonder beckoning-sky. Let us try to reach the big Banana Game for it can take you anywhere! These bananas are so beguiling, so sunshine-yellow, warm and smiling. They can bunch to take wing or peel to shed skin. If I win then I shall wear a banana crown. I shall wear it all around the town! There is a sudden grin on the grapes. At the machine's behest I let them spin to grant me a win. A modest gain purrs in, but life, need and irreverent greed are still leading me on to dare for a greater victory. Seeming reward can be punishment as the machine and I try to out-bluff each other as mechanized-pirates and human-banditos in modern-day recognition.

"You might have momentarily won, my fateful friend," says the flashing fruit, silver shark-machine, "But not more than me."

Spellbound, I sit in front of the mammoth, triple-linked community fruit machine. I am startled by such a sudden win. I immediately transfer the credit and put the gold back in. In speaking those words to me, is the machine being purely challenging or is it being cruel and mean? Am I under a curse of blindness or do I sit in a vortex spell-of-kindness? Are the machines helping me? Are they beneficent banks or just modern, one-armed versions of desperado you-and-me?

In the battle of wills, the machine and I engage in a virtual war of wants and peremptory needs. Am I too bound up in myself or is it a final face-off with life's fortune machine? I fear it is crazy-time. I guess I have to be fearless. I have to be tearless. In order to be so, I have to circle and survive the dark side of my scything Moon. Can I handle another night without light so soon? Our mutual cunning meets in a matter of dare to outwit each other. The outcome is not assured, but I feel my fate is not yet over. Only one of us can end up dancing in clover! To the victor the spoils.

You cannot beat the machine, but you can access its generosity by befriending its rainbow-fruit. It is a two-way system. Output needs input, so I feed the devourer with money and attention. It feeds me the opportunity to safely investigate my spinning madness. Yet what manner of madness do I confront and inhabit? Are these tumbling life processes merely a gambler's habit? Do I dwell in a benevolent universe or is life somewhat accursed, an illusion enthralling most of us? Do we all free-fall in impartial indifference – cool, cruel or casually caring? Will the machine pay out more if I pretend it is for sharing? But what if it is not? Will life really connect and join the dots? Will it respond to my idiot's intent or is it purely random? Am I in for the win or just for the playing? Only asking. Only saying. What stimulation is it that I truly seek? Like me, it is hungry for gold today – wild and unmeek! It snaps up and devours paper pounds like sticks of chewing gum. I think the machine knows what I am up to.

Each fruit has different identifying features. That 'Peter Perfect' pear has a strong, defining parting in his green, luscious wavy hair. With a strutting jaw and unfair physical advantage he is not at all like me. Meanwhile, the scarce, monocled succulent strawberries ogle and stare whilst those irascible grinning grapes chin-chin their middle-class fortunes and bourgeois wares. The red wild cherries come as laughing twins; cockney to mock me of any aristocratic pretensions and standoffish sins! They act as clackers, as humblers, but I do not need their poverty or the head-ker-banging violence of their stone fruit. Have I told you that the smiles on the lips of those impeccable plums have been getting to me recently? Well, they have.

Really, what have I left to lose? Apart from my sanity, what is left for me to choose? Right alignment? Which way up is that? My vertical hold is slipping. My horizontal centres are spinning. I am opening. Is this spice crisis or am I plum crazy? The fruit are ripe for picking, but they will not sit still. I must grab them all to take my fill. Yet they are such a mixed bunch running wild. The psychic strawberries stare and gang up on me, notwithstanding I am their friend. I am fashioned-old and true to this form I have selected an old-fashioned, slow machine. Can I win against the spiralling slots and the spinning mechanism within?

Another twenty pounds goes in for a further forty dizzying spins. The fruit and I all gather within this whirling madness, yet what manner of supernatural disturbance is it that seemingly descends from my soul to claim me? Are these oh-so-lucky lemons sent from Heaven, or do they intend to dash my hopes and try to make me the freshly squeezed? Can I escape the dire calculations and more drastic permutations? I must not end up sharp and bitter. Mean time is not meant for me. I want to be sweet and free – a sun-ripened blend! What variety of luscious fruit I wonder will Mother Nature send? Will Heaven come to my cool-aid? In my mind I turn some dour-looking lemons into sprightly, sun-shiny, zesty lemonade.

Yikes! Here come some apples and pears to push me down the spiralling stairs. That is not a winning combination. Some miserable grapes appear. They try to console. These sour fruit and my bad-loser's ungrateful whine will not make a cask or glass of any truly good vintage wine! I have to compute before I can compote them all. O lucky sin! Please grant me a win. Yet I must not focus on what I lack. At this rate I shall never succeed or get abundance back. Down in my pocket, but on with my rocket – my accelerated rainbow-struggle and glorious soul-return.

Suddenly, strawberries spin in a winner. Here comes the tenner I already owe! So I have won. Not a lot, nevertheless a bit. What of it? Where is the fun in winning so early? I stand defiant pursuing my bounty. I cannot walk away for I am in a daze. I am Billy-the-Whizz, disco kid, playing on an arcade game. I think I am slowly going insane. Fruitful. Should I collect or hit the wall? Am I truly a wind-blown fool waiting for such a haphazard windfall? Cash or bust? Who will do their worst? Is my laziness blessed or cursed? I work hard to win though to no avail, but then countless, casual, little lucky wins prevail.

I am as one in a dream. Small wins are only for cats that like to case the joint and skim the cream. What about my carnivorous lion within? In this Fruitopia even my vegetarian cannot walk away. I will scoff those strawberries and have my say. Hey! Let this slot machine pay my way. Am I playing with fire as I stoke the engine of my desire? I do not play to lose, but is it all right if I do? Win or lose — imposters both! That is what we have been previously told.

If I win, then I am winning for him at home. I shall be a sultan and he henceforth a king upon a comfy sofa-throne! I am in it for the perilous spin — madness and magic! If I win for him I shall buy him a brand new hat. Fancy that! In the bonkers Bank of Brazil the bonus builds, but profit margins slowly reduce. I challenge myself and the community fruit machine for the bigger, biggest, bestest win! At least enough to pay the monthly rent and our daily vittles shopping.

It feels uncomfortable now as I enter a near-despair dearth cycle. The machine knows exactly what buttons to press. This particular emotional-challenge comes to test all my lows by churning leftover feelings of all my presumed past hard-disasters. It questions my belief of entitlement, but I cannot outwit the machine. I cannot run any faster. So I fight away the old, losing, reeling feelings. I have to! For depression and devastation are here. Self-doubt and questioning-fear. The seeking of easy-money through lucky hunches and amateur magic ultimately becomes hard gambling work and a wild struggle with self.

It is a risky business treading water amongst the metallic sharks. How much can I afford to lose? How much am I willing to sacrifice? A week's wage? Two hundred smackers in a bundled bunch are easily eaten up in a five-minute throw of automatic two-pound play. A thousand-pound win is thrown back in only to be slowly devoured. I feel her loser's ouch! Sink or swim? It takes dedication and hours. Could she have walked away a winner? Should someone have intervened?

Everyone loves a harmless flutter – a bingo win, a horse's nose, a lucky find, or a lottery drop. In my childish innocence of the hound-and-hare on the greyhound track I would bet on the lure for the dashing hare always wins. So what assured furry enticement and pull is there here for me? Am I measly and risk-averse, or do I really want to pluck this ripened fruit and stuff it all into my empty purse? Who is it reeling me in to the machine?

In this house of fun and quick-city of iniquity everyone is perceived to be a sinner. We wander. We squander. A nimble-lazy way to earn the crust of the earthly-day. My pursuit? Is it trivial, criminal or high-inspirational art? Justice for crumbs or crime of my heart? Message – should my grabbing hands grab all they can or could they be some kind of creative fulcrum? These days we all need help to hold onto a crust even within God's present breaking of bread. We are hungry, alive, whilst our spectral ancestors are not dead! They are everywhere following me around this dusty-London's crazy town.

Now in my continuing spin I begin to hear old souls nattering. By my side Plato and Merlin appear, chit-chatting. As their kind scrutiny and unwelcome warm wisdom try to join in, so my rebel takes to arguing. They mumble and mutter askance. In the end I know I can only be left with infernal-eternal utterance. If they cannot tell me the winning lottery numbers or reveal the reels' winning combination, what is the point? So I shut them out like unwanted ghosts. Stupid old spooks! Thus relieved, I go back to the interminable game. Fun or money? Money or fun? What apprentice-wizard is it that I have so newly become? Pinball-student or arcade-fool? Or merely the incessant seeking of divine magic and help up against a financial brick wall?

For a while I play small for medium percentage stakes. Beware! Beware! The eyes of the snakes. I am smitten, not bitten. I am going to have to ride the waves of a gloomy, rainy Sunday in a fabulous wonderland Las Vegas arcade. I am on a sinking rider. Have I become a disappointing provider? There goes yesterday's lukewarm esteem and all the small change of the weekly housekeeping.

In the pursuit of fun and ever-mindless activity, I seek reassurance from the battering outside world. In my distress, there is a comfort in the whirling colours and delightful patterns of the machine's organized lights. Simplicity? Control? Something entrancing, yet restful, in the repetitive rhythms combines with the never-ending, roller coaster thrill. Is it astral foreplay or an addictive hit? Agitated-magic becomes wild when lit. Next to me Gandalf the Grey goes through a vanish cycle and re-appears as a wizard white! Merlin and Plato are still near at hand, but are they here to help or reprimand? I hear them cheer! Why am I always so touched by God's electro-magnetic presence, dear?

The surrounding watchful attendants concur, concluding that I am just a big kid. How are they to decipher if I am windward in-on-the-up or conversely sliding down-on-the-skids? Is it a symptom of a compulsive disorder or am I going truly bananas? I like the friendly attendants, and they like me. They offer me drinks – fizzy and free! Other attendants scowl and prowl, controlling the venue's flaunted security. Some clients pop in for morning coffee, a biscuit with snap-and-chat, whilst others arrive later for afternoon tea and free raffle after a senior's cosy-dozy nap!

By my side in our shared hermit-hole a paraplegic dwarf momentarily keeps me company. We nod and greet, but do not speak. Is this some form of solitary social? A secluded safe haven or an urban hovel? A random white rabbit passes by on a charitable concern. Bouncing behind, a tail-tied yellow balloon tags along. A pink panther and a golden lion follow after. I hear stealth and tinkling wings, witchy cackling, and crafty pirate laughter. I wonder where I am – in a wizard's wonderland or happy-ever-after? In the glinting arcade-cave anything can happen. Happiness, circumstance or serendipitous happenstance. Synchronicity, community characters or a gambler's growing chance, chance, chance.

Bazooka Joe pops in to say hello. Usually he busks it outside with a traffic cone. Didgeridoo-style – plastic drone! He plays for tourists for pennies and pounds. The community police kick him all around town. He happily keeps on moving on. He is fun, but only knows one song. Not "Sun Arise", but "I Should Be So Lucky". How funny! Is this amusement arcade the bank for bonkers people or is it the laundry of Chinese money? Some play hard and fast. Others play to keep warm. Some fend off household boredom to swell the coffers, a quick personal thrill before the latest supermarket offers.

Privileged good town living has become expensive. I wonder what the business-type men are doing here? Ever-thronging in city bars, exchanging tips and platitudes, with their egos and defences raised. Will they live to regret, or will they be lifted up in God's ultimate praise? Which side of life's street are they walking on now? Do they sail sunny-side-up or slowly spiral shadow-side-down? Whose tide is swelling and whose tide is sinking in this money-washed glitter town? Do we need bankers anymore?

Soullessly practising social disregard their professional business tips seem spun through with dice, chance and casino chips. Are they weary, avaricious piggies, lost and lonely? Perhaps they are waiting for the massage parlour next door where everyone malingers waiting to score. Bread-and-butter. Hope-and-flutter. Lady-bunny's honey for money. Is that funny? How our 'want' wants so much more! Searching for indiscreet, shady fun the businessmen readily apply fat sweaty fingers onto all the more fancy figures. Bikini-cover or bikini-reveal? Fiscal, statistical manipulation. Another greedy banker's steal.

The insatiable city is corpulent enough for us to cut its throat. Let us not kowtow. Let us do a jig and roast their pig! Is life so very different now? Let us make a toast. Cheers! Here is to their end and our thanksgiving. I am sure they will be generous and more than willing to be robbed, unstuffed and lend a shilling to every pauper's leaking shoe. Perhaps a gold coin or two like an old Christmas saint was often once wont to do. Am I at the heist or behest of wonderworker St Nicholas tugging at me from the world of saints? Where is the beatitude of my ingratitude? In spirit there is always "more" whilst on Earth the physical "more" can tarnish and destroy. Am I reincarnated as old Rob Roy? What is my depletion? Where is my restraint? I am warning you – in the final fill a saint I ain't!

Ordinary others play ruthlessly as well, watching you die; watching you lose from out of the corner of their scavenging eyes. Licking their lips, they are as lizards to flies. Hyenas on the prowl, glancing, advancing, are misfortune-aware. The vultures hover. The casino-hawks swoop in. People lose, drop away and disappear without much cheer. Here comes a cherry crunch! I have lost whilst playing that usual-unusual lucky hunch. I reel under their clobbering, but there is no stopping of the gambling-me. Those cheeky, common cherries knock heads like a cracking Glasgow kiss as some kind of wake-up call. Is this some kind of rebuke and reminder before my idiot's Paradise-fall? Or is there time left to acquire what I can – money, magic or wisdom for what kind of man? Am I the wonky wizard of Wonga playing for personal gain or am I actually plain insane?

Do I fear punishment from the machine or the system itself for my boldness and current dare? Do I fear reprimand? Do I care! I succumb to a disastrous cherry run. My dreams of a golden empire are falling. The circling vultures and stalking hawks quickly smooth-manoeuver. They sidle in to sit on warm seats to steal the money-filled machines like some well-rehearsed sliding, gliding hoover that will suck you dry. They are somewhat quick-of-heel, slick and well oiled. They are descending. Damn it! The machine informs me I have insufficient credit, just like the stacking reminders from my bank. Have I only myself to blame or thank?

I quickly 'reserve' the machine before the hyenas and other vulgar predators schmooze and sidle their own idle way in. Trust in Allah, but tie up your machines and camels first! They truly do not care. They want to take my lion's share. To them I am but a passing stranger and thus fair game. Is it me or is society to blame? Why cannot we all live for free? The industrious birds and bees all do, but I want money. Need money. On the Orwellian roundabout of oppressive structure I could be forever frighteningly out of proportion. What happened in the end to the monster-man? Did he grab himself a heart or did he grab himself all that he can? Neanderthal living means short cuts to survival, but what about compassion and care? Backfiring earthly karma is here. Gaia destiny, not people's personal hope and painful despair. May she "live long and prosper" in our evolving, deepening prayer.

Edging out through the arcade, I see people milling everywhere. Some bemused. Some killing time. Some with elbow-locked partners in afternoon crime, laughing, loving, egging on good fortune through economic hard times. I watch their laughter as I drown in despair and edge with disaster. Austerity smiles like a fallen statue made from alabaster. Un-giving. I have lost more than I should, but still I vow to play on in an imprudent fashion. What else is there for me to be doing on such an earthbound miserable Sunday?

On the way to the bank's hole-in-the-wall I pass shops and take stock. What to do if I should win? Perhaps at last I shall go shopping for jewels, a microscope or a mandolin. Some decent art for all my perilous and precocious sin. If I win I resolve to buy for thee. For the love of you if not for the sake of me. For the filling of our fridge I am prepared to climb insanity's precarious ridge! Yet there is something else happening here. Something subliminal, criminal, yet somewhat sublime. Something is taking me out-of-my-mind. Is it despondency or is it drop raining? Is this spin simply a first step in a wizard's training? I urgently follow my feet back to the loot-of-the-fruit. Should I be afraid to loop the fruit loop?

Returning from the cash machine with the last of my money, I notice divine whim, mirth and merriment are locked in fierce struggle with the poverty and need of my prevailing predicament. Back in Aladdin's cave of cash and gold I stare into the machine's highly polished soul and see my reflected, smiling face and needy heart. Greed or adventure? Who cares! Both are equally good places to restart. I settle down to the long game of survival and profit hunting, of out-smarting and out-manoeuvring. My quandary – detriment or destitute? I have to ride the rainbow waves of all of Nature's fortune-fruit. Until then, I will not be bullied into submission or be lulled into any false sense of insecurity.

I press 'play' and the game recommences. The whirring wheels click and fall into place. They help my wizard think. Help me! Help me! Look at me sink. I am sure that fleeting bell just gave me a-nudge-and-a-wink! The fruity faces are raising their eyebrows at me. Hark! The bells of Heaven are a-pealing. Something strange, yet stranger is revealing. Are those brazen bananas really unpeeling? Suddenly, my cloud-mind is crashing. My wizard is beat. Should I therefore quit and admit defeat? Far beneath the triple-reels-of-Hell I chase the cheeky cherry chaps in gratitude of anything. They have a toothy-goofy, widespread grin. I did not know that hidden beneath their enticing fruity smile were such carnivorous, capitalist teeth. The voluptuous fruits show me more than their external wares. Yet is not their acid bite both our fun and our enamel-eroding sweet delight?

Oh dear! Momentarily afraid of fruit sugars, I welcome in the alkaline. I abandon irrationality and give into common sense, yet still with a curvy, lustrous shine. I scrap big game advances for small, failsafe cash conquests. Desire gives into what I can see. Reason! I argue back unreasonably. Downtrodden, I am briefly chastened by a humble gain. A small, winning spin clicks in like a simple sunbeam.

Whereas a moment ago those insignificant juicy fruits were merely a sacrificial throw. Somewhere I feel as though I am growing a multi-coloured bow. Like comprehending clouds and glass, I have become an accidental Sun-catcher. Adrift in a dream who cares if I am no longer a homeowner under Margaret Thatcher! Some say I have lost it all. This spinning madness? Is it my jester's rise or my loony-fruit's ripened fall? Is this my rain's ignorance and my addiction to fun? Or do I follow the fruit back to where I was first begun?

My mood changes. I forgo another moderate strawberry win to let the world and the machine know that I am not in the mood for losing. To tell the truth, those stuck-up strawberries can be so aloof. Toffs and robbers all! Yet my mind is not quite so crumble-proof. Are my repetitive acts of stupidity settling in? Is this fun-on-the-run or just louche sin? Is it fateful? Is it wasteful? Am I grudging and ungrateful? I might be on the floor, but still I believe there is more. Yet in my present state of apparent privation is the "more" ever enough? I hit the heart-pedal and push my dissatisfaction on, testing the galactic system to check whether it is benign and idiot-proof.

Will Heaven help us? Heaven knows! Thus ludicrously caught I am forever spinning in a world of action and non-thought. My wizard destiny – to whirl and wheel within freethinking liberty? Or is this a re-enactment of a passing childhood, excitable habit? I must run fast to catch the elusive white rabbit! Playing recklessly fulfils some need for thrills, speed and excitement. The looping wormholes of all our strange desires. Half-completed ideas and magic-hat stuff. Hard coin pressing against fuzzy-white tails of feather and fluff! Streaming between the cloud-veil, our interactive human qualities and freedoms are those that Angels envy.

Angels, spiritual Masters, ancestors and treasured friends will be attendant to our loving needs. They also keep an eye out to ensure we pirouette on our dancing toes in the completion of our daily chores and earthly deeds. I wonder what they make of my impertinent needs? Should I listen to them and cut my losses whilst I can? Oh, go tell the oil-digging man! Are my natural resources for sharing or general profiteering? Where is my wealth? What is my sin? Ingratitude for such a meagre win or the fruitless war of my inner-dragon's ravenous wanting?

What point my socially fitting in when everyone else seems to be in it for their own gain? I go for broke and succumb to playing for deliverance from the chattering monkeys upon my back: simians, seraphs or just my devils-in-disguise? Is their jungle-cave blood red, cloud white or hellhole black? What peering Merlin's owl-wise eyes are these? What truly dissolves but my past history's brain-disease! Is it monkey-money or Plato's pure madness that I explore? Is it the want-divine or merely the greed of the more, more, more? Why do I need to know?

O Pharaoh gold – jewel and devil of the Nile! My Mayan princess is running wild. This is not "game over", but "game on". Near is not enough and my desire is growing strong. I could absolve myself and press 'auto-play', but have I divined the correct astrological day? I want to interact and at least pretend I have some small control on the passing of my ever-growing fateful way. Am I merely holding off my utter downfall? Life can be joyful, yet occasionally cruel. Here comes the collapse of cards. Here comes my gambler's ruin. That looked like a winning combination to me! I take to arguing with the machine. It is not fighting fairly. Sometimes it wishes me to advance like a friend. At other times it is a merciless archenemy – unwittingly annoying. Is all this really character-building or is it simply soul-destroying?

These fruit machines are designed to intrigue, to cough out coins, or else to make you stand-and-deliver. At some point my penny must drop – should it not? Abundance or recklessness? I feel the winning cash cascading and overflowing from all the other nearby, surrounding slots. I thought this was supposed to be an amusement arcade? I so desire to be included in their good-luck and deserved-win. Have I become hollow in this mercenary spin? If it is happiness that I truly seek should I be splashing in the shallows of Las Vegas-styled idle-money-taking-in? Materialism or pursuit of things finer and higher? Where lies the answer? Where is the unifying true desire? Please do not let it be wisdom and a mind-of-white! Yet the harvest of all my previous labour is subsequently swiped and wiped.

Here comes the fruit cake of my former crushed mess. I am burgeoning with berries. Am I truly mixed-fruit blessed? Trance-like, I slide onto a downward mega-death spiral. I strip the shirt from off my back. All quids in! How close can I sail to the perilous wind? Where I am going invincibility and earthly gold have no worth. I have a compulsive desire to climb and climb ever higher and higher. I have to crack the coconut to gain the rich-tasting monkey-nut honey. Will that lead to wisdom or leave just enough for monthly rent and pocket money? Do I have the tools and the wherewithal? I so desire a true-homestead to nest and lie in. Somewhere to put my skipping feet and tree-roots down, yet someplace to fly in.

Around me people are watching. People are staring. Do people beware such considerable daring? In my abandonment I do not care how much desperation spills into the air. I will supersede economic depression and any remaining emotional despair. I find recklessness is everything when you are a wizard-rascal and a ransomed fool's king. With all that said I instantly descend into a pit of anger with myself, a place of almost never-ending fear and spinning dread.

I am fighting. I am reeling. I am possessed by supernatural feeling. I am fixated. Yet people are nice. People are kind. In my luck what other luminous persons do I find? Where? Why? Over there is an eyeball watching down from the ogling sky. So many eyes all turned upon me. Is this affliction just addiction or are there chime and rhyme in spinning-reason? Is this idiocy to block out trouble and sadness or am I coming to terms with the restless world – the unknowable outcomes of all our madness?

With only 86% guaranteed returns, the remaining violent 14% rattles and spits, pierces, then breaks and burns. Yet reality is not at all like that: money, machines, life and spirit, the whole wide world – all that is damnable without and heavenly within it! The machine and I work fast now in coming to terms with all the winning and losing amalgamations; all the possible, plausible, logical, illogical, irrational, frustrating permutations. Still, the whirling slots are getting to me. In a terrifying quick-spin, I feel frightened, yet so alive. I try to pull up from a death-defying, frantic tail-dive.

Surrounding me, there are so many machines looming like giants and metallic mountains. Is God really hiding between the flashing yellows, reds and greens? Am I simply coming to peace with myself or is that really highest Heaven sitting on the big-win shelf? Far away, I hear the dull, dampening dissatisfaction of yet another losing soul-combination. There is no win. The leaden lack of luck in these situations can be quit deafening. I am running on near empty now. However, I will not let these fearless fruits diminish my spirits as I dare for a bigger, glorious life. Yet is it really Heaven's indestructible fortress or another brick-wall that tempts me to butt head?

Programmed and patterned, yet unpredictable, the machine eases and teases the game by prolonging the monkey shots out. Yet a banana is encouragement enough for my inner chimpanzee to climb and shout. Meanwhile, the rainbow faces keep tumbling and swapping places. Is acceptance all in my arcadia's success and fall? It does not matter, lose or win, for I learn attachment-detachment in the triumphant spiritual-love system that we all circulate within.

Perhaps I am Shylock tugging on a stray curl of hair? Or simply another Scrooge with a Christmas miser's shallow despair? Or just a grubby dodging-art without a mother's loving care? Do I waste my time and effort here? If I have to "pick-a-pocket-or-two" does it really matter whom? As for my Argonaut's grandest dare – a golden hind, a sparkling fleece or a whimsical, fleeting, spectral hare? Is this my former blood-money lender leeching or my present just-desserts a-preaching? If I were a rich and wealthy man I would be experiencing this and life so differently. Truly, what is a lot to me to him is meagre and measly.

This all sounds so strange, but where are the doors to the nearest stock exchange? Am I a would-be robbing hero here to redistribute wealth or am I flash-cash masquerading? What is that "love of money" saying? Do deeds of biblical greed and generosity interplay in instant acts of karma? Let us find out. Come on machine! Hand me a fistful of your ripe bananas. Yet why do I reach so for money's bliss? Is not my beast's climb after subliminal beauty's kiss? I secretly fear I play to win. Fun, experience, shame and sin. Perhaps it is a release of my inner kid's immaturity. Or simply back to basics – useful top-up for my social security.

If I play for fun, then of course I know the supposed outcome. Were I to play for fun and win – is that not better and most charming? If I play to win, but lose, then surely that is more alarming! Embarrassing too. I am the stupid fruit in an unrepentant fool's super-stew! All my kings and rascals too. Like coins, my remnants of cleverness go down the machine's silver-lined, hunger-flue. It is a bottomless pit. Yet within quantum entanglement only consciousness wins through. In the end I know only awareness will do. Yet where is my spiralling realisation? Is that the surprise? Is this my human downfall or my sleepy-soul's spiritual rise? I must reconcile the right amount of win and lose. I must go the distance and simply re-choose.

Can I cherry-pick along the way? Can I make the machine do my bidding? Is it worth the try? Are you kidding!

So, I break my bonkers bank and chuck in my final soul and crown. I throw in the last of my gold and put all of my mouth and my money down. Mesmerized, I find I have smashed all my watermelons. Running out of reserves, I am playing with Peter's pumpkin-felons! Borrowing. Extracting. Please God; assist me in all my aims here today. Dear God, do not make me fall to my knees to beg for alms and wretchedly pray! Please quench my loser's thirst before I bow and befall cloud-clown. Whilst spinning ever sky-high, I simultaneously spiral down, down, down. Eater! Defeater? Is it the machine or me? Where is the loving synchronized being?

Tired now, I have to focus, fresh blink and think. Both the machine and I are on the brink. Built around notions of fun and greed, it does not personally care about my need. Or does it? Boom or bust, I strive to ride the cosmic dust for as long as it takes. What were the original stakes? Manic-art, money or fun? Or is it a type of anti-social intensity with too much dunce and brain-ache density? Maybe it is an apprentice-wizard's alchemical-chemistry? Am I retreating from social upheaval? My hope and fear is that it could be momentary soul retrieval.

Then I suddenly hear a ghostly shout. Through life's tapestry my troubadour wanders in and out. I answer the call from around the corner of my future life. There I am rich and not so full of monetary woe and financial strife! Yet vast wealth is always on my mind. O Universe! Would that not be kind? Nonetheless, deep in the interior the vaults-of-God are securely locked. I hope you are not too greatly shocked, for I have my magpie's eye on them. Gold! Lots of gold. Pots of gold. A dragon's treasure. Wealth beyond wanting. Wealth beyond measure! A hoard! A heap! O for a prancing, dancing, lucky leprechaun's leap! Look there! A ginger beard, a feisty freckled face, a twinkle in his blue-roving eyes – one full of mischief, one full of grace. Giving it all of this and all of that! Green velvet jacket, waistcoat and buckled top hat. Jigging, come win or lose, in knickerbockers with buckled shoes, he has red-and-white striped stockings on. Here comes the charming-alarming leprechaun's song:

*Me: O lucky leap! O lucky leap! Sing me a song that is not too deep.*
*Tell me so. How do the dispossessed get to the end of the bow?*

*Leprechaun: Tell me. What truly begins to beckon and glow?*
*For both Sun and shower have to flow before such riches start to grow.*

*Me: If over love's rainbow I must fly to collect such gains.*
*Tell me. Where are the seven league boots and gold-diggers' light trains?*

*Leprechaun: T'is true! Through good fortune's arch-of-insanity you must go.*
*But why? Did all the prosperity trains leave? Did the sprite rockets not show?*

*Me: It's true; I am left standing here, tilting shamrock stalks with questing fear.*
*Yet know, I will with patience grow and by love be filled and not despair.*

*Leprechaun: Then luck be with you and let love be quick.*
*Be nimble or scorched! For you must jump the Devil's candlestick.*

*So follow life's curve around rainbow's bright bend.*
*For only with determination and resolve will you get to the golden end.*

In a distant field I can see a hundred million dancing leprechauns all called Sean, but not O'Casey! Now I am going shamrock-crazy. Is this Emerald-isle blessing or little folk curse to the pecuniary strings of my paucity purse? Is this truly divine madness or solely my poverty pursuit and economic anger? O good fortune! No longer be a stranger. O sky-big Mr G! Up in the clouds, are you really there to catch free-flying me? I know I have to let it all go before the bluebirds collect me from the edge-of-the-bow.

In a firmament-frenzy I play faster now. I have come to the edge of reason and danger. Yet still the same frustrating, repeated reel-failure. I am no longer sane. Here comes the mad-fruit again. Do I want too badly? Am I going to take it all? Where is the winning combination for this wizard's fool? There is no assurance in this love of madness running free. Am I at the mercy of fate or subject to the choice-forces of whirling liberty? A voice like a snake in the grass rattles at me from out of the machine in serpent's tongue:

"Let 'em spin! In twenty turns or less, by over-whelming disaster or fortune you'll be caressed."

What is this message so suddenly appearing? Is it truly success at last revealing? Stars above! Can I influence such paltry outcomes with gigantic love? The capitalist machine informs me of 'a guaranteed win!' let us see. Let us see. Big or little? Is my sanity so very brittle? Stepping back, I see myself in the reflective metal of the machine. Huge, yet vulnerable, the awoken astute is hidden deep within the ashamed mirror of behemoth-me. Where is my good will and sincerity? Is there no stopping of the mad-spinning-me? I so want to join the juicy-fruity, rainbow community.

Words of love. Words of truth. Words free-spilling through the roof. Words of wisdom. Words of heart. Words from wizards of an ancient manic-art. In this frantic-spin, body and soul both do part, but both assuredly come back together again. Does that need another spin? So what is it that is ascend-descending? Does it mean another ending? Do I need to chapter-change whilst caught up so in this rapture-strange? Improvement, so it is said, lies that way. I must be detached from these things that I do or say for my humanity is no longer the usual man's sanity. Here, reason has no sway.

Suddenly I am overwhelmed by glimpses of an abundant globe. Everywhere there are vertical lines streaked through with gold. Fortune, it seems, does favour those who endeavour bold. I grab hold and monkey-swing. What are the odds of unlocking such a bounteous God-win? Is it luck, work or poverty? Or is this another mischievous truth playing with my win and lose? It seems I have to let go of all forms of self-control to find the variegation of my complex soul. The heart-art of the matter? Is the one-true-reality really beyond the grasp of the everyday you-and-me? My mind chimes with ludicrous rhyme and crashes with preposterous poetry.

I have become word-absurd. Am I serious or just delirious? How have I become so Heaven-lured? Has my baseness been raised up or cured? There are 27 ways to enter the banana feature, but only one-way of catching the banana-eating monkey-creature. Could life be any easier or harder? I must sky-climb high to get to the flashing triple red banana. I am vexed. I am perplexed. If I am to become the monkey itself then who is to be the organ-grinder provider? There are skins to slip on everywhere. I am becoming suspicious, yet somehow yellow banana-aware. Auspicious or coconut-alert? I am going monkey-crazy. I am going banana-berserk!

I know I am a millionaire in many respects: love, life, and rich experience. Yet those evading missing millions have my name on them. Somewhere I believe I deserve billions and squillions. Of course I will care and share! I can hear monkey-money whooshing through the leaves of trees and through the concrete-jungle air. Telephone transfers or computer lines? Where are the lost diamond mines? Where are the fruits of the Midas vines? Where are the golden girls having unabashed good times?

Beware! Beware! My monkey devil does not care. Yet what is this? I am sure by now that you get the gist. A surprise series of extra holds lets me back into the big-bunched banana game. Here come the wild reels. Here arises the extra madness again, sheer and pure now. I let the inevitability of destiny and providence decide my outcome. If luck rubs off I do not need to grab, stuff or rob. There is magic in numbers and in the air. There is creative wizardry running through my fingers and through my curly gypsy-hair. There is Merlin-magic everywhere. I am a very lucky man, but still I fear the losses whilst I hope and strive for life's lovely gains. Is this not balance for financial-bankers, as well as those ordinary and criminally insane?

Zany does as zany do. Perhaps I am in Xanadu? Monkey-brains or monkey-charm? Funky-monkey or Hanuman? Here come the ancient Masters – magical munch-bunch or mystical masticators? To whom and to where shall I be sending my prayers? I reselect and stretch my stakes. I hope not to be thrown back down the spiralling stairs or stumble upon my past mistakes. Wisdom would want me to walk away a winner. Yet in this funnel-of-fortune I am just a spinner! A double monkey chuckle means some kind of fun, yet endless trouble. It fills me with cheer from spirit. Beyond I find is always oh-so close and with lots of lovely souls within it. Hey! Hey! With those Masters. Are they merely monkeying around? Am I a dizzy day dreamer or a true believer rescued and found?

Tish tosh! Spit spot! It matters not. For I have been divinely drawn to play upon the psychic slots. This is Delphi for the other-worldly wealthy. Yet this madness has some method and reason for is it not inspiration's shooting season? For those who dare do it, care to it, in final crazy-cracked development. Simply a good time or a spiritual white elephant?

In the fractured teapot of my mind, what is it that I truly find? What has been so secretly sought and what so urgently left behind? Spirit surges through me with love, life and leafy business. The Dormouse, Mad-Hatter and Hare are here, I fear. Which hat should I wear? Funny! This feeling is more golden goose than egg and runny. Have I been on a wild goose chase? Did I catch him? Grab him? Nab him? Did I make haste? Was it a red-herring rush or a stampede of truth? God or gold? Las Vegas is not daunted or so I am told. Welcome to my wonder world.

Still need and greed drive me on. Can nothing stop me? Are there boundaries to God's generosity? The dice are rolling. The plates are spinning. The fates are playing. I chase their ace, but what are they saying? That it is me? That I am a winner? No different then from the usual sinner. Whether I win or lose, triumphant victory or defining defeat, I have to re-choose. I must stand spiritually tall. Even in extremis within the profundity of the fall. The machine tries to shatter your confidence with false hope. The machine giveth. The machine taketh away. Can I cope?

It has to be said that those big apples are not as ambivalent as they look. Some are shiny with a poisoned hook. I must return what I mistook and took. These fruit machines are primed to ease, to trick and tease, even slide and scoop all your honey from inside of you. Honey-money – veritably that is not funny – from out of your wallet into their thick, quick, swallowing, capitalist gullet. Where is the common's bullion run? Where is the spirit of working-class fun? A final, unreasonable question from the voice beyond…

"Crackpot! Do you deserve to win Heaven's golden jackpot?"

O my! It suddenly becomes not about the money, but love universal. Pure consciousness in dispersal. Here, I change stakes amidst stupid mistakes, but I cannot stop. It is all in the adjustments. The stake? What I can give. And what can I forsake? Not only what I can take. The common denominator is here. The most high and the lowest – love and fear. The domination of denominators is all-powerful and will decide whether I ride its wave or have to hide my loser's gambling shame. Dear Ganesha, hear my prayer and overcome the obstacles in my dare. My banana brains get scrambled. In my indecision I cannot prophesize precision so I let the auto-nudge take over. Please let it be prosperity provision. I want it to be me dancing in clover!

I stare at the illuminating lights and pretty patterns. Are they all aligning for me? Here comes the triple monkey screeching. Here comes the fruit free falling from its tree. O whack! Oh crap! Have I trashed the machine-of-me? The lights are tripping and the fruit is flashing. I am surrounded by cascading cash, yet sounds of crashing. Is this break-through? Will I do? Enough is enough. Life is already tough. Am I desirous of all this fruit folly? I fear it is bank IOU, but o my God! I have won lots of lolly! Musa. Musa. Musa. A triple banana jackpot reels in. I hold the win. Again! And again! This is the much-vaunted rainbow-riches golden-game.

In the high branches of the banana tree I allow myself a millionaire's moment and laugh with delight. I am going truly insane! I have found the elusive, fifth green-fairy of the wondrous leprechaun's emerald-game. Of course! If I am over the fruit rainbow I must be in Oz.

"Ha. Ha. Ha. Ha. Congratulations! You're a winner!

Ha. Ha. Ha. Ha."

It seems we never know what is around the corner or dangling above our head – or what is hidden from our limited view and what might be suddenly shared! Yet in this moment within this spin, happiness overwhelms me from within. Coins spill out from metal tips. I touch cascading gold and lick my lips. Hurrah! I am buried in treasure up to my hips! I hurriedly bucket my coins and cash in my chips. These places play 24/7. I have been in reel-fruit-time, but do not know what real-time zone I am truly in. All I know is that it is momentary Heaven. Do God or Las Vegas ever close? I wonder whether you will still be awake to share in the glory of the growing household stake?

Here comes my gratitude and the monthly rent. Wondrously stolen or celestially sent? Is this my chattering banana karma? Curious monkey-reward for such a peculiar, precarious puzzle-climb? Or was it truly an irrational plunge, soul-lent, in search of pure madness divine? Was it time or money well spent? Was it monkey brains to pocket money and the lazy way of gain? Or is it Heaven's banker, Holy Host, playing a crazy, bottle-spinning chakra game?

I have stayed out on the chance of a God-hinted win; my mind's debris caught up in a twisting vortex castle – a travelling whirl-of-a-wind. Unconscious thought, art or craft? This soul mist within my grasp – Will-o'-the-Wisp or just a laugh? Did I beware the way-laying goblin asking for help and follow the fairies to Fairyland? Did I find Witch Mountain and somehow fly with Peter Pan? Has my wizard been battling with the sorceress forces of Madam Mim? Did I truly win within this most perilous plummet of madness and spins?

Old, inner incarcerating rivalries duel. Merlin might have been mad, but he was no fool. Has he been craftily playing to reconcile my peace within? Was Plato secretly praying for my deliverance from the world-cave's darkness and from all my greedy, grabbing sin? Want not? Want all? For all my wizard, for all my fool, it could not have been any different. I could not have walked out a winner or loser any sooner. So, in the end – a lucky chancer's true God-send? My gambler's whirl it seems was a further shine of my lustrous pearl. Fun or money or unconditional love? Base metal of mine or gold from above? My own loving living-allowance or the growing appreciation of an integrated self? Truly, if this is all about peace through acceptance then I grab myself a pocketful. What a glorious abundance of golden wealth!

As generosity gently practises on me so I practise reciprocity. I buy Bazooka Joe and his dog a bed for the night and leave a trail of gold coins behind for other people's lucky finds. Walking home I am not alone. Under a Crystal Moon, Plato and Merlin accompany me. Plato recalls his prayer to Pan and re-counts all of his philosophical cave wisdom. Of course I do not listen. What knowledge need I of caves when I have brass in pocket? Merlin mocks me for my magic's mediocrity and mutters of magic most mysterious yet to come. Who cares! Life is for him who dares.

I spend the money.

I bring the madness home.

# 2. ANNUAL REVIEW

## a duologue

*Scene: <u>Cloud Nine</u> - a floating Cloud-Office scuds high in the sky, somewhere over our shoulders. At various points a glorious series of starbursts, meteor showers, rainbow bridges, dragons, a phoenix, buddhas and blue gods, angels and birds, flying elephants and carpets, and a plethora of winged creatures and enchanting cloud-shapes pass by in a joyfully distracting manner.*

*Mr G is a misty figure who can transform and shape-shift in a blink of an eye to intrigue as he desires. He can conjure elemental cloud-vapours to perform tasks as necessary. Basically, Mr G can be, do, summon and speak tongues at will. Mr G has a floating 'Personal Assistant' cloud called 'Dextera Domini' otherwise known as the Almighty Hand - about the size of the Incredible Hulk's hand, but with dexterous magical powers - to assist in menial chores.*

*Me is a working-class, laid-back, casual type of mortal in pursuit of an education, yet with an anxiety string running through him. Due to a recent 'travelling vortex' event and an 'over the rainbow' experience, Me's 'Light Wings' and 'Inner Lightworker' have become involuntarily activated. Me is a handsome, curious fella who fears he might be about to be stretched out of his comfort zone by some sort of oncoming responsibility. Me has a Highlander's hip flask filled with a volatile, triple rectification absinthe-brew that occasionally escapes as a Green Muse Fairy, and a snuff pouch hidden about his person. Somewhat stupid, somewhat smart, Me is a reluctant new recruit, and is slightly apprehensive about his first meeting with his new line-manager - Mr G - after the Universe's recent restructuring.*

31

**Me** *(slightly dishevelled and flustered, trying to straighten hair and appearance, hovering by the office door)* – Hello. Oh sorry, you look rather busy. Am I too early? *(trying to get out of it)* Can always come back another time!

**Mr G** – And a grand good morrow to you. No, you've got your timing right.

**Me** *(somewhat relieved, somewhat not)* – Phew! Well then… A resounding good morning straight back at ya.

**Mr G** *(kindly)* – Did you travel light, or did you bring your old apoplexy, apology and defiant inconveniences with you?

**Me** *(miffed)* – Oh! By that do you mean I'm a little baggage-heavy and possibly overdue?

*(Me tries to ensure his hip flask and snuff pouch are suitably hidden from view, but within reaching distance if required. For a moment, Mr G stops busying with a stack of Cloud-Office files and stares silently at the incomprehensibility of Me. Feeling as though he is being x-rayed, Me becomes even more disconcerted)*

**Me** – Sorry! Didn't mean to offend. What I meant was - am I really on time, or am I a little bit early or late?

**Mr G** *(sagely, pulling out some dusty files)* – The fruit falls when it is ripe.

**Me** – I know. And nobody wants under-ripe or rotten fruit, right?

**Mr G** – True. None of this ripen-at-home nonsense.

**Me** *(inanely)* – Fresh. Branch-to-bowl. That's me!

**Mr G** *(not really listening)* – I know exactly what you mean.

**Me** – It's just that I can't quite get the hang of these new-fangled wings, and the time differentials are strange in these accelerated Light Planes and Tachyon time-zones.

*(Me folds in his wings. Mr G ignores the flapping of Me and sings distractedly to himself whilst sorting out Me's paperwork, "Hi-diddle-dee-dee. An actor's life for me. Om-diddle-dee-pom. I've forgotten the rest of the song." Mr G laughs)*

**Me** *(nervously)* – Anyway, forget it. I didn't want you to think I was tardy or anything. *(As Mr G continues to ignore him and rummage, Me politely changes the subject)* By the way... You sound perky!

**Mr G** *(looking up)* – Only if that makes you Pinky!

*(Mr G laughs again. Acting on a silent command his Personal Assistant, the floating Almighty Hand, roughly scruffs the top of Me's head with his large knuckles. Simultaneously, the word 'Knucklehead' emanates through the air into Me's mind. After Me's initial surprise, sparkling energy runs down his spine in a pleasant, tingling manner)*

**Me** *(rubbing his head)* – Ow! *(reconsidering)* Oh! That's really rather nice.

**Mr G** – Thank you, Domini, that's enough. Back to work.

*(the Almighty Hand sets to gently polishing the interior of the cloud, which is somewhat grubby and cobwebby in places. Mr G stares at Me in manner that could be considered accusatory)*

**Mr G** – You know a little Fairy Dust does wonders, but getting stuck on the intoxicating states... *(Mr G pauses as if waiting for Me to confess to something. Me says nothing so Mr G politely changes the conversation)* Anyhow, I miss those childhood shows - there were some very magical creations. I even over-shadowed 'Watch with Mother', encouraging children to enjoy TV, whilst deflecting fears of bad mothering.

**Me** – I suppose. But you're referring back to the Golden Age when the BBC was a bit more wholesome, and the mesmerising goggle box wasn't your greatest enemy.

**Mr G** – Now, now. We all grow up and become corrupted.

**Me** *(relieved)* – Really?

**Mr G** – Up here it's called 'relative occurrence' and is one stage of the renewal cycle. I do look forward to hearing all about yours.

**Me** – We call it 'unsettling experience' down on Earth.

**Mr G** – Indeed! But 'selective' good TV watching can be artistic, educational and fun. As for the plight of Sunday school dropouts…

**Me** *(enthusiastically, but somewhat annoyingly)* – That's me!

**Mr G** *(sighs)* – …and those preoccupied by the love of TV, money and Mammon *(Me is about to say, 'That's me too!' but decides to keep schtum)* I've got my secret creative recruits in place to lift their eyes.

**Me** *(seriously)* – I'm beginning to realise that now. Doctor Who's got a really interesting Time-awareness-string. Plus all the glorious nature and space programmes that are so amazing and healing.

**Mr G** *(nodding)* – Ah! The revitalising regenerist-mist and the good old, great outdoors. *(knowingly)* Yet certain things are still bigger on the inside. It's all part of Gaia's current natural spa regeneration programme. Cosmic rebirth… Earth's Springtime…

**Me** *(whimsically)* – Oh for the life of a Time-Traveller's wife! All very inspirational. Tantalizing Moon-giants… Star-filled, spectacular night skies. Culturally there's been some great comedy, enchanting fairy tales, not forgetting Star Trek, Star Wars, Harry Potter, Middle-Earth and the Super-Heroes stories are really advancing well into film.

**Mr G** *(still searching amidst a pile of files)* – Marvellous!

**Me** – It really is TV geeksville Nerd-vana at times!

**Mr G** *(knowingly)* – All fodder for the rise of the fans.

**Me** *(pleasantly surprised)* – Oh, that's good to hear! Shall I come in and sit down?

**Mr G** – Yes, please do. Take a perch. No point hovering around the door whilst I'm sorting the lost bits of paperwork. Pull up a small cloud. They're deceptively tricky and confusingly transformable, but comfortable once you get the knack of them.

**Me** – Okay, as long as they're not too moist or precipitous. Is a cloud chaise lounge too informal?

**Mr G** – Up to you. Suit yourself. Now, where is your file?

**Me** *(concentrating intently conjures up a chaise longue)* – Hm! Not really getting to grips with this cloud thing. *(Me puts his feet up, but slowly sinks through)*. It keeps curling round the edges and I keep falling through.

**Mr G** *(unimpressed)* – I can see.

**Me** – It's a little bit damp too.

**Mr G** – Just add your own sunshine and I suggest you bolster your silver lining. *(Mr G wiggles his fingers and the Cloud-Office shimmers)* Here, we consciously employ the various colours and aspects of light to aid us in our work.

**Me** *(tantalized by the variety of rainbow light and the mind-boggling complexity of the Cloud)* – Wow, cool! How many shades of silver are there?

**Mr G** – It's self-reflective.

**Me** – Er… So?

**Mr G** *(patiently)* – How many different shades of solitude and crazy have you experienced?

**Me** *(trying to recall and finger-count the many types of Life's loneliness and madness he has so far encountered runs out of fingers)* – Well… Um…

**Mr G** – Dexter*a*! *(Mr G not wanting to be there all day, signals to the Almighty Hand who pulls down a Moon-phase Star-chart of Me's current life-trajectory and progress)* According to your chart about 25, going from Cosmic and Flash-Grey through to Moon Mist and Star-Silver. Not including Light Wonderment and Planetary Pearlescence of course.

**Me** *(relieved to give up counting and trying to remember)* – Of course! Silly me. Who could forget those! *(Me is still rapidly sinking through the chaise longue and worries that at this rate he might sink through the Cloud-Office floor)* Er, can you break silver linings? *(as a courtesy the Almighty Hand picks Me up and plonks him unceremoniously back onto the amorphous chaise longue)*

**Mr G** – You can't, but you do need to be careful with some of the gods. Thor might be able to. Vulcan foolishly tried. Zeus and Hephaestus could, but I don't see much of them these days. Too busy getting their Cloud-Hollywood makeovers. *(Me is still having trouble with his chaise longue)* Perhaps an upright chair would be better? Less incline than your attempt on a TV slouch-couch.

**Me** *(agreeing)* – How about one of those swivel chairs that turn and recline! *(at the thought of enjoyment, Me instantly conjures up an office swivel chair and begins to spin)* See… You can propel yourself from one side of the office right to the other. *(as he does so Me notices the clutter, the cobwebby ceiling and slightly dusty chamfers which the Almighty Hand is gently rubbing clean)* Whee! They're quite fun.

**Mr G** – As I said, up to you. More fun for some, but possibly more annoying to others.

**Me** *(remarking)* – I must say, it's a bit gloomy and cobwebby in places up here and there's quite a bit of clutter.

**Mr G** – As I said, the cloud is self-reflective. *(as Me still fails to understand Mr G spells it out)* It's your cloud!

**Me** *(thinking, but not realising)* – I see. Is that good?

**Mr G** *(briskly)* – Well, clutter usually means you're creative.

**Me** *(brightly)* – Oh!

**Mr G** – Right! *(pulling out a large sooty file and blowing the dust from it)* Found it. Can you believe those Recording Angels placed your file under "Sulky Old Disaffected Soul!"

**Me** *(attempting a joke)* – Bloody typical! More Sod's Law than God's Law these days, right?

**Mr G** *(pause, staring, slightly dumbfounded)* – But as you know any ongoing quick or ill-temper can be converted into affection given enough time, patience and the right amount of long-suffering.

**Me** – Didn't you bury Monkey for 500 years under a mountain?

**Mr G** *(reminding)* – He did eat almost *all* of the peaches from the Garden of Immortality!

**Me** *(oblivious)* – You've got to admire the cheek.

**Mr G** *(looking at notes on Me's file)* – Whilst your own 'living burial' was only a matter of months.

**Me** – I suppose our mountains are mere molehills to you?

**Mr G** – Each to their own suffering. Huge achievements to some, just desserts to others! *(the sound of Me groaning is covered by the sound of Mr G laughing unto himself)* But punitive fruit puns aside are you ready? *(Me is caught off-guard looking out of the window as a smiling, rotating Cloud-Buddha drifts by. Me waves. The Buddha laughs, rubs his stomach three times and waves back sending kisses and good wishes like butterflies through the air)*

**Me** *(absently)* – I suppose so. Are we ever? Past appraisals on Earth have been a bit intimidating. Paperwork sitting around for years, unattended action points, the laborious who, what, when of self-evaluation within ever-shifting goalposts, the endless justifications, debriefs and, of course, the usual lack of constructive follow-up.

**Mr G** *(helpfully adding to Me's list)* – Not forgetting the current socio-political conditions, climate shifts and Gaia-changes.

**Me** – Too true! A lot of doing, getting it wrong, and wondering what to do with all the accumulated staples, gripes and paperclips of Life.

**Mr G** – It's called becoming proficient.

**Me** *(remembering his cycling test)* – All a bit unnerving, unnecessary and over-rated, particularly for us kind-hearted, wobbly-ones.

**Mr G** *(checking file)* – Yes! Your early attempt at cycling proficiency wasn't great.

**Me** – My bike was too big. I was side-lined, then sent home for being too young.

**Mr G** *(kindly)* – Not your fault. You couldn't help being the youngest of the year.

**Me** – A Leo's luck. I suppose I was to grow into her.

**Mr G** – It says here *(tapping file)* that your bike was made from scrap?

**Me** – Dodgy brakes, but I hand-painted her myself.

**Mr G** *(smiling)* – You were never going to outsmart the Virgos, but in a battle of wills and social heart skills you're going to get your own way in the long run. Still distrusting the dust of unsettling past experience?

**Me** – Tell me about it! Wishing you had trusted your first instinct and hadn't given others the benefit of the doubt. No experience preparing you adequately for the next. Sometimes it's all a bit much.

**Mr G** *(nodding in agreement)* – Particularly where knowing meets the incomprehensible Cloud of Unknowing.

**Me** *(attempting a pun)* – I know. How effin' ineffable!

**Mr G** *(proudly as lights twinkle like a star-cloth through the cloud)* – Indeed! How very dare I. But it's all to do with my Virtual-presence in creating the cosmic Grand Elegance… *(the Almighty Hand tuts, but continues to clean industriously)* …with a little help, of course.

**Me** – You mean the unknown, but suspected non-physical reality?

**Mr G** *(laughs)* – How mean of me to hide it! It can be a tricky business at first, but it's all part of the great unfolding mystery.

**Me** *(trying not to be fuddled)* – The so-called plan? *(the Almighty Hand helpfully scratches Me's head. Me brushes the Almighty Hand away, but passes through him like elusive mist)* Which reality is that again?

**Mr G** *(laughing, ignoring)* – The truth is out there, but things aren't always what they seem. Talking of which… *(Mr G swirls a cloud-cape around him and disappears)* Do you like my Cloak-of-Invisibility?

**Me** *(politely)* – Lovely. How very Ali Bongo!

**Mr G** *(irked)* – I was being Houdini!

**Me** – You could make David Blaine disappear if you really want to help!

**Mr G** – Why? Is he considered the most annoying?

**Me** *(wary)* – Apparently. But Invisibility Cloaks are very popular these days. Everybody wants one after Harry and Hogwarts.

**Mr G** *(still in stealth mode)* – It's great for general marauding and sneaking about in people's secret dreams.

**Me** *(unsure of Mr G's whereabouts)* – And great for stealing food for midnight feasts I imagine. But as I was saying… Work! Endless bureaucracy and administrative adherence. Then there's the whole round of re-inventing policy and procedure.

**Mr G** *(enquiringly)* – Is that like repetitive stupidity?

**Me** – Oh, don't talk about that! I've been there too many times.

**Mr G** *(sneaking up behind Me)* – But at least you're able to laugh at all your foibles and folly in the Springtime comedy of your 'relative occurrences'. *(Mr G tickles Me rather roughly in the ribs with both hands)*

**Me** *(doubled-over whilst laughing painfully through gritted teeth)* – Ow! Stop that! Do you mean the balancing of my virtues against my sins?

**Mr G** – Your virtuosic re-consideration of the all and everything. *(Mr G removing his Cloak of Invisibility bows in a lofty Shakespearean manner)*

**Me** *(uncomfortable, yet annoyed)* – So? Is this to be some kind of Comedy-of-Errors account?

**Mr G** *(smiling)* – Perhaps a double-act if you let it, but different from your recent Winter's grief. See it as part of your 'Ealing comedy! *(Mr G laughs heartily. Me does not)* If it's any consolation, in forming the early Universe I started out very dense too.

**Me** *(continuing obliviously of Mr G's puns)* – Well, work up to now has been very frustrating. All about dealing with dingbats, wombats…

**Mr G** *(patiently)* – Yes, I've noticed you like your bats.

**Me** – …bats with no clue. Management not listening to what's said. The relentless overuse of established 'icebreakers' when everyone in the room already knows each other!

**Mr G** – Cursed times indeed.

**Me** – Enough to break anybody.

**Mr G** *(peering at Me)* – Yet many do come with a considerable amount of ice and concrete to be broken.

**Me** – Tell me about it! The endless re-conceiving of 'strategy' after 'strategy' without addressing the real issue.

**Mr G** – Whilst overusing the strategic 'S'-word inappropriately! And then you that time - caught off-guard, daydreaming, looking out of the window at that whirlwind I sent.

**Me** *(remembering)* – Oh! Was that you distracting me? The one with all the lovely swirling leaves inside it?

**Mr G** – Yes, I noticed you liked your distractions. It whipped up your boredom, exasperation and desire to run out to play all in one. I thought it was funny.

**Me** *(terse)* – Did you now?

**Mr G** – I noticed someone 'strategically' placed a Christmas Comic-Relief swear box outside the meeting room for anyone overusing that particular 'S' word. 'Plan' I find is a better term than 'strategy'.

**Me** *(not missing a trick, but forgetting Mr G's favourite joke)* – 'Plan' for this, 'Ploy' for that…

**Mr G** *(humorously)* – Your personal tactics were more 'tic tacs' than anything else. I do find people's long-term plans for success nothing other than fascinating. Don't you?

**Me** *(ignoring, relentless)* – …the sharing of systems that worked the first time round before they tried to fix it. You know, square pegs… Round holes… Work became a joke!

**Mr G** – Your inability to conform was spectacular. That's because your soul is a future prototype evolving the new realm of spiritual triangles. And rather nicely if I might add.

**Me** *(perplexed)* – Well, there sure are some squares about if that's what you mean! Anyhow, I could go on listing all day.

**Mr G** *(peering at Me)* – I can tell.

**Me** – Life! You know, it's quite a lot of stuff to take on board in these quickening days of yours.

**Mr G** *(nodding)* – Particularly when your personal details seemingly get stuffed in the bottom of a cabinet and forgotten about. But Life shouldn't be all about lessons.

**Me** – I'm glad you said that because at times it's really been very overwhelming and frustrating.

**Mr G** – But you do need to grasp the social-spiritual basics and that can be quite hard in the pressure-cooker of modern-day, city-living. *(Mr G scans Me's notes and flicks quickly through several pages)* Yet you seem to have fun running around.

**Me** – I try to, but things do get aggressive at times.

**Mr G** – So dog eat dog?

**Me** – Greed, gain, austerity. It brings out the worst in people.

**Mr G** *(humorously)* – And my all-time favourite knockdown situational comedy… Control, control, control.

**Me** – I know! It's all very annoying.

**Mr G** – Yet still so many good people.

**Me** – True, you mustn't forget the important everyday heroes.

**Mr G** – Listen to you! You'll soon be talking about the weather, harking back to the good old days whilst harping on about how you miss the old views.

**Me** *(peeved)* – Well things have changed, haven't they? I'm ageing…

**Mr G** – Maturing I'd like to think. How old now?

**Me** – 48 and a bit, give or take a few million years or so.

**Mr G** – Not so young in sin anymore then. Looking back at the Land of Youth whilst getting ever closer to Eternity.

**Me** – I suppose I do look back with a touch of longing, but not too much remorse, whilst looking forward with a bit of trepidation.

**Mr G** – Ah! The body's infirmity as the spirit within keeps growing and reconciling the passing of decades. That's if you're lucky.

**Me** *(honestly)* – More aches and pains than the dinosaurs, but hopefully not quite so Jurassic.

**Mr G** *(referring to file)* – More Plodosaurus than Plateosaurus these days! *(a distant light rumble of thunder rolls through the cloud as Mr G laughs at the slowness of Me)*

**Me** *(recollecting)* – That was a good life as far as I remember.

**Mr G** – Brought out the vegetarian in you! But don't tell me. In today's speedy living you sometimes feel rather old and left behind?

**Me** – Are you mocking my trouser-rolling, paddling inclinations?

**Mr G** – Your inner turtle affections and tortoise afflictions meant you were born old. Still suffering the twinges?

**Me** *(agreeing)* – True, progress has passed me by, and there are 10-year-olds more up to speed than me!

**Mr G** – Ah! The indigos. And some of the more active pensioners and super-grans are streets ahead too.

**Me** – Now, now. Laughing at other people's grumbles will only set the clouds to rumbling, and I've had enough rain and thunderstorms to last a lifetime.

*(a drum set appears in the corner of the Cloud-Office. Like 'Animal' from The Muppets, the Almighty Hand quickly grabs a cloud-cotton, padded drumstick and hits cymbals, timpani, and wobble board to reproduce the sound effect of a distant, rumbling storm cloud. The Almighty Hand ends his solo on a gently diminishing, soft thudding drum-roll)*

**Mr G** – Now, now, Noah. You mean my sympathy storms?

**Me** *(puts finger in ear and wriggles it)* – Sorry, all a bit deafening. Was that my misery, sympathy or symphony storms? *(the Almighty Hands hovers above Me's head, clenching his fist to produce a light-sprinkling of rain)*

**Mr G** *(chuckling)* – Domini, that's enough.

**Me** *(sodden)* – Perhaps I should've worn my sou'wester?

**Mr G** *(smirking as the Almighty Hand swings away back to cleaning and sorting)* – Only a passing shower, but don't confuse the dark-winged, angelic chorus for storm music!

**Me** *(trying to get on Mr G's good side)* – Is that your favourite?

**Mr G** *(being drawn)* – Well, I do like some of the architectural space compositions. The grand choral cloudscapes, cathedrals-in-the-sky, star-gates, organs with a dash of orchestra and canons to stir the soul and loins. *(Mr G laughs as the Almighty Hand abstractedly conducts some* *inaudible piece of air-music that suddenly accumulates into a loud breaking crescendo)* And some of the old Baroque-'n'-roll was fun.

**Me** *(placing his hands over his ears)* – Still, one man's music is another man's noise!

**Me** G – Not that I don't enjoy some of the modern, wild child music, but some of it is a bit jagged and pained in the wrong way... You can't really listen. It's partly to do with the Technosphere distortion, which has warped some of the melodic frequencies. Music is both mathematics and emotion, but whatever happened to real world instruments?

**Me** – I know!

**Mr G** *(deliberating)* – The plain song and monastic chants guided by the over-shadowing angels in the Medieval Dark Ages still send shivers throughout the galaxy. A fine example of across-the-veil collaboration. And of course I do so love the sound of nature.

**Me** – Me too.

**Mr G** *(reminiscing on Earthly sound delights)* – The chatter of rainforests, the beauty of bird song, the humming of bees, the summoning of bells, the wind through the trees, the fall of water, tropical downpours and tidal flow. Still, I find the cosmic wind and the eternal humming of the background Om very comforting.

**Me** – More reassuring than white noise, I suppose, but not as good as Bollywood. *(Me does an unscrewing the light bulb, patting the dog Indian dance routine)* Ching-ba-da-ching! Ching-ba-da-ching!

**Mr G** – You're right. More Bollywood less Hollywood, but not forgetting the sitar and Krishna chants.

**Me** – I like pop, indie and folk myself. Nice voices, piano and guitar, the occasional disco strings.

**Mr G** *(nodding, Mr G signals to the Almighty Hand to retrieve something)* – Easy listening, but also something to move and groove to. Some whacky Bush-rhythms for the feet, a few mystic chords for the heart and some emotive lyricism for expressionistic arm-waving. I do understand. There have been some great musical poets in your time. *(the Almighty Hand returns holding a tuning fork)*

**Me** – I like my easy listening.

**Mr G** – Me too. Something soothing with an impulse to sway. It was what you were rocked and comforted to by your mother as a babe-in-arms. Lyrical suits you. *(the Almighty Hand taps the tuning fork and places it to Me's head whilst Mr G listens to the reverberating note)* Ah! D major… The key of glory, but coupled with 2 sharps and indicative of tonal difficulties.

**Me** *(attempting a pun)* – As long as it's not A flat minor…

**Mr G** *(cutting Me short)* – No, we all know that involves a piano being shoved down a mineshaft. Ha! This links into you not minding a challenge, but being disinclined to challenge others. *(writes a note on Me's file)*

**Me** *(nodding vacantly)* – Does it? Tone deaf myself.

**Mr G** – Particularly those in authority, but you're getting better. And you are, by virtue of me, naturally challenging.

**Me** *(already confused)* – Oh! I thought I was convivial?

**Mr G** – Indeed you are that too. As for your muffled hearing, it isn't particularly helpful when you can't hear the difference between sin-eater and Sinitta in a publicity marketing talk! *(kindly)* Time to consider a hearing aid?

**Me** *(miming holding an ear-trumpet)* – Or an ear trumpet.

**Mr G** – And a bath chair with a blanket for your knees?

**Me** – Honestly, I don't know what to do with myself. It's a good job I'm not a hypochondriac.

**Mr G** *(examining Me through the tuning fork)* – No, just a tad neurotic.

**Me** – Some days I feel so old and weary it's hopeless. Yet other days I feel fresh as a daisy…

**Mr G** – Ah! The elusive 'élan vital'. Keep catching the Sun, but don't be afraid to enter the dark. *(knowingly)* That's all I can say at present. So, all in all, growing up a bit then?

**Me** – Sort of.

**Mr G** – Talking of which… How's that half-baked, suit-yourself, ad-hoc diet and fitness programme coming along?

**Me** – What? Fit for 50?

**Mr G** – Still a general disinclination towards the gym?

**Me** *(irked)* – Always. Lazy feet and more interested in writing than working for others. More a sofa-coffee-biscuits kinda guy these days.

**Mr G** – Yet, now summoned up, you're back on the improver's slope I'm pleased to see… But walking to the bus stop is not one of your five-a-day! *(Me says nothing)* So apart from your on-off appointments with self, your specific moans and groans, your general laziness…

**Me** *(complaining)* – I work hard, particularly given the current instability of my situation!

**Mr G** *(tapping file)* – True. It says here 'Industrious, but with ongoing grumbles'. So, how are we? Life falling into place?

**Me** – Kind of.

**Mr G** *(warmly)* – Wait until you get to 81 when you become free from the magnetic dream spiral of archetypes and patterns.

**Me** – Yes, the wonderful 9 of 9s, but frankly I have to leave all those numbers, fractals and geometric pattern things to the higher mathematically-minded. *(Mr G laughs)* Really not my thing. I'm more of a wordsmith than a spiritual-scientist these days.

**Mr G** – Perhaps try integrating the different strands. *(Mr G mumbles out loud as he writes on Me's file - 'Re: ability to new approaches of learning. Not sure if Me thinks he's too old, above or beneath it all or simply can't be bothered')* There! *(pleased)* Something to consider as an action point.

**Me** *(sighs)* – Oh! Will there be many of those? Should I be taking notes as well?

**Mr G** – Up to you. Who's counting in the developmental stages?

**Me** *(puzzled)* – I don't know? Is that anything to do with the length of a piece of string on a swing with a roundabout?

**Mr G** *(sighs)* – Yes. As many and as long as you need them to be in the encountering. Yet you can't balance your scales until they've been fully utilised and suitably tipped.

**Me** – Oh, is that like confronting the last hurdle of self?

**Mr G** – Sort of. As for your thoughts and feelings, all are automatically recorded… *(Mr G points to an electro-magnetic, rainbow-recording device that surrounds the cloud)* Here, you know, you can mention anything. It *is* all private and confidential.

**Me** *(facetiously, looking over at the saintly Almighty Hand dusting)* – Perhaps your useful sidekick can jot important points down on a 'Post-it Note' and stick them to my forehead overnight when I'm sleeping. Then I can read them in the mirror when I shave in the morning and won't forget.

**Mr G** *(pleased)* – Genius! But why wait? Let's implement it with immediate effect. From here on in I'll get Dextera to put anything important in writing on a Post-it note for you.

*(Mr G looks to the Almighty Hand who is dextrously buffing each fingernail with the pad of his thumb. The Almighty Hand holds out his fingers for inspection, then rapidly gestures a series of precise hasta-mudrās designed to impress, before going to Mr G's desk drawer to find Post-it notes and a quill pen)*

**Me** *(unenthusiastically)* – Seriously?

**Mr G** *(enthusiastically)* – Consider it a part of your 'Idiot's Guide to Consciousness'. Dextera!

*(the Almighty Hand writes a quick Post-it note with the words 'read and remember me' embossed upon it and slaps it firmly to Me's forehead. Me peels the note off, reads it and tuts as he throws it into the bin)*

**Me** – By the way, talking about important and troubling things, this isn't some kind of sneaky Neptune report is it?

**Mr G** – You really do need to consider that aspect of yourself.

**Me** – Or even worse, an early second Saturn-return? I hear they can all be a bit tricky.

**Mr G** – A boot up the backside to move you along, you mean?

**Me** – It can all be very disconcerting. Health, home and happiness up for the reconsideration again?

**Mr G** *(amused)* – No. Today it is just you and I having a review chat for your Storm Report.

**Me** – Do you mean the tempest of my recent snake 'life event'?

**Mr G** – Yes, everyone has a follow-up debrief so no need for off pat answers. I also have a note from the Moon here somewhere *(rummages through a pile of papers)* but I seem to have misplaced it. Easily done in all the recent cloud chaos and ranting wars. Anyway, first things first. Ready?

**Me** – Yes.

**Mr G** – Then let's begin. *(pause)*

**Me** *(confused)* – What? I thought we had! *(pause)*

**Mr G** – What?

**Me** – Already begun.

**Mr G** – Ah! You mean my preambles and pleasantries. *(smiling)* See those as a kind of informal icebreaker.

**Me** – Really?

**Mr G** – Oh yes. Could go on forever…

**Me** *(slightly defiant)* – Only if I let it!

**Mr G** *(graciously)* – Still thinking you have some choice in the matter?

**Me** *(concerned)* – Er…? *(longer pause)*

**Mr G** *(slowly)* – So…

**Me** *(uncomfortable)* – Oh! Are you going to use that word a lot?

**Mr G** – Maybe. Is that a problem?

**Me** *(sincerely)* – To be honest, a little. It's a bit expectant and too 'onusy' if you get what I mean… Like you're somehow expecting me to know what I'm doing whereas I'm relying on you and the Universe to supply a few answers.

**Mr G** – Yes, the Universe said she'd received quite a few unopened requests with 'return to sender' on them… Plus a sack full of personal entreaties and ego-demands.

**Me** – As I said, 'over to you!' I thought petitions and prayers were meant to be one-way correspondence? *(Mr G wisely stays silent. Me becomes uncomfortable)* Likewise there were some vocal distress signals I sent out that seemed to be ignored.

**Mr G** *(recollecting)* – Was that the annoying squeaking noise?

**Me** – That was my cat being a bit of a frightened mouse. Or come to think about it *(thinking about it)* perhaps it was my mouse meeting your black cat?

**Mr G** *(enigmatic)* – Ah! The dark Alpha and Omega chakras. And what about the parrot squawking?

**Me** – That was my pirate captain abandoning ship.

**Mr G** – Either way, too much screeching for my liking and hardly a harmonic tone for the universe to respond to.

**Me** *(touching his receding hairline)* – And a fair amount of hair has fallen out. I've turned grey in the process.

**Mr G** *(pleasantly)* – My suggestion? Stop flapping! However, I did receive some of your more powerful roars and drones.

**Me** – That was probably me emerging through the auric-egg.

**Mr G** *(reading file, shaking head and laughing)* – Snake, turtle, eagle, angel… It was quite a toss-up!

**Me** – And there must be a stack of unheeded wishes and unattended desires I sent to the universe lying around here somewhere.

**Mr G** – Material manifestation? Join the complaints queue!

**Me** *(trying it on)* – Is it very long?

**Mr G** *(cheerfully)* – No, but it's right next to the spinning Fate's office that you visit prior to picking up your chits for the next incarnation!

**Me** – Cheers, thanks for that reminder!

**Mr G** *(genuinely)* – You're most welcome.

**Me** *(sighs)* – I try to be as interactive with you as possible. If it makes me quite demanding, well… I'm sorry, but there's always more.

**Mr G** *(leaning forward)* – But your requests are mainly about money.

**Me** – The lack of it you mean! Plus other things. Shall we look at them?

**Mr G** – No, we're focusing on your personal and professional development in this session, not outdated shopping lists of desires, personal wants and changes of mind. I'm not Father Christmas.

**Me** – Oh, my ongoing survival needs, I think you mean! That errand boy of yours, Hermes, was getting a bit quick on your universal demands so I asked him to slack off a bit whilst I sorted myself out.

**Mr G** – And have you?

**Me** – What?

**Mr G** – Sorted yourself out?

**Me** – Yes, I'm in a much better place now, thanks for asking.

**Mr G** – Bigger, perhaps?

**Me** – Yes, bigger and better I suppose. Freer. I'm becoming more qualitative than quantitative in these things. *(pause)*

**Mr G** – More expansive?

**Me** – Size matters?

**Mr G** – Of course. On all forms of life and functionality.

**Me** – I suppose in not wanting more responsibility I'm just waiting for the thrusting of greatness.

**Mr G** *(amused)* – And mine's not inconsiderable.

**Me** – I get restless at times, then nothing happens and I grow listless.

**Mr G** – And easily distracted, but all good things in their own good time. Yet by size I meant space.

**Me** – More space?

**Mr G** – And, all things considered, more time as well. Particularly on patience, cheeriness and heart-expansion.

**Me** – But that's not always quantifiable.

**Mr G** – Indeed! Life's not a spreadsheet, more of a vibrational motion study… And being beyond all space and time you do need to get your head, heart and imagination around that. *(smiling)* So…

**Me** *(terse)* – Okay, okay. Life's not a standardisation or fitting in exercise.

**Mr G** *(beaming)* – Quite the opposite. *(briskly)* So, how about we start with a quick overview of the past year or two?

**Me** – Hmmm… That's been difficult. Being attacked on the work front. Resignations. My dad dying. Working on the treadmill for less than I was worth at the agency. Losing the flat because we couldn't keep up the mortgage payments. Having to move twice in one year. All the destabilising madness of others, which, I might add, helped capsize my rather splendid plans.

**Mr G** *(instructively)* – The trouble with human plans is that they can often collapse whereas the true realms of realities do not. It all depends on the foundations.

**Me** – Oh! So?

**Mr G** *(sighs)* – So, less planning and more adaptive interaction with the true realms of realities.

**Me** – Then I was sick through the stress of it all. Now living in no man's land.

**Mr G** *(correcting)* – An oasis, you mean?

**Me** – Yes, absolutely lovely, but the energy's not very green.

**Mr G** – Beginning to tire of the city? At least it's quiet where you live, which is good for writing. See it as a useful containment exercise as you integrate the different strands and aspects of your work.

**Me** – Thanks!

**Mr G** *(smiling)* – My pleasure.

**Me** – Then you set that rather epic hermit project on top of my heartbreak. It was mind-boggling and extraordinary, but honestly, it's all been a bit brutal.

**Mr G** *(sagely)* – More than some, yet not as much as others. But I get your drift. It's been a tough year or two. Perhaps best to draw a line under those. This year's looking better. How's the new electricity and heart centre I sent going?

**Me** *(cheerily)* – Oh! Very nicely. It's fantastic in fact. Two hearts, one central unifying compartment, two new Light Wings connected front and back with their own jet power-pack. Plus, all the pneumatic air pressure plates around the body feel great.

**Mr G** – Technically that's called a 'space suit'. It only gets fully released once you're through the compression chamber of karma and back in balance with yourself. The pressure valves and seals of the liberty heart activate it. Have you got it fully operational yet?

**Me** *(unsure)* – Oh! Well, it's all very pleasant, interesting and rather intriguing. What's it for?

**Mr G** – Mainly for discovering far away space fields and star travel. You know, bouncy Moon Base landing then kick off with compassion from there.

**Me** – Oh! It's very whizzy, but I'm not sure I've fully got the hang of the wings yet!

**Mr G** *(beaming)* – You see... As a star child you don't need a spaceship to get to the other side of the galaxy. The space suit also helps if you feel any sudden onslaught of electro-magnetic particles.

**Me** – I do sometimes feel overwhelmed.

**Mr G** – I know, blinking particles! What can you do? Light elements are quite busy. Perpetual motion. Fizzy molecules...

**Me** – It certainly does get hectic at times.

**Mr G** – It's the multi-dimensional qi. It acts like miracle dust. You just need to activate the quick silver-skin on your spacesuit.

**Me** – And how do you do that?

**Mr G** – Through consciousness. The reflective surface protects you from any light-heat and unwanted particle bombardment. That way you can dance on the edge of sunshine without too much damage and avoid solar burn.

**Me** – Nice!

**Mr G** – And of course avoiding vaporising cosmic-storm damage.

**Me** – Oh, that doesn't sound pleasant! Should I be expecting some?

**Mr G** *(smiling)* – No more than usual. Ultimately, as your elements are absorbed back into the source, you will feel incredibly light. Unburdened of karma and secrets, the different energies and frequencies redistribute and a sense of weightlessness develops.

**Me** – Sounds delightful!

**Mr G** – The space suit has an anti-gravity factor so you can become psychonautic whenever you want, but it also has a useful earthing mechanism. Meanwhile, I suggest you sit back and enjoy the ride.

**Me** – You mean relax more?

**Mr G** – Let the galactic system take the strain.

**Me** – Oh, I like the sound of that!

**Mr G** – I'm sure you do. Being massless, light particles can be here, there and everywhere whilst containing useable, fundamental energy.

**Me** *(casually)* – Multi-dimensional chi, you mentioned.

**Mr G** – All operating within the natural laws of course.

**Me** *(bemused)* – Is that like being all the God-particles at once?

**Mr G** *(smiling)* – Sort of, but no. You just need to experience them whilst allowing yourself to become more holistically light.

**Me** *(scratching his head, lost)* – Okay.

**Mr G** *(helpfully)* – Dextera!

*The Almighty Hand starts writing out a useful note…*

*Light consists of massless particles acting as electro-magnetic energy transporters.*

*Pockets of light are packed with frequencies and information all struggling to inform and align.*

*These become colour-coded sources of emotion and thought in your biological, human, social prism-matter-dimension.*

*Colour is a good way of exploring the multi-verses. That way I can probe the many worlds and dimensions through the prism of your auras and the light fields.*

*Gathering light-information is the same as having curiosity and interest in your environment.*

**Mr G** – Your home world is full of sensory processing combined with a new emerging spiritual intelligence. It's a very interesting place. Incarnated souls become a more useful, clear crystal lens for dispersing light once they've walked the 'gauntlet of shame' and are free from guilt by having struggled with it, owned it and forgiven it. Each has their personal over soul connection to explore and tell.

**Me** – Oh! Was the life event I experienced recently some kind of 'Shadow Walk' thing?

**Mr G** – Yes, partly. It was more of a universe 'Infinity Gauntlet' challenge that you picked up. It was about forgiveness, reconciliation and the un-mortification of your many selves.

**Me** – You mean stop playing the blame-game of experience?

**Mr G** – Ah, the dagger or the duck.

**Me** – Sorry?

**Mr G** – It's often to do with the way you experience the different elements of life's many events and how you approach change - the way of metal or the way of water, for example.

**Me** – A stab to the heart or letting it flow like water off your back?

**Mr G** – Indeed. Part of your trouble is that you don't fully know who you are yet. Consequently, you don't know how to allow yourself the freedom to be that fully integrated soul-person. Now, life and the return journey become much more light and lively.

**Me** – Well, at least that part sounds more pleasant!

**Mr G** – It's called Nirvana understanding and is an antidote to ignorance, attachment and aversion.

**Me** – Stuck 'inside-out' pain? I tried investigating all that through the healing-counselling services.

**Mr G** – Very wise. Unfortunately, the general employment of most limited human psychoanalytic systems work solely on this life's memories and events. The vibrational wobble I sent you dealt with all your lives simultaneously. Different thing entirely.

**Me** – Oh! I see. Wow! *(pause)*

**Mr G** *(good humouredly)* – As for the space suit, you can wear it down the shops if you wish.

**Me** – Okay, thanks. Like an everyday costume thing?

**Mr G** – Yes, but it's for space cadets, not airheads. I'm presently recruiting them alongside peace warriors and rainbow wizards for the new Gaia accord. *(wanting to tick a box on Me's file)* So, which should I put you down for - space, peace or wiz?

**Me** – I'd be interested in a wizard position. What types are there?

**Mr G** – Well, there's your basic warlocks, witches and wand-bashers, then there's your astronomical star crafters, whilst individual wizards come as planetary, pearl, gold, emerald, or sapphire… Oh, and of course the wonderful.

**Me** *(bemused by the overwhelming choice)* – Oh, I'm not sure. They all sound tempting. Can I get back to you?

**Mr G** – Certainly. *(pause)* So…

**Me** – Sorry?

**Mr G** – So, worth it all in the end then… All that new electricity and magnetism you experienced as surrendering your old conflict, grief, fear and pain?

**Me** – Oh, definitely! I didn't mean to sound ungrateful. Honestly, in retrospect, everything's fine. It was just on top of the year that I'd already had, plus that 'Snake Book!' and then the life event… Well, I'm pleased to be moving away from it all.

**Mr G** – Pleased to be more incorporated on this side and not that?

**Me** *(considering)* – I suppose. Generally, things are looking more hopeful and getting more exciting.

**Mr G** – Indeed! You've still got that big surprise to come…

**Me** *(tired by the thought)* – Not another life event so soon, I hope? I seem to have had so many.

**Mr G** – Yes, it certainly is all packed in the precarious heroic life.

**Me** *(boldly takes a pinch of snuff)* – Not much of a hero really. Just another poet "slouching towards Bethlehem".

**Mr G** – Partly understanding disorder in the golden dream, partly the epic homecoming.

**Me** – I suppose we all have to leave the Emerald City at some point.

**Mr G** – True. Getting here is one thing, the journey on another, but this is something else. More to do with…

**Me** – No spoilers please! I like surprises. Good or bad, I'd rather not know. Unless I specifically ask, of course.

**Mr G** – Well, all I will say is that it concerns the unifying of a certain form of love and grace that a few of you are holding within the heart centre frequencies, but I won't say more than that… *(unable not to say anymore blurts out)* Other than it's pink, white and gold in colour and will energise you for the next phase of development and work.

**Me** *(annoyed)* – Okay, thank you. Enough!

**Mr G** *(smiling)* – Anything to suit your personal anxiety plans. Now, you remember what we said about plans?

**Me** – Yes, yes, I remember. No plans. Mice and men, that kind of thing. I get it, I get it.

**Mr G** *(scrutinising Me)* – Sure? I'm not convinced that you do.

**Me** *(scratches head)* – Sort of. It's very difficult. Plans? No plans?

**Mr G** *(clarifying)* – It's all right having plans, but not ones that limit you from a Venus love angle. Similarly, plans have to be helpful with achievable practical goals when looked at from the Mars angle.

**Me** *(none the wiser)* – Oh?

**Mr G** – Sometimes it's best not to have any plans, but surrender to the inspiration of the Mother and Holy Ghost, and then improvise.

**Me** *(reflecting)* – I had some really good plans though.

**Mr G** – Indeed you did, but instability and forces beyond your control scuppered them.

**Me** – You mean other people's unsolicited dramas, madness and some reprehensible, unprofessional behaviour!

**Mr G** – Ah! The unfolding of the hidden tragi-comedy. A stepping-stone to where you are now. Remember to use your space suit and re-delve the frontiers of your space.

**Me** – Re-find the dream?

**Mr G** – It's all about vision and will. Your previous plans, which were good, didn't help your situation at that time, but that's not to say flexible, positive, future plans and mini achievable goals aren't sometimes a good idea. You had to push back a few boundaries and challenge a few conventions along the way first. Peace doesn't come from avoiding life, as you now realise, but you're doing fine.

**Me** – Do I need contingency plans this time?

**Mr G** – A good question. *(surprised, but pleased, Me sits upright to listen)* If you have the right Sun-dance partners your projects will take off and soar. You might want to borrow my business head if it helps. All projects need financing, particularly sacred ones! Remember to be romantic in affairs of the heart and matters of life, but not in the concerns of business.

**Me** – In equal weight and measure fair?

**Mr G** – Precisely! Invest in people justly. You cannot talk to others about Truth if you haven't confronted your own. You have to face yourself honestly and conclude that you are your own success and saviour.

**Me** *(randomly quoting)* – "Nothing is impossible to industry".

**Mr G** – For good or ill, unfortunately.

**Me** – More on your toes in these shifting times?

**Mr G** – Yes! And you do like to dance.

**Me** – True, I do. But if I can't dance with, then I'd rather dance around than confront, but hey ho… In the end.

**Mr G** – "Beware the fury of a patient man!" Give yourself a clean slate and a new chance. The power of forgiveness is a mighty thing. In the end you crossed some authority lines…

**Me** *(crossly)* – Some unacceptable impositions you mean?

**Mr G** – You became reactive and consequently were left trying to outsmart some difficult divorcing forces at work.

**Me** – To try and stop a work culture being created that had no rhyme or reason to exist.

**Mr G** – Sometimes nice people end up being dumped on. Generally, you are moderate and reasonable, sensible and kind, which means you get lumbered more than the sharper knives in the drawer.

**Me** – Yes, I've been told before my Sword-of-Truth is a bit blunt. I suppose I see myself as more of a spoon really, ladling out love.

**Mr G** – Spoons are not so good for cutting through things.

**Me** – Not even runcible ones?

**Mr G** – No, sharp, precise, well-utilised knives, swords and scalpels are best for that.

**Me** – In that case perhaps I should reconsider the whole cutlery drawer of my beingness?

**Mr G** *(indulgently)* – Only if you really have to.

**Me** *(enthusiastically)* – Well! My fork's pretty good at picking up the pieces and spreading thoughts around.

**Mr G** *(humouring Me as a parent does a child)* – Yes, forks are good for catching hold of tender morsels and for the distribution of ideas. Yet pitchforks are more fun for rounding up devils, bats and rats though.

**Me** – Spoons are good for scooping out softness.

**Mr G** – Yes, ice cream and the conical delight of light, but it was your knife that you needed and it wasn't as sharp and fit for purpose as it could have been. 'Easy going' doesn't have to mean the accepting of situations that are unpleasant or unreasonable.

**Me** – It got to me in the end, so I removed myself, as the person with the problem should.

**Mr G** – Let's say you were riled and got more emotionally expressive than you usually do, regardless of the consequences.

**Me** – You mean the 'fuck it' factor? Throwing caution to the wind?

**Mr G** *(cheerfully)* – Swearing in meetings is always fun. The 'flying profanity' usually denotes the end of someone's tether and imminent downfall and exodus. Many individuals and institutions have seen similar breakdowns and experienced the betrayal of trust you felt.

**Me** – Too soul-destroying.

**Mr G** – Unhappy, exploited, disaffected staff make for unhappy students and uncared for patients. It would have been too compromising a position for you to stay in.

**Me** – The situation was very unstable.

**Mr G** – All the players had cards to play. Some decks are a bit wilder than others; some hands are weighted higher or lower.

**Me** – Couldn't you have sent a thunderbolt from out the blue?

**Mr G** – I did, but sometimes you need to learn how to box clever.

**Me** – Oh!

**Mr G** – However, galactic-guidance and explosive heavenly-dynamic-supply are not on demand. As humans controlling it would be an absolute recipe for disaster. *(staring intently at Me)* Good intentions or not. Best to let life unfold in accordance to its own natural and supernatural laws whilst keeping your hearts, eyes and minds lifted to the cosmic God-of-Good.

**Me** – I see. The way of no control.

**Mr G** – Your limiting ideas of self had to be overcome. You're not small. In fact you'll find yourself to be less of a person and more of a yellow, beckoning star cluster once you've zoned in properly.

**Me** *(baffled)* – Really? Any particular one? And is that why I feel I have so many aspects?

**Mr G** – Of course! Your particular cluster is of the 'globular' kind, somewhat old and gravitationally bound. That's why you're secretly envious of the more 'open' clusters - younger, freer and with fewer affiliates.

**Me** – Oh, so not the twinkly second star on the right, the one just before morning?

**Mr G** – Ah, the wishing star that stirs belief and magical desire!

**Me** *(hopefully)* – Yes?

**Mr G** – No, you're not that one, but everyone's different. Ultimately, until you're connected to universal flow and divine consciousness, no plans or human house can stand the test of heavenly-weather.

**Me** – You need to storm or be stormed?

**Mr G** – One begets the other. Once you're there…

**Me** – Where?

**Mr G** – Having left the homeland, over the rainbow, past the Emerald City, then far, far away until you finally arrive back home…

**Me** – Oh.

**Mr G** – Then you can guide yourself with an occasional divine prompt from one of the winged team.

**Me** – Lovely, but I'd like to put some roots down now. All this drifting is getting to me.

**Mr G** – Yes, so? *(pause)*

**Me** – Er!

**Mr G** – So, what are you going to do about it?

**Me** *(struggling)* – Plan a little more?

**Mr G** – Keep working toward your highest vision that you had as a child. Remember the vision quest?

**Me** – Yes.

**Mr G** – Well, you've been busy setting yourself a few new personal challenges. Now let the universe operate and guide you to the next. Manifest from positivity and without the anxiety.

**Me** *(wearily)* – It's hard to fathom when you've got gravy for brains!

**Mr G** – True, but you're more of a jacket potato head. Aren't you?

**Me** – Oh! I do like those.

**Mr G** – I know you do. Is cheese and coleslaw with garlic butter still your favourite?

**Me** *(concerned)* – That's very personal. How did you know that?

**Mr G** *(tapping file)* – It's all down here. It comes with the 'Omni' part of the job. Apple crumble, rhubarb pie…

**Me** *(sighing)* – I like those too. Sometimes you just need to tuck out! Well… *(nostalgic)* Back in the days when I was slimmer.

**Mr G** – Yes, you have a different body now.

**Me** – Fuller.

**Mr G** *(kindly)* – More rugby build. *(tapping file)* It's all down here. Your gravy instinct reveals a need for home making, cooking and baking… A family life of feasting and sharing. Isn't that what you want?

**Me** – Yes, partly. I do like my creature comforts though.

**Mr G** – Nincompoops, Bears and the Mermaid-Moonstruck have a bigger heart life than those with clever, set know-it-all minds.

**Me** *(brightly)* – Oh, okay! I guess they do.

**Mr G** – So stick to your heart-path and manifest that. Be the success you already are, right now, today, in everything you think, do and say.

**Me** – Thank you. It's just sometimes I have a self-doubt day.

**Mr G** – That's all right. Everyone has one once in a while. Even whilst working on their good and better humour! Use it to your advantage. Re-group and align yourself to your soul's purpose, but remember… You can't please them all so best to please yourself and see who follows and wants to join in.

**Me** – Such difficult times and circumstances for so many. Yet what allows you to fully engage with the current world struggle?

**Mr G** – Another good question. *(Me cannot believe his luck as Mr G puts a double tick on his file)* Many spiritual-samurais and warrior-knights are currently being awakened to guide the incarnating spirit children and fight the world evils. World questions need local answers and battles. Heart-centred administration and organisation are required. Right now, you need to be meditating and reflecting upon the appropriate universal question-directions and then apply your answers. *(pause)* So…. Where do we go from here?

**Me** *(stunned)* – Not sure. I suppose we could do a "SWOT" analysis?

**Mr G** – Oh! Do you mean like a fly or a bit bookish?

**Me** – Recently it has felt more "SWAT" than "SWOT", but on Earth they use it as a reflective guide. You know… strengths, weaknesses, opportunities and threats.

**Mr G** – I'm not sure those conventions as judged by the mind are terribly useful. It's difficult to assess heart processes when you're all busy individually experiencing the manifestation of your own unique universe. It partly depends on how much you've conformed or how much you've allowed your creativity to inform you.

**Me** – Interesting.

**Mr G** – Reality is so different for each of you. And that partly depends on the hierarchy of your senses, the sensitivity of your perception and how you've re-ordered your personal conceptual imaginal-worlds.

**Me** – "A fool sees not the same tree that a wise man sees".

**Mr G** *(grinning)* – Yes, it's all trial and error. Everyone's experiencing the world and interpreting life quite differently. Whereas I thought you were referring to "SWAT" the "Sikh Welfare Awareness Team".

**Me** – Oh, are they doing good work?

**Mr G** – Indeed, as do a lot of the evangelical inner-city mercy missions. It's all in the City Angels' monthly report I receive *(tapping a rack full of monthly reports and magazines with quirky angelic art on the covers)*

**Me** – Well, I hardly meant the "Special Weapons and Tactics" unit.

**Mr G** *(suddenly serious)* – No, true. The archangels are rather busy at the moment at the other end of the multi-verse. I sent them there on a secret mission, but how did you know that?

**Me** *(flummoxed by his uncanny ability to pluck things out of thin air)* – Er! Just making it up as usual.

**Mr G** – I didn't think you'd need them so soon considering you've recently disarmed yourself. Yet if you're ready to re-engage with the world struggle and fight, the Archangel Michael is always willing to lend a hand and a sword or two. I can send him in if you wish as most of the tyrants in the recent cloud-world wars have been toppled and banished on this side of the divide.

**Me** – Big guns indeed! I wasn't expecting to need that kind of help. *(Mr G says nothing)* But I take your point. I'll seek out the Sikh in me.

**Mr G** – Or try and find the inner swami. That was a useful life.

**Me** – I was thinking of releasing more of the Mad Merlin.

**Mr G** – It's up to you which masters you want to work with. Depends on whom you can catch or who is willing?

**Me** – Oh, okay. Is that a you or me thing? I don't want to be lumbered. Which one overshadows and cooks the best food?

**Mr G** – You and your international appetite!

**Me** *(deliberately mishearing)* – Inspirational appetite?

**Mr G** *(sighs)* – Let's try another approach.

**Me** – Okay, how about doing one of those 'hundred day impact' assessment type things?

**Mr G** *(breezily)* – Is that like re-inventing the wheel and the kind of repetitive stupidity that you were talking about earlier?

**Me** – Sort of. More to do with managing change and executive implementations regardless of whether they're needed or not.

**Mr G** *(swivels in his chair to watch the unfolding of the early universe on the Cloud-Office's large, white screen)* – I thought I'd already done that deep impact-thing?

**Me** – Alignment and approach, not meteorites and planetary collisions. Something smaller and more useful. Helpful ways toward a more harmonious life in these discordant days.

**Mr G** – You mean like my personal intervention to some of the earlier races and species? That did everyone a favour.

**Me** – I don't think the abominations and dinosaurs were quite so appreciative.

**Mr G** – There's loads of impact-information floating about right now. You don't need more, but rather to select and apply the good stuff. I'm more interested in what you need to do to fully realise yourself in 'this life'. *(Mr G mimics Yul Brynner in an offhand manner whilst the Almighty Hand gesticulates in a royal manner)* "Etc. etc. etc."

**Me** *(sighs)* – How very grand!

**Mr G** *(smugly)* – Thanks, I'm a natural. But part of this review is to check that there's nothing still holding you back. As for the 'hundred days impact' theory… Well, personally, I tend to take my time. That creation thing wasn't done in a week, you know. It took a long time to consider it all, let alone start creating it. The substantial universe didn't come first by any means. It took me thousands of years of deliberation. Personal notes to self, laboratory research, then manufacturing the dark-light universe through the layering of the sub-dimensional membranes of consciousness.

**Me** *(joking)* – Oh! Did you have time as well as space on your hands?

**Mr G** – No, time was the follow up awareness-through-the-planes-and-dimensions programme that I set in motion whilst allowing the natural evolution of species to occur. *(peering at Me and smiling)* Like you, I was at first divinely unconscious.

**Me** *(staggered)* – Cheers! I'm working on it.

**Mr G** *(helpfully)* – And I'm trying to help. Dextera!

> *First desire created stirring-impulse which then met first thought. Together they created motion and brought forward first fire-idea.*
>
> *Through touch and plasma contact, the spark of ignition-friction begat first light-seed that led to causal impact, or what you know now as the original super nova starburst of elemental existence.*
>
> *There were many inter-connected bubble universes created simultaneously.*

**Me** *(exhausted)* – Phew, there's nothing like a good secret teaching!

**Mr G** – It's hard for your species to re-call, as the vaults of the guardians of deep space knowledge are locked to all but a few. There are many concurrent universes within those specific space co-ordinates. That's why the astronomers are now beginning to find the multi-verse bubble-bruising. I was not separate, but my first question to myself, 'Who am I?' enabled me as Father-God to inseminate that part of me which was Mother-God who in turn gave birth to elemental matter… then bingo! Bump, dump, ba-da-boom!

**Me** – You mean the big bang was you begetting with yourself?

**Mr G** *(smiling, joking)* – Kind of. The old black magic of dark matter. I was unified until I spilt the milk of my way and split. I became supernatural father and the universe became elemental mother. The physical components of your universe are from the same source expanding through super-accelerated cosmic inflation from the same startling vast force, which was love born of desire giving birth.

**Me** *(baffled)* – Is that why the whole thing seems so inexplicable?

**Mr G** – Exactly. You also have to know that yours wasn't the first elemental existing creation, plus there are other physical universes and a whole host of alternative dimensions to discover. Dark matter holds the initial energy key, but consciousness is the living force from which everything was propelled - and that was born from joy.

**Me** *(flummoxed)* – Er! I'm sorry. You'll have to forgive me. It all sounds delightful, but is way beyond my limited comprehension.

**Mr G** – Precisely! It's meant to be. Having instantaneously explored everything and every state-of-being past, present and future the answer echoed throughout the universe, 'I am God.' Simple really. You're all emanating and resounding from that beyond-point catching up in the yearn and return. Does that help?

**Me** – Not really! It's too big and metaphysical.

**Mr G** – Yes, it certainly is all in the stretch! But I thought we'd already decided that substantiality matters and that you liked that?

**Me** – Proportion and size?

**Mr G** – From your side of the cloud the imponderable ratios have often seemed hidden. Likewise, in the humanitarian Age of Aquarius the sacred mysteries are going to be locked as well.

**Me** – Oh?

**Mr G** – The nature-of-consciousness in that age is going to be different and more about the exploration of en masse global amiability. So there's not much point discussing the mystical aspects anymore until they are re-awakened at the beginning of the Age of Capricorn when the next, huge planetary initiation takes place.

**Me** *(mystified)* – I see.

**Mr G** – For thousands of years humanity has been involved in an exceedingly speeded-up world project of which consciousness, love-awareness and universal joy are now the rewards. The past mysteries were all part of a process to save Gaia and the human inhabitants from a type of space invasion that occurred at different points in Earth's history.

**Me** – Was it Mars by any chance?

**Mr G** – Partly, but well done.

**Me** – I know my H G Wells. *(reconsidering)* Or was it David Bowie?

**Mr G** – It all started during the Lemurian-Atlantean crossover. The most invasive form was the Romans from the Red Planet, whilst the most recent was the inner realm attack of the giants. That formed the Middle Earth violence you experienced in the culmination of the Second World War as a result of the corruption of the Age of Pisces through the Crucifixion.

**Me** – As channelled and depicted in 'The Lord of the Rings' trilogy?

**Mr G** – Yes! Beautifully crafted and a little, light reading before bed.

**Me** *(utterly poleaxed)* – Impenetrable! Perhaps we'd better stick to looking more at personal reflection, peer and group feedback and mentoring after all. Something more on an ordinary human scale.

**Mr G** *(cheerily)* – I thought you were enjoying our friendly, little one-to-one? A few verbatim minutes and action points from me now and then to last you a few lifetimes, wherever you end up, plus a chance to construct a space in which fellow space cadets, peace warriors and world wizards can inhabit when the time is right.

**Me** *(reluctantly)* – True. I do like a good chat when I'm in the mood, but sometimes, just sometimes…

*(Me shakes his head muttering something about 'being impossible' and wishing for something to anaesthetise his brain. Me thinks about taking a swig from his hip flask, but looks out of the window instead. A passing floating Japanese Blossom Tree kindly points an encouraging leafy-twiggy finger back into the room)*

**Me** – So… *(apprehensively)* Any particular path, purpose or direction to the rest of our meeting?

**Mr G** *(jauntily)* – Other than for you to reflect and review?

**Me** *(trying not to look out the window)* – Not *more* reflective practice.

**Mr G** – You'll be pleased to know that I do have a few general areas to cover and there'll be time for questions and feedback at the end.

**Me** – Fine.

**Mr G** – Let's start with the recent inner work and self-discovery. *(tapping file)* It says here that you've spent some time realising your divine child.

**Me** – Is that the same as releasing my inner child?

**Mr G** – No, not really.

**Me** – Yes, well, I had to! Just to keep up with that familiar of mine.

*(Mr G writes on file: 'Confusion between the different human-psycho and divine-psyche reality zones. Client seems unsure of the difference between Muppets and men, cartoons and characters, animal guides and totems, people and partners')*

**Mr G** – It's not a competition to see who can have the most fun.

**Me** – Could've fooled me. Tell him that.

**Mr G** – What totem has he incarnated as this time?

**Me** – A bear, a bit grizzly lately, but there's been lots of laughs…

**Mr G** – Releasing the inner child is one thing, the unleashing of annoying and demanding baby-adults quite another! I think you're mistaking it for the release of the inner brat.

**Me** *(helpfully)* – The inner bat?

**Mr G** *(sighs)* – That's an altogether different sonic process.

**Me** *(joshing)* – Could be worse. Could be my inner diva!

**Mr G** *(not to be outdone in the sweeping melodramatic stakes)* – Ah! The sweet tones of the adorable Bianca Castafiore - the Milanese Nightingale! She was one of my great earthly loves, you know. I would turn into a swan for her any day. Oh to be a diamond necklace nestled against her charming breast! How kind of you to remind me.

**Me** *(regretting bringing the topic up however unintentionally)* – That's me - always an uncanny knack of disturbing something best left buried. Quite frankly, I often find that most people's inner child needs to be locked up and their inner diva needs a slap or two!

**Mr G** *(getting back to business - writing and mumbling, 'Used to be such a nice boy, but doesn't always play so well with others these days.')* – Oh good, I'm glad you meant that. People's inner brat is only a slight step on from their spiteful child. Yet the loving, willing children of the cloud of mystery, divinity, applied imagination and vision are never in short supply on this side of the veil.

**Me** *(rolling his eyes, but glimpsing the view through the window)* – Inspiring qualities I'm sure! It's just that everyone on Earth wants to be a superstar these days. *(the forms of different Muses laughing, singing and dancing float by on a neighbouring cloud, gently tumbling in a poetic round. Me is enchanted, yet distracted)* It's a different ball game entirely down there.

**Mr G** – Ah, the celebrity class!

**Me** – Criminal!

**Mr G** – People need to break though the cloud-divide and grab hold of the more inspirational light qualities, colours and sounds.

**Me** – That's not always so easy as most people forget.

**Mr G** – That's partly due to the in-built amnesia-system and partly due to the overwhelming clamour of social ambition and status-demands on your side of the cloud.

**Me** – True.

**Mr G** – Then there's western humanity's strange creation of the concrete mind-mantle disabling proper veil-penetration. I find all these factors, particularly when considered alongside the current mainstream chorus of spiritual discord, conspiracy and general mind-disapproval of the lovely heart-encouragement that's around...

**Me** *(interjecting whilst still looking out the window)* – Not to mention all the added glamour of entrenched hierarchy, high society and position.

**Mr G** *(trying to complete his sentence)* – Plus the ongoing surge-purge turmoil within the recent Gaia-transition…

**Me** *(pointing, outlining the shapes of some passing clouds)* – Tell me about it!

**Mr G** *(exasperated, but finally finishing his sentence)* – …Has all added to humanity's sense of natural chaos, disorder and presumed disaster. Then, hey presto! *(Mr G, noticing Me's preoccupation, summons the Almighty Hand to click his fingers in front of Me's face and asks loudly)* But what do you think?

**Me** *(caught out, responds in an automatic, but inane, second-guessing way)* – Et voilà! Instant apocalyptic outlook and negative approach.

**Mr G** *(distinctly unimpressed)* – I thought you'd dealt with all of your 'conflict aspects' otherwise you wouldn't be here? Any remaining problems I can put on the list of 'emotional homework'?

**Me** *(turning back into the room)* – Oh, no! Do you have to? I'm sure it's nothing. Any aches and pains, moans and groans, are simply leftover niggles not enjoying the reminders of current light scrutiny.

**Mr G** – Residuals all on the way up and out to full release I hope?

**Me** – The inspection and review process isn't always so enjoyable down there on Earth. I'm sure you'll agree that it's some of the mind-inspectors who need re-attuning!

**Mr G** – Yes, true. Gaia evolutionary-education is a gift of the heart not the mind, but cynicism has dealt rather a blow in certain areas.

*(Mr G starts humming a Pink Floyd tune, "Hey! Government inspectors - leave our heart-teachers alone." As Mr G begins to write suggestions down on Me's file,*

*he telepathically transmits them to Me via the inbuilt me-cloud message storage system: 'Try listing leftover negative thoughts and see them as weeds that need pulling from the mental body. Follow up with visualisation practice. Spend time feeling into the emotional biorhythms of the energy field and talking beneficially to heart-self on a daily basis. Keep up the purification processes')*

**Mr G** *(pleased)* – There, another action point. We're doing well.

**Me** *(grouchy)* – Oh, that's unfair! That's not one point, more like three.

**Mr G** – See it as value for time and money then.

**Me** *(sighing)* – I hope this review isn't going to be all lists, targets or performance-oriented action points. Carrot and stick, old-fashioned quota-incentivising… Not really keen on those things. Achievement and motivation isn't everything, right?

*(Mr G writes on Me's file, 'A tendency to drift listlessly. Client uses daydreaming as a form of avoidance and shows little interest in right alignment. Unsure if he understands the difference between motivation, intention and purpose')*

**Mr G** – What would you suggest?

**Me** *(put out)* – Encouragement and understanding the core of me.

**Mr G** – Which is what?

**Me** *(boldly)* – Fun and adventure!

**Mr G** *(smiling)* – Oh, I'll make a note of it immediately.

*(Mr G does nothing of the sort, but continues reading Me's notes whilst occasionally guffawing unto himself. The Almighty Hand kindly turns the pages of what now appears to be an ever-expanding file before going back to cleaning a particularly stubborn gloomy patch in the shape of a thistle in the cloud's corner)*

**Me** *(fidgeting)* – Does that file have many other things to say?

**Mr G** *(not looking up)* – Such as interesting insights, notes and tendencies of self?

**Me** – Sort of. You know, I *have* been quite helpful. It can't all be bad!

**Mr G** – Do you consider me hard work or not worth the effort then?

**Me** *(defeated)* – No, of course not! You're always a joy.

**Mr G** *(still reading, appraising)* – Glad to hear it.

**Me** – I meant is there anything else in that file that I need to know before we proceed? You know more about me than I do!

**Mr G** – That's true! It says here *(tapping file)* that you are prone to being argumentative, somewhat contrary and given to parsimony.

**Me** *(punning like Basil Brush)* – But generous with it. Boom! Boom!

**Mr G** *(over-seriously as though to make a point)* – Being generous with parsimony? Isn't that like the sin of prudence - "a rich ugly old maid courted by incapacity?"

**Me** *(sighs)* – You would say that! Somehow it's like you know how to read my mind, get to me and stir up my confusion.

**Mr G** – True, I *do* like a bit of a collective chat and scrap! It's my controversial taste for topical satire, ruthless kindness and social libel.

**Me** *(incredulous)* – You wouldn't necessarily expect it of you!

*(Mr G acts out a mock doppelganger fight with the Almighty Hand beginning with a Snagglepuss impression, "Heavens to Murgatroyd! - even," followed by the Cowardly Lion, "Put 'em up! Put 'em up!" routine. The Almighty Hand flutters around excitedly wanting to join in hoping to use Me as a punch-bag)*

**Me** *(slapping the Almighty Hand away)* – Are you sure you're not the devil in disguise?

**Mr G** – Certainly not! That quote was merely a little poet joke.

**Me** – I like those.

**Mr G** – I know, that's why I'm putting them in! I'm terribly good to you despite all your moaning. I tend to improvise and mix it all in with a touch of fantasy re-enactment as a reminder to sail close to the heavenly-winds. Of course, Lucifer and I are very good friends.

**Me** – What! The cat from Cinderella or the real one?

**Mr G** *(ignoring Me's oblique reference)* – You know, the world's notions of a devil are all quite man-made. A useful fear-control construct for some, I suppose, but a pretty nasty device for others. Whereas the real Star-Lucifer and I have daily, early morning meetings.

**Me** – How very dawn-breaking, must be nice for you both!

**Mr G** – Now, now. Just because you're still dead to the world doesn't mean others aren't already up spreading the emergent light.

**Me** – That's true. Mornings and me don't always get on.

**Mr G** – Occasionally we even get to have tea and biscuits in bed if one of the attendant angels isn't too busy.

**Me** – Perks of the trade I suppose, but I thought prudence was about time and consideration, a form of patience that grows from consideration into wisdom?

**Mr G** – Mentally perhaps, but not emotionally. What would the galloping horses-of-desire or Pegasus say to such restraint?

**Me** *(reflective)* – Oh, of course. Impulses as a horse, but what happens if you can't keep hold of your horses?

**Mr G** – The careering strong stallions? Imagine what you could do with one of those put to good purpose.

**Me** *(thoughtful)* – Break or befriend?

**Mr G** – Every horse is different depending on how frisky and well-treated they are. You need your horses-of-desire for how else will your charioteer steer the cosmic sky into new adventure?

**Me** – Oh! So let them be free, growing strong until they're needed, then rein them in and point them in a different direction?

**Mr G** – For unrestricted freedom-of-living you have to open the desire box and know all the informing creatures within. Similarly, understand that each of your light bodies operate in a different way, but one telling the other off is no good.

**Me** – So in that case, befriending is best.

**Mr G** – Eventually desires, like horses, should be bridled and utilised by wisdom in search of the greater happiness of the galactic good. What's worse? A horse wild and out of control or one broken and left to neglect?

**Me** *(considering)* – Neither sound good.

**Mr G** – Unbridled passion always gets interesting to the novice and dualistic-desire to the new charioteer feels like a bucking bronco.

**Me** – I've certainly been thrown from the saddle a few times.

**Mr G** – Can you imagine galloping like a centaur with the arrows of star-craft and the bows of sky-wisdom by your side?

**Me** – You'd need a very large trough to feed the desires of such a fabulous creature with two stomachs!

**Mr G** *(laughing)* – Sometimes it does take a lot of wine. The wise-horse has an appetite for feasting and sex, but knows when to rest, study and be philosophical as well as have fun. And where else would the apples-of-desire be if the horse hadn't upset the apple cart?

**Me** *(baffled)* – Not so rolling away and stuck in such strange places?

**Mr G** *(laughing)* – But you like the strange. That's often where your best inspiration comes from. On the whole I discourage physical excess, but each to their own and you don't know your limit until you get there. *(foresighted and hinting)* I think you'll find the extremes rather electrifying, but then again, that's where all new life usually begins.

**Me** *(oblivious of any hints)* – Oh! So, bottom out and kick-start?

**Mr G** – Follow your impulses until they each find their wise doom and reconfigure from there. Remember that your subtle bodies can find themselves at energised oppositional points until you love yourself as much as Mother Nature and I do.

**Me** – Is that a process of integration and synthesis?

**Mr G** – Right. Dextera!

> *You are here to synthesise yourself through the combining of serenity, love, wisdom and trust in things higher. Until that point you are held by Nature's laws and love.*
>
> *The balancing of the acknowledgement of world hardship, human condition and people's pain with personal peace and acceptance is crucial. After that, you are free to fly-drive your own auric-bubble or chariot as you please.*
>
> *Remember that it is an imperfect world where you currently reside and that it is impermanent, not firmament.*

*(the Almighty Hand having finished writing in his best script slaps the Post-it note brusquely to Me's forehead)*

**Me** – Thanks Hand. *(reading it)* Very worthy!

**Mr G** *(allowing himself a light chuckle)* – Domini! *(the Almighty Hand goes back to cleaning duties)* Whereas in reality, it is the spiritual astral Summerland where you will ultimately reside.

**Me** *(scratching his head and taking a sneaky pinch of snuff)* – Oh, okay. So do you ever let go of us?

**Mr G** – That would make you like a balloon let loose into the sky, or a drop of water individually picked up from a pond before being placed back within it at death.

**Me** *(lets out a long questioning sigh)* – Soooo…?

**Mr G** *(twinkling)* – Dextera!

**Me** *(beleaguered)* – Not another note so soon?

> The experiencing of the individual life-arc within the sky-or-sea-of-consciousness is both reality and illusion. You truly never left!
>
> The seeking and acceptance of the glorious life, with all of its phases, include the sought after, many merry and varied light-tones of joy, as well as the often avoided sombre, serious and sober timbres that create sorrow.
>
> I permeate the cosmic-water and etheric-air as well as all the elemental kingdoms. I am the dappled in unification. I am the black-and-the-white as well as the shades in-between.
>
> In return, I am the ultimate integration of all colours. Any sense of separation you experience during incarnation is an illusion.

**Mr G** *(pleased)* – You truly are residing within my dynamic energy fields. Likewise, my many wondrous realms are all available within you.

*(the Almighty Hand rubs and polishes Me's emerald-heart modem as a gentle reminder, which swirls and hums in a particularly warming manner)*

**Me** *(comforted)* – Oh, that's nice! It's like a cat's purr. *(the Almighty Hand scratches behind Me's ear and chucks under his chin as though Me were a cat)*

**Me** *(feeling slightly humiliated)* – Humph! Is there no escape?

**Mr G** *(smiling sweetly)* – No, no escaping from the true nature-of-reality or its repercussive laws.

**Me** – Including death and re-birth?

**Mr G** *(grinning)* – Or from the eventual meeting with me.

**Me** – Great! So where do we go from here?

**Mr G** *(reminding)* – The elemental system your consciousness currently operates within is one of immersion, yet is universally cohesive...

*(Bored, Me begins to drift and looks out of the window distracted by a passing Unicorn. Unimpressed, but not perturbed by Me's lack of interest and inability to grasp the multi-verse subject matter, Mr G politely changes approach to something smaller and more personally rewarding. Mr G reads from Me's file...)*

**Mr G** – Now, it says here that you're quite hot-headed, prone not to listen, often impatient in asking for universal assistance, and yet seldom acting upon it as you think it has arrived too late.

**Me** *(laments)* – That's not fair...

**Mr G** – Growing fickle?

**Me** – Picky, perhaps, but I know who has the superior intelligence!

**Mr G** *(correcting)* – Stronger force-of-consciousness...

**Me** *(oblivious)* – It's just… *(Me is lost for words and rapidly loses the will to explain)* I don't know, I can't always rationalise or act on things.

**Mr G** *(smiling)* – Remember that I am the stronger force, it is for the greater good and that you don't have all the answers.

**Me** *(helpfully trying to re-engage)* – I know, but I do try.

**Mr G** *(laughing, tapping file)* – Yes, it says here that you *are* very trying. *(suddenly very serious, Mr G gives Me a Yoda, "No! Try not. Do, or do not. There is no trying", type of stare whilst the floating Almighty Hand performs a Vulcan mind-meld on Me)* You have much to learn.

**Me** *(sighs, trying to understand the point, but robotically repeats back)* – I know, I have much to learn.

**Mr G** – Remember, this is all about humour.

**Me** – Or rather the lack of it! I'm not coming out of this terribly well.

**Mr G** – Oh, I don't know about that! Your mind-body split is hilarious and as a consequence your humanity towards yourself is increasing on a daily basis.

**Me** *(begrudgingly)* – Thanks.

**Mr G** – Now, now, don't be like that. Haven't you realised yet there is no winning?

**Me** – It certainly seems that way!

**Mr G** – No winning or losing, only the glorious experience of re-incarnating existence. And no taking of positions either.

**Me** *(surly)* – Great, most helpful!

**Mr G** – Remember that you're a human 'being' first and foremost. Now… *(removing a slightly dented circular object from an envelope at the back of Me's file)* It says here that you keep returning your halo.

**Me** *(politely)* – Sorry.

**Mr G** – It's not a frisbee.

**Me** *(unapologetic, brusquely)* – I know, I know. I never petitioned for it. As far as I'm concerned, prayers are a one-way request rather than any form of dialogue or correspondence.

**Mr G** *(smirking)* – Yes, you just need to beseech and petition me with your whole heart and I will be there.

**Me** – That's a good trick.

**Mr G** *(pleased)* – More of a magnetic principle really. Right now I'm answering your prayers - that's why you're here.

**Me** *(slightly mock-surprised, testing)* – Oh! So… Is this going to be some kind of ongoing dialogue?

**Mr G** – You? Me? Us, in ongoing unconscious-conscious collaboration? Would you like that?

**Me** *(cornered and quickly weighing up his options)* – Could go on delightfully forever I suppose! Does it take up much personal time?

**Mr G** – Indeed! Remember, once you're awake to the rainbow dream look out for the yellow brick road.

**Me** – All roads lead to Oz…

**Mr G** *(meaningfully)* – But who is the wizard?

**Me** *(ignoring)* – Funny, but keep pointing me in the right direction.

**Mr G** *(innocently)* – Would I do anything different?

**Me** *(unsure)* – Hhhm! Sometimes I do wonder.

**Mr G** *(warming up)* – From here to Eternity and a little bit further.

**Me** *(pleading, fearing the worst)* – Please don't get mathematical on me!

*(Mr G quickly recites the first 100 numbers to the π sequence simply to show off and give a little glimpse of infinity. The Almighty Hand helpfully finger counts)*

**Mr G** *(generously)* – All right. I'll alert you to some of the places you need to be, and to some of the ideas that you might need to consider.

**Me** – Thank you.

**Mr G** – On one level you're a social-cultural composite of sorts. All processes now need to be future-friendly and recycling is a very good place to start.

**Me** – Is that why there are so many reprocessed ideas floating around my head these days?

**Mr G** – As far as I'm concerned there is nothing new under the Sun, only your personal new-perception, fresh-conception and individual fusion in the discovery and artistic re-telling. Remember, life is there to serve you, *(tapping file)* but you've already unlocked that particular mystery. So… *(the Almighty Hand kindly offers the halo to Me)*

**Me** *(takes back the halo and starts fiddling with it, musing)* – I'm not keen on sainthood if that's what this is all about. Where's the fun in that?

**Mr G** – The halo effectively keeps the brighter colours together and is a super-absorbent way of organising the finer hues and shades…

**Me** *(quizzically)* – Oh?

**Mr G** – Particularly the much sought-after silver and gold of the crown chakra in break-through. It's part of the space suit operation.

**Me** – Yeah, but halos often come with a faint whiff of burnt martyr and that's one thing I'm not too keen on repeating!

**Mr G** *(warmly)* – Made you more magnetic and more giving.

**Me** – Nevertheless, it's too sacrificial and makes me struggle with the selfish art gene.

**Mr G** – In your own polite, introverted way your megalomania is coming along quite nicely. It says here though *(tapping file)* that you think a crown would be more fitting.

**Me** *(placing the halo in different positions about his head to find the jauntiest angle)* – Well, yes… sort of. I've got quite a theatrical hat-head and a crown could be fun!

**Mr G** – How very royal. Self-bequeathing?

**Me** – Of course! Hardly by popular request. I don't see anyone else giving it to me. Some things you just need to take. I presume a crown would come with more instant majesty?

**Mr G** *(nonchalantly turning the pages of the file and reading a note further down)* – Still lusting after power?

**Me** *(quickly in case of reprisal)* – Influence - perhaps with a pinch of personal empire building!

**Mr G** – Fair enough. Perhaps you'd like my job for the day?

**Me** – Yes please, but only if I can intervene and sort it all out!

**Mr G** – Sorry, the job comes with a non-intervention sub-clause.

**Me** – Is that like being a passive Santa? He was a bear, right?

**Mr G** – Funny! More of an über polar bear and a wonderful saint in reality. Remember the world doesn't need sorting out.

**Me** – Oh, I forgot! From where I stand it all looks pretty messed-up. *(wistfully thinking and wishing, 'If only I were God or king for a day…')*

**Mr G** *(reading Me's mind, writes a note on Me's file)* – Still have complexes I see.

**Me** – Only the interesting ones! More fantasy than anything else.

**Mr G** *(reads a note on Me's recent arcade escapades)* – How about a hat like Carmen Miranda for your monkey brains? Flowers, fruit, bananas?

**Me** *(shaking pretend maracas as a passing parrot flies through the room)* – Totally tropical, but a bit nuts. How about a Viking helmet?

**Mr G** – Ah! Noggin the Nog and the noggin of nogs!

**Me** – Could be cool?

**Mr G** *(moving quickly on)* – More interestingly, it says here *(refers to file)* that you've released and realised your inner daemon. Right, time to talk about the shadow work.

*(Me gurns through the halo using fingers to indicate Devil Horns then throws the halo back onto Mr G's table)*

**Me** – Was that the recognition of the dark stuff?

**Mr G** – Yes, sort of.

**Me** *(recalling)* – It's a good job your shadow's attached to your feet.

**Mr G** – Yes, it's not going anywhere until it rises up and engulfs you.

*(Mr G picks up the halo and extending his arm looks askance at Me through it. Some passing tropical yellow, orange, gold and blue sky-fish fly-swim behind Me to gaze in, but then dart off shooed away by the Almighty Hand. Mr G takes a photo through the halo's luminescent porthole to update Me's file with a recent headshot picture. The Almighty Hand hovers at the side in the form of a boxing-glove fist waiting to throw a punch if Me should be tempted to peek through the halo. Fortunately, Me shows no interest. Mr G staples the photo to the file in such a way as to place a Harry Potter wizard scar on Me's tilted, smiling face)*

**Mr G** – Sometimes it can express itself as wanting to remain hidden or the over love of your 'little monster'!

**Me** *(confidently)* – Mine's very rogue, but totally cute and lovable. Not sure about other people's though! Is my 'LM' any different from my inner deviant and slacker?

**Mr G** – Not too far removed. On a more serious note though… *(throws halo into the bin appraising Me's response)* …The aspects you have to particularly watch out for are the inner tyrant and the inner despiser. Particularly if they're masquerading and acting out as unresolved abuse or childhood damage.

**Me** *(agreeing)* – Doesn't sound at all pleasant.

**Mr G** – No, not very pleasant at all. *(pause)* On a lighter note how goes your inner courtesan and personal junkie these days?

**Me** *(elusively)* – Not sure. Hopefully busy concocting some dubious, yet delicious dish to surprise me with!

**Mr G** *(reading from file)* – Scrupulously unscrupulous, somewhat attendant, strangely assisting whilst also self-serving. That's a bit of a confusing mix.

**Me** *(shrugging)* – Tell me about it!

**Mr G** – It's all to do with the frequencies of your juvenile funky-Monkey and lusty old-goat having to balance with the refining activity and alchemy of the sky Kunda-birds.

**Me** – The raven, the swan, the peacock, the pelican, the phoenix?

**Mr G** – Exactly. Well done!

*(Mr G is so impressed that he passes a gold merit-badge to the Almighty Hand who goes to pin it on Me. Me is horrified at the thought of a merit-badge as it reminds him of his reluctant school prefect-days and his dislike of anything remotely suggestive of 'joining-in', 'system-monitoring' or conformity)*

**Me** *(desperate)* – But not forgetting the cuckoo!

*(Me's face becomes glazed as he executes a rapid, repetitive and rather annoying 'cuckoo-clock' impression peeking between his opening-and-closing hands. Mr G stares intently at Me and instantly rescinds the merit-badge. Pleased at Me's juvenile behaviour, the Almighty Hand does a Roman-arena thumbs-down and gestures for Me to be instantly beheaded doing everybody a favour)*

**Mr G** *(offish)* – Well, apart from needing your head examined I thought you could put it with your disco-medals!

**Me** – Thanks! At least they were real achievements. The other stuff happens and you're left experiencing it whether you like it or not!

**Mr G** – It's called master break-through!

**Me** *(defiant)* – Oh! Sounds as bad as getting your halo.

**Mr G** *(dangerously)* – Gratitude is the best attitudinal approach I think you'll find, however immature you've judged your inner impurities and personal insecurities to be.

**Me** *(begrudging)* – If you really want to give me any type of award it should be for becoming an 'honorary homeless person'.

**Mr G** *(turning a page on the file)* – Well… *(considering)* True. I did see that listed somewhere here too.

**Me** *(sulkily)* – Glad it wasn't overlooked. The rest was just research.

**Mr G** – Ah, the itinerant stance. Very touching helping him and his dog out like that. Any chance you're getting smart-in-the-heart?

**Me** – Doubt it. I'm not particularly smart in anything… except perhaps braver-in-love. More of an enthusiast really.

**Mr G** – Yet you were interested when the true alchemy-of-birds was upon you and the Goddess Kunda came to claim?

**Me** – The search for knowledge and alchemy is another matter entirely!

**Mr G** – True. The laboratory-of-consciousness is an interesting place. *(kindly)* Particularly the phoenix cycle.

**Me** *(intrigued)* – Was that when the new purifying energies met the embers of my dying flame?

**Mr G** – Yes, a form of self-combustion, death, re-ignition all in one.

**Me** – I wish they had taught alchemy at school. In my precarious state I could've blown myself up!

**Mr G** – In a roundabout way they did - at Hogwarts.

**Me** *(musing)* – That whole vibrational-wobble-life-event thing was very difficult. God-awful really!

**Mr G** – God-awful or your awfulness and faults stirred and God-inspired? *(chuckling)* Yet I suppose all that 'aspect conflict' descending at once can feel a bit explosive.

**Me** *(pops up like a jack-in-the-box)* – "Flash Jack ka-boom!" *(Me laughs. Mr G does not)* I know, I know. You end up fighting your better nature and all that jazz. Stop telling me things I already know or asking about things I don't. It could be considered very annoying.

**Mr G** *(momentarily looking volatile)* – Half known, but mainly forgotten! Are you accusing me of not knowing the difference between grandmothers who can and cannot suck eggs?

**Me** *(moodily)* – No.

**Mr G** – The power of the correctly turned question is an almighty key to unlocking certain doors-of-mystery.

**Me** *(quickly)* – I thought those were shut?

**Mr G** – And if I repeat things it's because you could be considered borderline remedial!

**Me** *(twitters nervously)* – Ah, yes! The dis-remembering of self so one can re-member.

**Mr G** *(seriously)* – It's called 'discovery', 'retrieval' and 're-collection'. And if there's any dismembering to be done I'll be the one to do it!

**Me** *(perturbed)* – I get your drift. Go on, I'm listening.

**Mr G** – Until matter becomes finer, sexual chemistry for species-survival has found a wonderful ally in love. The feminine often tries to combine the two whilst the masculine often wants to keep the two apart. *(laughing)* Seed, spawn, begat and be gone! I know I did.

**Me** *(trying to be alert and helpful, but remembering seed dispersal from both sides of the relationship equation - leaving and being left)* – Tell me about it! But I presume that your comment about the masculine and feminine was a bit of an over-generalisation?

**Mr G** – Yes, because I was also referring to inner qualities of masculine and feminine - gods and goddesses, generation and regeneration - sexual themes of fertility, not just sexual identity as you reincarnate as both genders. When overly focused on sexual gender arguments can be equally self-serving and unfair. In Nature, you see, there is no war between the sexes. In Divine Nature the energies love interacting with each other: foreplay, interplay, and after play.

**Me** – Oh, you and your tantra mahamudras.

**Mr G** *(smiling, but serious)* – Sex is a great gift. People should certainly be encouraged to play with their sexual energies! However, any present mistreating of the feminine or of Gaia will not be tolerated.

**Me** – Good, about time!

**Mr G** *(helpfully)* – As for any unwanted offspring of the sexually active young resulting from such early, exciting sexual encounters… Share them and the duties of care. Nature loves a good, socially diverse sprawl. Unfortunately, humanity has got a lot of its laws, attitudes and approaches to living wrong. Heart and sex know best! Right… *(Me sighs)* Dextera!

---

*For the love of diversity, Mother Nature's gene pool is naturally promiscuous and bounteous.*

*Unlike the biological needs of thirst and hunger, which if unfulfilled can lead to death, the sexual urge and procreative drive for life are first of all physical desires, combining physiological, psychological and soul factors.*

*Sex is a touch therapy for expressing love, for fun, for play as pleasurable exploration, and involves the spontaneous magnetic arts of attraction and repulsion. Touch and physical contact are very important to human development.*

*Sex naturally includes certain sacred mysteries: the unconscious 'la petite mort', the fulfilling Tantric 'golden glow' and the eventual Kundalini serpent's rise and flow.*

*Sex is an arena for physical release and emotional sharing as well as the evolution of loving energies.*

*It is a harmonising art. Sex is for sharing and the impregnation of joy. Sexual energy is for healing and to help bring you back to the heart home.*

---

**Me** – Wow! That was a big one! And sex for offspring and children as our re-incarnational roots?

**Mr G** – Bingo Einstein! Well, until you evolve the spirit-matter transportation system. Then you won't need to physically incarnate.

**Me** *(joking)* – What? Jaunt or beam down to the Earth Realms and pop in for a cup-of-tea when you feel like it?

**Mr G** *(smiling)* – Yes, exactly.

**Me** – Oh. I tend to find people are going to do whatever they are going to do and usually that's whatever suits them most at the time.

**Mr G** – Indeed, it is going to be as it is going to be. As for the re-balancing of your personal psycho-sexual-spiritual nature I suppose the old adage rings true…

**Me** *(trying it on)* – What? "You can take a w-horse-arse to water but you can't make him think!" Ba-da-boom! Ba-da-boom!

**Mr G** *(sighs)* – No, that "Energy is the only life". Body and soul are not separate. Everything from source is good until corrupted and wrongly controlled by improper earthly influence. Why? Are your desires, habits and addictions dissimilar from the ordinary adolescent or 'delinquent' rebelling against the conformity of social norms?

**Me** *(bemused)* – Doubt it! But is that why I've not been acting my age?

**Mr G** – Partly catch up with your masculine-feminine imbalances, but your proclivities aren't any different from those caught up in survival from a blinkered society so recently exposed and finally expunged during the convulsing death-of-days?

**Me** *(trying to connect the dots)* – Gaia's Winter exhaust cycle, you mean?

**Mr G** – Yes. Residual ill intent, planetary-invasion and imperial control, long before the Romans and the Colonialists decided to follow suit, were all purged recently from Gaia's soul.

**Me** – A lot of fag ends of discontent then?

**Mr G** – Desires and seeming coping-mechanisms of survival all got mixed up. Do you wish to be releasing more of some kind of unassailable, inner sex-god?

**Me** *(taking a quick swig of absinthe)* – No. I'm not interested in acting-out sex under imperial-command or the role of the rampant emperor! I know his fate. He gets head-butted by some very feminine pigeons, rolled up into a carpet-circle of completion, stuffed in the boot of Thelma-and-Louise's car and driven off to be sat on a bench in a park to watch the birds in bewilderment with a blanket over his knees wondering what on earth happened to him!

**Mr G** *(chuckling)* – Very droll! So, apart from some "late-flowering lust", integration of rising snake energy and the s-s-s-ex-pression of yourself, how goes it?

**Me** *(amused)* – Well, as you put it like that I don't think my sins, sex-gods and earthly appetites are very different from anyone else's really!

**Mr G** – Ah, but this particular life of yours is all about balance and the journey home. Energies like to flow - both ways. High to low. Above. Below. In. Out…

**Me** *(doing the hokey-cokey)* – And shake it all about!

**Mr G** – Precisely! And vice versa. The movers, groovers and shakers all have a certain something, but you have to know 'who you really are' to have universal fun as a divine child.

**Me** *(eagerly)* – And who's that then?

**Mr G** *(regarding Me)* – You tell me.

**Me** *(exasperated)* – Really?

**Mr G** – Try some of your famous summoning-up magic.

**Me** *(sighs and scratches head)* – Well, I now know that I'm a beckoning star cluster gradually experiencing the unfolding all-and-everything.

**Mr G** *(amused)* – Sort of true.

**Me** *(hopelessly clutching at disappearing straws and vanishing castles in the air)* – But other than that, I'm really pretty clueless.

**Mr G** *(helpfully)* – Indeed! That's why I provide the many mysterious symbols and signs along the merry way to help and guide you.

**Me** – I know! It's like being part of the Hardy Boys mystery team.

**Mr G** *(smiling like a recently polished silver-lining)* – They're sort of built in from this side of the cloud-equation before you were born.

**Me** – Er! So… Well?

**Mr G** – I'll give you a clue, Nancy Drew! Who are you in the 'Being Human' stakes?

**Me** *(perking up)* – The TV series? As far as roles go, you mean?

**Mr G** – Yes.

**Me** – Well, I am the ghost living with a werewolf and a vampire.

**Mr G** – A curious, modern but common assorted creature collective. Remember the Three Musketeers?

**Me** – Mickey, Donald and Goofy - all for fun and fun for all! But weren't there four of them?

**Mr G** *(ignoring Me, whilst reading housemate profiles)* – Hmmm! On second thoughts perhaps you're more like the Three Stooges - lost souls familiarising yourselves in amidst the farcical fall-about, yet all the time befriending.

**Me** – It's been quite vaudeville if that's what you mean.

**Mr G** – Still… *(considering, then helpfully)* At least you know where you stand with a vampire! As for the moods of the werewolf… *(tapping file)* Perhaps time for a quick review of your current living situation. So, what have you learnt about your inner nature?

**Me** *(thinking)* – Well, our collective-appetites are all very diverse. In having distinct needs and personal desires to consider, we can't judge and we have to look out for each other in unusual ways.

**Mr G** – So know your own nature, the nature of your appetites and consequently understand your enemies, weak spots and addictions.

**Me** – The blood? The love? The Moon? The doorways?

**Mr G** – The cravings and excess if not all things bright and beautiful! Even more reason to be honest with yourself and with your desires in a collective way. As a spook what did you learn about your tribe?

**Me** – No-one gets left behind, we try to live in a caring, sharing way, but take no prisoners in the name of love and truth!

**Mr G** – It is not one thing, this or that, but all things combined. Strive towards balance, yet there must be no bars to realising your immortality. The altered states are fun when not a habit.

**Me** – For some it's a neuro-hobby or trashed way of life!

**Mr G** – Go tell Bacchus! I'm always dragging him out of the bars, but there's a method to his intoxicating madness. 'Sober' does not always mean 'better'. However, the worship of Bacchus in stuck drunkenness does not help either. Remember, in old time, you all needed to release the Dionysian maniac and the inner desire outlaw at some point.

**Me** – We did?

**Mr G** – Otherwise you remained bound and constricted by human conditioning when you needed to be released and 'twice born'.

**Me** *(rolling his eyes)* – At least.

**Mr G** – The initial impulse for release and to be free of restrictions is a good one. Yet it really *is* all about seeking the spiritual path of return. Dextera!

> *Being 'broken' or 'fixed' is a comparative viewpoint and often regarded and judged from people's own distorted perspective, depending on which side of those two worlds they, seemingly, belong to. Neither are necessarily mine!*
>
> *Go between the altered states with ease, but do not use one realm as an excuse to escape from or not properly inhabit the other.*
>
> *Be time-space-awareness-appropriate.*
>
> *Ultimately, you need to become silent and alert. Let your light body be filled with light.*

**Mr G** – The history of your planet's olden days is not what it seemed, but you're in new time now. It says here *(reading from file)* that you've experienced six or seven rebirths in this life already.

**Me** – Well, if you include dipping underwater in the foaming bath tub with the glug-glug bubble-frogs in pursuit of the Kraken, swimming with the golden quacky ducks to avoid the Sirens…

**Mr G** *(helpfully cutting short)* – No, I don't count those.

**Me** – Oh! Well, that leaves the stumbling initiation dramas and those God-awful Herculean tasks…

**Mr G** *(tickled)* – You never did like cleaning out the Augean stables.

**Me** – The smell of the Stymphalian birds was worst, but I'm much better at toilet duties these days after the capture of the Cretan Bull!

**Mr G** – Indeed! Generally, though, you do your labours with love.

**Me** – Shucks! Just Cinderella services again. *(quickly grabbing at an opportunity for another tick)* Doesn't that deserve a merit of some kind?

**Mr G** *(beaming)* – Well, apart from making you an excellent tea boy, no... It's an artistic, aloof, past-life imbalance you're correcting. Remember, all problems have their merit and worth in the end if they help you find Cloud Nine...

**Me** – Is that some etheric-air cosmic-water thing again?

**Mr G** – Some fly in, some ride in upon foaming white horses, whilst others just glide in upon the cosmic wave like the Silver Surfer. Depends on the magnetic nature of their desire and creative perception. *(staring at Me)* Some I have to tug hard on their angelic-balloon string and see what the cat drags in. Dextera!

> *Desires, like the Hydras-of-old, are there for a good reason. They guard the entrance to your powerful Underworld and help express and transmute the inner drama.*
>
> *Your hero needs to do battle with the world-of-your-self. Fantastic power or hideous release? How else would you value and re-evaluate the experience of awaking the immortal timeless beast?*

**Me** – Cor blimey!

*(the Almighty Hand having slapped the Post-it note to Me's forehead hovers as though to joke-poke Me in the eye. Me peels the Post-it note off his head and sticks it to his burgeoning hip flask. Me decides to take another quick nip)*

**Mr G** – Perhaps not all of your values were previously known to you. Only in experience did they become revealed. You desired a bite of the golden apples of Hesperides.

**Me** *(brightly)* – An apple a day to keep the doctor away! They had "eat me" written all over them.

**Mr G** – Only you took a bite to find one of them poisoned. It was a bioflavonoid-of-love - a secret, healing apple. You 'think' you bit off more than you could chew, and bit yourself in the process rather like my alchemical pet snake here.

*(Mr G draws a misty picture of a snake biting its own tail and places it around Me's neck and shoulders. Demonstratively, the snake starts to constrict as it slowly engulfs itself. Me shrugs to try and dislodge the snake which now tightens around his neck and throat in its endless gulping coil)*

**Mr G** – The ouroboric-serpent bites its own tail to release poison that heals itself into wholeness. It was for your own self-healing, encompassing your own and others personal relationship karma until you got the choke... I mean joke.

**Me** *(restricted, breathless)* – Oh! I see...

*(the Almighty Hand slaps against an invisible hand. There is a loud thunderclap 'booming!' sound and the snake disappears)*

**Mr G** – The world is caught up in the current renewal of creational time. In the West, most ordinary humans had no tribal culture to connect to or possessed no natural environment to relate to, so some created their own spiritual clans.

**Me** – The dancing warriors?

**Mr G** – The gallivants and gadabouts were all seeking the lost harmonic chord that raises you up. It was released recently at the Moon conclave of space cadets, peace warriors and planetary wizards.

**Me** – Sounds very timely and magical!

**Mr G** – Time's a great healer if you allow it.

**Me** – I thought love was the great healer?

**Mr G** – Yes, but can you experience love without space and time?

**Me** *(apologetic)* – They are both so vast and awesome, but I'm afraid it's all a little abstract and incomprehensible to me.

**Mr G** – Welcome to my world - the world of essential being.

**Me** *(helpfully)* – I'm getting better within my own awareness and the realisation of the great inter-connectedness if that's of any use.

**Mr G** – But not forgetting your singularity. Perhaps that's why you're sat here presently speaking to me?

**Me** *(trying to grasp the bigger picture)* – Is there much difference between us all?

**Mr G** – Yes and no. There's not much difference between your seeking and anyone else's if that's what you are asking. It's just that everyone's at different points of the journey.

**Me** – Struggling to get through the sieve of time?

**Mr G** – That's why so much crumbles about you. Fast change is best, so shake yourself loose, salvage yourself and your useful antiquity, and work with what you've got rather than bemoaning your falling lot. *(innocently)* It's not that I'm asking you to build an ark or anything!

**Me** *(suspiciously)* – That's a relief.

**Mr G** – Let go of the chaff and let the seed within do its developing.

**Me** – Collective wheat or individual star?

**Mr G** – It's difficult to tell from where I sit, as there are so many of you running about these days.

**Me** – I know, we really do need to bring the population down.

**Mr G** – As a collective of one type of species-consciousness it's easier for me to glean energy en masse, but everyone has to do it for themselves individually. Each has their own personal string. That's why I sent the universal farmer down a few years ago.

**Me** *(excitedly remembering one of his favourite childhood shows)* – Oh, oh, Farmer Barleymow! To reap and sow? *(Me starts humming the theme tune and practises doing 'the walk')*

**Mr G** *(laughing)* – Less Bod, more odds bodkins really! But through the cloud-mist I keep my eye out for those souls with exploding auras, the ones filled with fireworks like pollinating sky-blooms.

**Me** *(hitting the side of his head with the heel of his hand)* – Of course! The propulsion and pollination of ideas into the sky-mind alerts the cloud-mind that we're ready.

**Mr G** – It's all about cross-fertilisation. The human aura is both masculine and feminine.

**Me** – Oh! Is that the day-mind and the night-mind?

**Mr G** – More of the gay-mind and fright-mind with you!

**Me** – Charming!

**Mr G** – Dextera!

> *The physical body earths the sexual characteristics.*
> *Emotions are by their nature bi-sexual to allow for the*
> *myriad types of personal inter-relationships.*
>
> *On Earth, rational and seemingly irrational aspects of*
> *the mind are governed by the Sun-Moon energies. Each of*
> *Gaia's hemispheres, East and West, contain unique*
> *energies that need to connect and blend.*
>
> *Holographically, each one of you is attached by energy-*
> *threads through all your many simultaneous selves, the*
> *Light Worlds and trans-migratory species back to the*
> *Monad through me. Once triggered, your soul starts*
> *sending beams that are recognized by their colour back*
> *here to your slumbering spirit self.*
>
> *Then you awake.*

**Me** – So, once though the thorny thicket, having met a dragon or two, you wake up your sleeping princess with a kiss from your dashing hero?

**Mr G** – Part of the epic-voyage of the romantic-heart. Then you can partake consciously of the dream.

**Me** – I see… I think?

**Mr G** – All in the journeying. Good souls. Bad souls. Ah! Souls…

**Me** *(giggling, but trying to contain himself)* – Reciprocally "tedious or charming", do-able or not, accordingly!

**Mr G** *(unimpressed)* – You're all just risible-delights to me. Some are more afraid than others to fly high into the altitudes of love and seeming pure madness. Until that time, you're all amusing energy balls running around getting the hang of it.

**Me** *(containing himself)* – You would have to say that wouldn't you? Handfuls I'm sure!

**Mr G** – You're not the leanest of societies, yet apart from the unnecessary neurosis, the tendency towards self-destruct and the splintered societal violence, you don't live in bad times. And you're not as noisome as some of Gaia's early offspring, so be grateful. Those on the destructive dark path take longer to come back to full absorption, but they will. What else is there to do? Where else is there to go? Where on Earth are you trying to get?

**Me** *(shrugs shoulders)* – I don't know.

**Mr G** *(ever helpful)* – Well, the answer is Nowhere.

**Me** – Oh! I remember a song about that road.

**Mr G** – Very enjoyable.

**Me** – But Nowhere? Where's that?

**Mr G** – Precisely where you are.

**Me** – Oh! That's handy.

**Mr G** – What I really mean is non-where. Beyond space and time. The answer of course is right here, right now.

**Me** – Back to beingness, I see. I *am* trying to become more of the 'be' in 'being' within the quantum streaming.

**Mr G** – Ah yes, the eternal you.

**Me** – So, this is-ness business? Is that suchness or muchness?

**Mr G** – Ah, well. As that's a trick mind-question you can figure it out for yourself. Remember that the solar, galactic and cosmic systems are impersonal. Plus the universal Logos still keeps begetting. You experience it as constructive light interference on the hierarchically structured bubble-verse. Imagine?

**Me** *(does not really comprehend, but is willing to try it on for a laugh so makes a 'boing' noise as he hits the side of his head again. The Almighty Hand wishes he could join in)* – Boing! So, at a stretch and with the rule of light inflation...

**Mr G** *(playing along)* – 15 orders of magnitude larger than the observable universe...

**Me** *(struggling bravely)* – Being 93,000,000,000 light years in diameter...

**Mr G** – Divided by the current 17 known initiations...

**Me** – Over how many lives?

**Mr G** – 8,400,000 lives, but not forgetting to carry the universal 8 which is the average amount of lives people have to scrap before they get an inkling of The Way of the cosmic path...

**Me** *(eagerly)* – And not forgetting to divide by the current multiverse degradation...

**Mr G** – You're getting good at this. Remember there are 72-dimensional energies interplaying within the 18-dimensional universe responding to the 13 galactic tones. So in total...

**Me** *(exhausted)* – That leaves quite a lot for the head to get around.

*(the Almighty Hand scratches Me's head like a befuddled Laurel whilst Me does a Hardy impression, "Well, here's another nice mess you've gotten me into!")*

**Mr G** *(laughing)* – Not the head, nincompoop... the heart! But I appreciate the effort and at least you're getting slightly more entertaining.

**Me** *(crest-fallen)* – Oh, it's all too difficult!

**Mr G** – Life is there to serve the heart-you in whatever way suits the soul-spirit-you best. Love yourself more and give yourself everything love would. *(beaming ridiculously brightly so as to fill the cloud with dazzle)* Remember, there are a billion blazing paths of return, but only one source.

**Me** – For better or worse, we struggle to come home. I suppose there's a little bit of naughty and wicked in us all?

**Mr G** – In the current conflict of your middle-aged, situational-comedy, yes! Most people do this in their teens.

**Me** – Oh… So I'm a late developer?

**Mr G** – Yes, which means you've got it all ahead of you now. There is a lot of altruism, fear, selfishness and a whole host of yo-yoing tensions to help sort the war of your opposites out. Otherwise there would be no choice, no intricacy and no struggle.

**Me** *(exhausted by the thought)* – It's all a bit exhausting.

**Mr G** – Human society divided the virtues and the vices whereas they co-exist as transmutable energy packages. But how can you explain the non-dualistic outlook to others who are dualistic?

**Me** – Er?

**Mr G** *(helpfully)* – The expression of the Yin and Yang in harmonious completion. Unfortunately, the endless splintering of the soul and different aspects of self cause difficulties for some.

**Me** – So many realms to hide within and explore I suppose?

**Mr G** – In the end you need to find your self.

**Me** – Wherever we've put it…

**Mr G** *(smiling)* – Then understand your self.

**Me** – Even though each one of us is same-different?

**Mr G** – Precisely! Then retrieve it. Why do you ask? *(brightly, enquiringly)* Have you been running amok with diabolical intentions and leftover guilty remains?

**Me** – Touché! But I haven't done anything wrong, have I? Perhaps a bit feral and late in catching up on some way-laid impropriety, but my inner urchin likes scuffing around cities getting up to no-good.

**Mr G** – And you're not quite ready to give it all up and unsure as to what's next! I'm not PC Plod, but there are many ways to tame your inner ruffian. Perhaps it *is* time to put away some of the more childish things? *(the Almighty Hand prods at Me's hip flask and snuff pouch)* It's your choice, but know that it has to come from you. Unwilling sacrifice is such a whining bore!

*(Me ponders and is silent. In the encouragement of freethinking and not wishing to tell Me what to do, Mr G continues…)*

**Mr G** – Anyhow, back to your Review. *(taps file and turns page)* Next section: Future Plans - hopes, fears and sweet dreams. *(the Almighty Hand leafs through Me's file and hands Mr G a sheet of paper)* Are you ready for the next big release?

**Me** – Is that a trick question?

**Mr G** – No.

**Me** – Then probably not. I seldom am.

**Mr G** – Well, do you want it or not?

**Me** *(considering)* – Is it monstrous or nice?

**Mr G** – That's for you to decide afterwards.

**Me** *(musing)* – Well! I thought it would be great if I could release my inner playboy millionaire.

**Mr G** – Ah! Desire for the mobility of the modern, international rich?

**Me** – Yes please!

**Mr G** – Life as a leisurely luxury cruise?

**Me** – Too right!

**Mr G** – You and everyone else! Get in line.

**Me** *(petulant and annoying)* – Ooh! Not even a little? I haven't experienced that yet and I'm sure it would help me gain my balance in the greater scheme of things.

**Mr G** *(sighs, giving in)* – You mean like Hefner or Bond I suppose?

**Me** *(perking up)* – Sort of Bond, but without the killing if it can be helped. More the love of art and leisure with a twist of excitement.

**Mr G** – *(transforming into Sean Connery)* "My name is Bond. James Bond…" *(pause, then transforming into the real James Bond)* "Ornithologist and writer".

**Me** – You were dying to do that!

**Mr G** *(grinning)* – So you want to be a playboy millionaire with the intrigue of a super-hero or a high-living spy. Is that right?

**Me** – A swimming pool. A tennis court. A helicopter. Cocktails.

**Mr G** – I didn't think you'd like a life so shaken or stirred.

**Me** *(bravely swirls his hip flask and takes a swig of absinthe)* – No! Let the good times rock-'n'-roll.

**Mr G** *(peering intently)* – Hhm… Something to fulfil your need for thrills and for sofas.

**Me** *(eagerly)* – Yup! Speed and slowness somehow combined.

**Mr G** – By the sounds of it you just need to get out a little bit more.

**Me** – True. I *have* been stuck indoors the past 2 years.

**Mr G** – Very imprisoning in some ways, but I'm afraid that's what writers do. Anyway, I thought you wanted to work towards a more family life? *(writes on file, 'Seemingly wants it all, doesn't know yet that he can't')* Best be yourself. Don't try to emulate.

**Me** – We're all very impressionable down here.

**Mr G** – Yes, all running around seeking some kind of strange, mutually reassuring, instant gratification. Dextera!

> *Mimicking is good for learning, but it depends under whose sphere of influence you are choosing to select from.*
>
> *Social comparisons, self-defeating cognitions and maladaptive ideologies do not help the emotional wealth of a person, societal group or the spirit of a nation.*
>
> *Particularly damaging is all the cosmetics-cult and body image pressure, especially for women and the young.*

**Me** *(reading the note)* – Fair enough. And as we're on the subject of family life and homes, can I have two or three?

**Mr G** – Children or homes?

**Me** – Homes of course.

**Mr G** – Wanting to lay claim?

**Me** – Yes please. How about one in the city and one by the sea?

**Mr G** *(from an overhead curl-of-cloud the Almighty Hand pulls down a location map and circles four places)* – Broadstairs, Brighton, Bognor or Bermuda?

**Me** – Oh! Are they the best locations for a world hero or super spy? I don't want to get too cold or lost. I was thinking somewhere warmer on the Med with a yacht.

**Mr G** – Were you now! *(the Almighty Hand unfastens the map that quickly snap rolls and releases, disappearing back into the Cloud-Office ceiling)*

**Me** – Yes, so I can head south for the winter like the swallows!

**Mr G** – You do know how to get on my better side when you talk about birds. *(Me smiles and takes mental note of useful titbit)* Actually, I was going to introduce the 'golden joker' card to your life-mix next. I can only add what's permissible on your file to your current life.

**Me** – Oh! I thought you could do anything. You know, think and act outside the box.

**Mr G** – I can. It's just that you can't.

**Me** *(quickly)* – 'Yet'.

**Mr G** – Sorry?

**Me** – You mean I can't 'yet'.

**Mr G** – Oh, I see what you mean. True, but you're always going to be on the receiving end in catch-up. I'm merely checking that you're ready to deal with some of the finer detail of your soul contract as well as the connected thinking-and-doing required to switch on your blueprint of future possibilities.

**Me** – If that 'golden joker' card means I get to release my inner magician that could be fun. Does it come with any super powers?

**Mr G** – It does, but I thought that miracles and the incredible were part of your daily lot anyway?

**Me** – Is that the same as labours, tasks, trials and ordeals?

**Mr G** – The implausibly improbable, not your routine chores.

**Me** – If it's rods for backs… *(Me pauses whilst he takes a pinch of snuff for each nostril)* I don't do those. Isn't there some more of the good stuff?

**Mr G** *(slightly stunned)* – That was the good stuff. You have to be totally unprepared for something as big as that. Now the vision, integrity and intention can arise. The universal synchronometer *is* busy building and aligning the collective energies as we speak.

**Me** *(trying to remember the recent calendar advances)* – Is that part of the new 13 Moon-cycle, radial-ratio clock?

**Mr G** *(impressed, but now with a disinclination to merit)* – Yes, the new synchronometer is slowly generating and regulating the necessary natural energies. Love is time-released! You should be preparing to get good and ready, strong enough for the responsibility of re-entering the system on your own spiritual terms.

**Me** *(flicking his fingers as though emanating magic)* – Does it come with the ability to cast spells and hex?

**Mr G** – You mean alter the laws of physics and the probability lines?

**Me** – Yes, hocus pocus and a spot of telekinesis?

**Mr G** – So you can turn light switches off so you don't have to get out of bed after reading?

**Me** – Yeah, cool…

**Mr G** – Couldn't you just get a reading lamp?

**Me** *(oblivious, listing)* – Or change TV channels from the sofa. Or even better, command the phasing of traffic lights so you can have universal road flow. Oh, and some instant teleportation wouldn't go amiss when you're over-tired and want to be instantly home in bed.

**Mr G** – Like a jaunt belt?

**Me** – Fantastic! Or the power of camouflage.

**Mr G** – Ah, your inner chameleon. The power of blending in and not being seen.

**Me** – Or a spot of walking through walls.

**Mr G** – Hm! The party tricks. Not sure about those. There's some electro-magnetic vortex and purple light-stuff I could share with you if used for universal good.

**Me** – Neato Magneto! Does it come with an invisibility cloak?

**Mr G** – For stealth I suggest you use the infrared spectrum, as the purples can become a bit radioactive and leave a trace.

**Me** – Couldn't I just borrow your cloak?

**Mr G** – No. What I really want to talk about is your own personal development and stuckness. Your individual review and appraisal rather than gifts and the possible needs of others.

**Me** – Oh!

**Mr G** – More inventive solutions to living in relation to your own natural abilities. You know, love, encouragement and mutual admiration - those things that spirit and nature do best.

**Me** – Okay, I suppose. You're the boss.

**Mr G** – Right. *(tapping file)* Brief discussion of your relationship area.

**Me** – You mean my familiar and partner in crime?

**Mr G** – Yes, the escapades of the bat-brained and bird-minded. When you work as a team you're quite the dynamic duo: Ping and Pong, exuberance and exacerbation, live and let live.

**Me** *(proudly)* – The Impossibles - that's us!

**Mr G** *(smiling)* – Remember, whilst love is the best problem to have, all problems have roots. Sometimes your strands become twisted with misunderstanding and you have to unkink them.

**Me** – Oh!

**Mr G** – The answer lies in smooth compromise, cosmic understanding, and knowing that suffering has three roots: ignorance, attachment and aversion.

**Me** *(considering)* – Er… Our problems are probably a mixture plus a bit of avoidance, or is that a sub-root of aversion?

**Mr G** – A poultice for the patient, please! You're mentally breaking things down instead of re-constituting beingness back into holism.

**Me** – Sorry, old habits die hard.

**Mr G** – Reductive, analytical dissection and criticism are still over-prevalent mind-crimes of western culture, as they are not fully engaged with the heart. That's where love-wisdom and I come in.

*(Mr G beams such a huge, sun-shiny type of smile that golden rays bounce off the shimmering Cloud-Office silver walls, which now glisten with extra 'zing'. Me feels momentarily uplifted into a new way of being)*

**Me** *(appreciative)* – Oh! That was nice. Thank you. Anyway, my problem's not me, but him.

**Mr G** – Really? I find that hard to believe. Are you sure it's not an excuse for non-adaptation of the mind to relate to the heart?

**Me** *(suddenly reconsidering everything)* – Er… In that light you might be right. Have I got all of my perceptions wrong?

**Mr G** – Not all, but see it as an opportunity to become more loving, discovering new ways to communicate and approach each other.

**Me** *(humbly)* – Which can only be a good thing. Apologies. I didn't mean it to sound like an excuse.

*(Me, forgetting Mr G has x-ray vision, puts up a mental cloud-shield whilst reprimanding himself in an attempt to pull things together. 'Listen more. Talk less. Think before speaking. Don't look out of the window. Be polite. Try to be more interesting in what you say and take interest in others.' Me's thoughts start to drift. 'Perhaps a monastic life of silence and meditative retreat would have been better after all, but where's the shopping and sex in that!' Mr G, instantly seeing through Me, writes on the file, 'Amateur attempt at cloud-blocking - basic skill level. Somewhat disappointing.' The Cloud-Office becomes a little soggier and duller. Meanwhile, the diligent Almighty Hand wags a finger at Me and starts to peel away the finer layers of mist that have gathered around Me's mental body. Using his swirling index finger, the Almighty Hand collects the cobwebs and the greyer cloud drapes like candyfloss. Old and dusty words like 'bad listener', 'unclear communicator' and 'mental chatterbox' all clump together in a sticky mess. Mr G peruses these amassed thoughts by stabbing them with a sharp pencil and holding them up to the light shining through the Cloud-Office window. Adroitly, he rubs them out with a sunshine gold eraser. Afterwards Mr G writes a series of notes on Me's file whilst mumbling a word that could be 'reprobate', 'evaporate' or 'disintegrate'. Mr G draws a large question mark over the whole 'Relationship Review' page whilst adding the words, 'unfathomable, but fun… must be the junk and disorderly one of the lateral Taijitu lot')*

**Mr G** *(getting back to business)* – Now, obfuscating really won't help! It merely veils your problem.

**Me** *(deflated)* – Oh!

**Mr G** *(helpfully)* – Which is?

**Me** *(brightening to any offer of help)* – Presently, their stuckness and inability to find solutions.

**Mr G** – Ah! The problem of problems and how to manage and help with other people's pain? Hm! *(rolling his eyes)* Sounds all too familiar, but it's always tough for the nearest and dearest.

**Me** – I know *You* know, but I find it hard to cope with other people's inability to cope. Dealing with emotional delay, catch-up, taking flack, stressing over the stress of it all which, when combined with the relentless 'ongoingness' of life, laundry and other household activities, sometimes puts me into a role I'm not sure I always want.

**Mr G** – Ah, a woman's work! That merits more than a tick. Dextera! *(the Almighty Hand graciously presses a gold star onto Me's file)*

**Me** – And a role that I don't know whether helps or hinders.

**Mr G** – An effective enabler-disabler, you mean? Your own 'aspect conflict' has finished, but you're still inclined to sort other people's stuff out.

**Me** *(nodding)* – Align, fix or heal it if I can.

**Mr G** – Recognising it is the first step, but are you absorbing, compensating or correcting? *(Me silently considers. Mr G helpfully adds)* Does he have a backlog or have you been mollycoddling?

**Me** – Not sure. Is that about my power-of-sponge or my blunt-sword kind-of-a-thing?

**Mr G** *(smiling empathetically)* – Perhaps now's a good time for you to retrieve your halo and consider its implications. *(Me mock-scowls, but does not move to pick it up)* I'm sure it's all permissible in the fine print.

**Me** – Oh, the tit-for-tat, dog-and-cat, blatant disregard!

**Mr G** – The allowable Mr and Mrs Smith? How very Hitchcockian!

**Me** *(confused)* – Alfred or Wild Bill?

**Mr G** – More handcuffed-lovers, written in the stars, attempting their death defying acts of love.

**Me** – Two Toms tied together by the tail you mean!

**Mr G** *(laughing)* – Desire is stronger than reason and there's certainly no reasoning with cats. The challenge area is that your wild child and inner gypsy simply won't be told!

**Me** *(lamenting)* – And I'm not as good at lifting others up as you are.

**Mr G** – Nobody's as good as me, but you're getting better. Another action point! *(pleased, the Almighty Hand writes a note on Me's file 'to-do' list as Mr G dictates: 'More practice on love, kind-heartedness and understanding required')* But familiars such as yours are an essential rogue element. They have to be. Bewildering, but magically independent.

**Me** – Daft as a brush you mean!

**Mr G** – And a great test for patience! *(pause)* Talking of which, how is yours going?

**Me** *(suspicious, not wanting to add anything further to the 'emotional to-do' list, whilst trying to avoid being tested on his least favourite subject)* – Okay. Slowly getting better…

**Mr G** – Remember, it's a reciprocal system. That which you exact from me, which I might say is considerable time, love, tolerance and patience, you can utilise for others. Yet, I do notice that you have been in a detached, housework, self-preservation space recently.

**Me** – I have to when others' madness all gets too much. Survival instinct kicks in. I'm fine, but thanks for asking.

**Mr G** – Someone has to absorb the flack and fall-out, and better you than them. Mopping up amateur magic spills is a wizard's task.

**Me** *(considering)* – Perhaps that's one of my better superpowers?

**Mr G** – But you do have a tendency to look at the rest of the world as if they were you. Button pressing, limiting boundaries, and self-sufficiency aside, it's your trouble with triangles again.

**Me** – Is it? *(scratching head, but not wanting to know)* But what can you do when people are so far out to sea?

**Mr G** – You have to be in order to find me. It's the soul's attempt to cross the cosmic waters to reach the celestial shore.

**Me** – Sink or swim - another case of "not waving, but drowning"?

**Mr G** – And them not understanding why you hadn't rescued them.

**Me** – It's a bit like the Owl and the Pussycat recovering the dream?

**Mr G** *(laughing)* – Yes. It was a similar *green* boat-predicament that they found themselves in, but you take it in turns to scupper and bail. For a moment, let's concentrate on your own learning. Part of your trouble is that you don't want to let people down which is difficult because sometimes you have to. *(smiling helpfully)* More practice?

**Me** *(despairing)* – No, not particularly! I hate letting people down.

**Mr G** *(cheerfully tapping file)* – And rarely do.

**Me** – But I don't want to be stuck in a parent role either.

**Mr G** – Particularly not of the critical kind. You've worked very hard to rid yourself of that aspect.

*(putting a tick on Me's file, Mr G chuckles to himself and does an Eric Cartman impression, "How dare they disrespect my authority!")*

**Me** – People are always asking and not listening.

**Mr G** *(exasperated and muttering to himself, 'No shit, Sherlock! Go figure!')* – Well, there you go. Just remember that the fruits of the Poison Tree lead to the destructive states. Got that?

**Me** – Er! *(the Almighty Hand helpfully draws a diagram on a Post-it note and hands it to Me)* And the fruits have roots. Gotcha.

**Mr G** – Meanwhile, on a more personal note, I want to discuss the use of your invisible energy Light Wings…

**Me** *(interrupting)* – You mean bat, bird, or angel? They seem to transform with the different phases of the day.

**Mr G** *(continuing)* – However you see them, put them to better purpose rather than standing around aimlessly staring into space.

**Me** – You mean stop being a tit-in-a-trance in front of a slot machine?

**Mr G** – One contained expression of the gregarious you! Mindless activity and Darwinian dumbness are useful if meaningfully directed.

**Me** – I certainly have a lot of it.

**Mr G** *(mutters to himself, 'Oh! The want of a proper education, but I do choose them!')* – What can I say? Softly, softly, catchy monkey. *(Me says nothing.)* Yet going beyond the current would-be espionage of your banana-brained street urchin and the Tuinal of your bandito native-youth, I must admit you *are* one of my favourite blockheads.

*(the Almighty Hand rapidly taps Me on the head like a woodpecker tap. A hollow sound echoes through the room)*

**Me** *(perkily)* – Oh! Does that mean I'm going to be a real boy soon?

**Mr G** *(smiling)* – That depends on whether or not you pass this review or are put on extended probation. Once you're off Pleasure Island you'll have no strings.

**Me** *(does Superman impression)* – "Up, up and away!"

**Mr G** – Indeed! Into the engulfing cosmic darkness - the final frontiers of yourself and the mysterious beginning of the galactic dynamic. To achieve this requires some mode of transportation…

**Me** – Like a Bat-mobile or a cape-of-steel?

**Mr G** – Something to take you over the rainbow like your 'Light Wings' or a 'vortex event' if your wings haven't been activated yet.

**Me** – "To infinity… and beyond!"

**Mr G** *(correcting)* – From Here to Eternity and beyond.

**Me** – Like Atom Ant or Secret Squirrel.

**Mr G** *(considering)* – Invisible ink with stealth? Hmmm! Sounds more Squiddly Diddly than anything else.

*(impressed by Mr G's knowledge of fascinating creatures and superheroes, Me considers offering Mr G a merit-badge of some sort. On hearing a subliminal, 'No thanks', Me decides against it)*

**Mr G** – And remember there are many different avenues of life to explore and enjoy rather than being tied-down to work or taped-up with the bureaucracy of it all, like your last few jobs.

**Me** – Less A4 paperwork, photocopying, systems management and more adventure and love?

**Mr G** – I think that about sums it up. More me. Less you. Now, *(flicking through file)* Brazil wasn't it?

**Me** – Yup! Name, nut, country and coffee.

**Mr G** – 'Nut by name, nut by nature.' Was that a catchphrase?

**Me** – Tough to crack, but worth the effort I hope.

**Mr G** – Yes, but I saw you giving one of the Masters a bit of trouble.

**Me** *(remorseful)* – Sorry about that. Please apologise to her.

**Mr G** – Winning against a Master!

**Me** – Not so proud of that.

**Mr G** – They were only trying to help. It was for your own good.

**Me** – Yeah, I get that now!

**Mr G** – A surrendering of will…

**Me** – And an over-identified ego thing. It was a bit tricky *(pretends to draw out a light sabre and practise thrust and parry, Vwomm! Vwomm!)* She should have tried more koala cuddles than battling wills!

**Mr G** – That's not her style or what was required at the time.

**Me** – I know, I'm sorry. What was I supposed to do? I bumped into her by accident and it took me by surprise. Anyhow, *(changing tack slightly)* I noticed in the banana climb there were a significant number of masters helping people out at present.

**Mr G** – Optimus Prime, Prime Merlinian and the Unnamed Wizard Number 3 are all facilitating the current descent of pure madness.

**Me** – That Merlin sure does get everywhere!

**Mr G** – His ubiquitous Welsh Magic, alchemical-influence and resonance are certainly helping souls to cross the cosmic waters.

**Me** – And not forgetting all the wonderful hugging-Mothers.

**Mr G** – Absolutely, but when I was referring to Brazil I was going to mention that lovely film.

**Me** *(touchy)* – Oh! So not about me.

**Mr G** – Not everything is. Strangely, it mirrored your eventual escape from the evil clutches of paperwork, but gives us a chance to review the next section - Previous Work and Leftover Harm.

**Me** – Oh, *that* damage!

**Mr G** – I've not really spoken to you since the fallout from your last job. You performed some good work. It brought out the teacher in you and earthed you, yet managerially it didn't do much for your auric colour scheme. I did warn you it would have a bad outcome.

**Me** *(agreeing)* – You did, but it was a truly unpleasant ending! Was it really necessary?

**Mr G** – It had to be emphatic to get you out of there, but at least you got a chance to look at life from both sides of the human-consciousness coin.

**Me** – Ah! Well, that new crowd wasn't really me in the end. I was treated badly and they were rather unpleasant.

**Mr G** *(reading from the 'incident' file)* – Not up front in their dealings?

**Me** – Hardly above board! It was all about oppression and survival.

**Mr G** – Tricks-of-the-trade put to cutthroat advantage and ruthless pursuit. All part of the ongoing austerity squeeze endorsed by insidious, fiscally minded governments and management. Even some of the charitable institutions are at it.

**Me** – Terrible onslaught. They had a lot of people over the barrel.

**Mr G** – Professionalism as a veneer to social bullying and vandalism? That kind of culture only leads to victimisation and reprisal.

**Me** – The feeling of acrimony it created seemed pretty extreme.

**Mr G** – Of course. The last battlefield of divorce is often like that and "Nobody expects the Spanish Inquisition!"

**Me** – They knew what they were doing.

**Mr G** – Yet animosity helps separate people, which is sometimes necessary when extricating the different players.

**Me** – It was all very Machiavellian.

**Mr G** *(peering at Me)* – Not something you're particularly skilled in?

**Me** *(joking)* – Lack of parental skills in my childhood, I presume!

**Mr G** *(smiling)* – Perhaps you were a little naïve. You're either taught or have to read the right tactical books. More homework?

**Me** – No thanks. The Art of War was enough. Those situations are tricky, riling and bamboozling.

**Mr G** – Ultimately it freed you from the race of rats, slaves and ogres. It says here *(tapping Me's personal file)* that you could have taken them out, lined them all up and shot them!

**Me** – Well, figuratively speaking. It was very unjust and vexing.

**Mr G** – Gruelling, but it brought out your warrior-spirit even if you did lose your sense of humour. *(Me 'hmphs!' but says nothing)* And I presume with no thanks? *(peering intently)* The temerity of *those* people.

**Me** – Ambitious and ruthless. And me…

**Mr G** *(sympathetically)* – Poor you.

**Me** – And Me, left trying to point out to them…

**Mr G** *(nodding)* – Wicked them.

**Me** – I know, but I'm glad you understand. It was all very horrible.

**Mr G** – And far from the renaissance you had hoped for. Violence begets violence and its escalation, and likewise fear only begets betrayal. Their "Rule of Wrong" established a "Felony Tree" - thus your consequent desperate need to escape. *(smiling)* At least you got to practice your glorious 'hard done by' expression.

**Me** *(frowning, Me places his chin on his hand and slumps his demeanour into his favourite 'not again', 'fed-up' pose)* – I see. Thanks.

**Mr G** *(brightly)* – Yet ultimately you were forced to artistic freedom by 'letting go, letting God'. Now, in our conversational chat, we can explore this particular warrior-wound and give voice to those who have experienced similar things.

**Me** – Oh, like the spreading of communal hope and support?

**Mr G** – In this instance, more about approaches to change and ending personal suffering than comfort and joy. But all can now tap into the collective spiritual latency for healing and love. You fought valiantly so can be proud as well as disappointed, but remember ongoing happiness requires constant adjustment.

**Me** *(thoughtfully)* – What else could I do? I was so unhappy, but defeat is so defeating.

**Mr G** – Only if you let it. This is more about balancing righteous truth and compassionate regard toward personal misfortune than too much empathy and sympathy for your own or others' pain. Somehow yours became all wrapped up in a revenge of the Were-Rabbit type of thing.

**Me** – Confound it. Was I framed?

**Mr G** – Certain of society's structures and people's personal caught-up situations can be very imprisoning and frustrating, and events can lead to thoughts of revenge.

**Me** *(dissatisfied)* – I get that, but… Well…

**Mr G** – It's more important to end the contract, let go of the thought form and conclude your own suffering, then get on with your life.

**Me** *(sighs)* – True, but with the usual 100% hindsight I am so much better off being out of that situation.

**Mr G** *(tutting)* – Oh! So at last you reach that conclusion. I am glad.

**Me** – I tend to suffer in silence…

**Mr G** – And drag things out, but the rage of your inner volcano needed venting.

**Me** – It did become a bit Snoopy/Red Baron…

**Mr G** *(cheerily)* – Ah! The dogs-of-war. Fighting against injustice…

**Me** – In the end I gave up caring for Lent.

**Mr G** *(amused)* – I noticed that. It was an unfortunate management combination that you experienced as a triumvirate of hostility.

**Me** – Between you and me it was set up as a bit of a bitch fight.

**Mr G** *(nodding)* – Unprofessional, but true. But at least your sleeping hero got to fight a triple-headed Hydra. *(Mr G puts a tick on Me's file)*

**Me** – Thanks! They were very severe and fierce.

**Mr G** – What were their final cognomina?

**Me** – There were several bandied about. The Terror. Psycho-Nutter. Eek. Squeak. The Terrier. The Old Dragon.

**Mr G** – True, something canine was exposed and sometimes you do need to fight fire with fire.

**Me** – Another case of bulldogs and lipstick, but this time without the lipstick. Frightening.

**Mr G** *(wanting to tick a box)* – So, was it a Pylraster 243, a Task Master disguised as activity leader or a great, big Tyrannical Monster?

**Me** *(considering)* – More of a T-Rex with the snappy attitude of a Velociraptor and a fire-breather, but Godzilla by any other name.

**Mr G** *(pleased, ticking a box)* – They can be very ruthless and predatory, but demonstrative offspring of the Demon Spawn often are.

**Me** – I suppose it was just another normal day for you orbiting the dark side of 'The Office' looking on?

**Mr G** – True. A lot of management went over to the dark side in the name of fiscal management and severity cuts. Part of the temporary dominance of aggressive and ambitiously cruel management teams around the world.

**Me** – There certainly was a disturbance in the Force. Unfortunately, I couldn't get out and make it to the Dagobah System in time! Couldn't you have sent the Rebel Alliance in?

**Mr G** *(serious)* – Why? Were they secretly shielding a death star?

**Me** – Possibly. It was all very insidious, brutal and smug. On one level I could only feel sorry for them. I mean what had happened in their past that they hadn't resolved to become like that?

**Mr G** *(tapping a series of other files)* – I think you'll find it was unresolved sexual control and mother issues combined with some displaced, ancestral persecutory complexes.

**Me** – It certainly was worse than the attack of the killer tomatoes!

**Mr G** – They certainly had combative personalities, which resulted in some illegal and unprofessional practices.

**Me** – It was like the invasion of the annihilating nuns.

**Mr G** *(amused)* – Ill-treatment plus a very command and control style of management.

**Me** – Abrasive and positively prosecutory!

**Mr G** – It certainly was a collection of horrible experiences from aggressive, insular, controlling women.

**Me** – You mean a cunning clutch of hutched, bunny stunts?

**Mr G** *(laughing)* – Indeed! It says here *(tapping file)* that you often produce your best when you need it most. Quite the fishwife. Well done!

**Me** *(trying to read his file upside down)* – I tried my worst, but inspiration from desperation is not my preferred modus operandi.

**Mr G** – Mine neither, but you should be glad you weren't up against "Hypno-Toad" or Pixie-Slug again.

**Me** *(sighing as he considers previous nemesis toads and bullying trolls)* – True. Those were difficult days too.

**Mr G** – Well, you'll be pleased to know that there are a lot of slaves across the world like you rising at this point.

**Me** *(holding up a pretend sword-of-truth forged from his unfortunate shackles-of-experience)* – Excelsior!

**Mr G** – You kept chanting that song title like a mantra. What was it?

**Me** *(quoting)* – "Be good or be gone." Yes, I drew a line in the sand.

**Mr G** – In the closing tussle it was a combination of game playing, towing the party line, being micro-managed and following the draconian dread or feel the full force of the punitive whip!

**Me** – Sounds terribly political when you put it like that.

**Mr G** – Unfortunately, it was "game over" for a lot of people and Compassion has taken quite a bludgeoning. All in all though, it was a brave and gutsy performance that brought out your inner Spartacus. *(ticking a box on Me's file)*

**Me** – I gradually came to accept the inevitable. Yet the nature of the non-responsive, slow-changing, control situation was like…

**Mr G** *(helpfully)* – Like meeting a Gorgon - saxifying?

**Me** *(practicing sword and head slicing manoeuvres)* – Yes, exactly! I could've cut off their heads they were so brutish and rude.

**Mr G** *(grinning, puts a big tick on Me's file)* – Insult and injury, but another heroic encounter. No wonder you were disillusioned.

**Me** – I suppose you can't win them all.

**Mr G** – You had them on toast, but were disinclined to eat them.

**Me** – In the final squidge they looked very unappetising.

**Mr G** – Lack of killer instinct, letting them off the hook or a wise move on your behalf? Plus you forgot the 'B' word.

**Me** – What? 'Bitches', 'bastards' or 'bullshit'?

**Mr G** – No, 'boundaries'. It's all right to have boundaries. Are you at the whim of everything or are you the master of your misery?

**Me** – Probably more at the kindness of gods and strangers.

**Mr G** – Hm! Not so good. *(Mr G puts crosses next to 'inner dodo' and 'inner ostrich' on Me's file)* On the other hand, at least you had the chance to enact out the exciting roles of 'fly-in-the-ointment' and 'sacrificed son'. *(smiling, places two handsome ticks on Me's file)*

**Me** *(not knowing whether to be pleased or not)* – Oh, I just go with life's flow avoiding as many trip-wires, mouse, mine and booby-traps as I can. I'm better at walking on other people's eggshells these days.

**Mr G** – Look at the current world turmoil. Explosions everywhere as hundreds of years of fighting history are being compressed into a few years. Well, in terms of societal dynamics, you were all at the storming stage and you, quite rightly, exited stage left.

**Me** – Pursued by an orc! Upwardly managing bad situations because I could meant that I was trouble-shooting all the time. You know, I'm not always very good dealing with the 'A' word.

**Mr G** *(kindly)* – What? 'Arseholes' or 'avoidance'?'

**Me** *(laughing)* – No, 'assertiveness'. Particularly the applied sort against aggressive people.

**Mr G** – Another action point?

**Me** – Nooo!

**Mr G** *(kindly, but writing it down anyway)* – Perhaps 'ambivalence' would be a better choice in dealing with future cases?

**Me** – Shrug and walk away you mean or show the other meek-cheek?

**Mr G** – We could all work on that... and by that I mean having compassionate regard for the other person and the situation that caused their behaviour, not being masochistic.

**Me** *(putting up his fists)* – I wanted to punch their lights out!

**Mr G** – You were still feeling "don't get angry get even". It was a puncher's chance your inner praying mantis and internal pugilist couldn't resist, but one that your prayerful man abhors. Perhaps "don't get angry get strong" might have been more appropriate.

**Me** – A Parthian shot kind of thing?

**Mr G** – It was an understandable reaction to a passive-aggressive management style, but there were mixed intentions all round. When it comes to departures clean breaks without any threads to tug on are best. Unfortunately, you were an old broom...

**Me** – And they were keen on a new sweep.

**Mr G** – Requiring a certain brand of loyalty! If you had stayed you would have wanted to rip their throats out for such behaviour. It was an oppressive stranglehold you felt from their boots-on-the-throat tactics. They destroyed your trust. That's why we have to untwist the twisted now. It's got to be released.

**Me** – It was all rather bruising though. I couldn't turn my mental flick switch off. Was it that funny?

**Mr G** *(flicking through pages of another file)* – Accusations of perspicacity, executives disappearing on financial magic carpets, veiled notifications, the consultation of insults, the poisoned chalice...

**Me** *(mumbling)* – Obviously not poisoned enough!

**Mr G** – All laid out in the steamroller method. Priceless! You couldn't buy all that experience, but if you fancy a little more practice there's a whole list of inequalities and issues I can send your way? As for the World's 'generational grievances' being dragged through the ages... Well, loads of those to mop up as well.

**Me** – Whoa! No thanks. I'm not a Gaia sewage worker, am I?

**Mr G** *(not answering, but smiling)* – You see, it's all in the resistance.

**Me** – I thought that was futile?

**Mr G** – No, it's actually useful, but ultimately I'm only ever interested in your eventual surrender.

**Me** – Our defeat?

**Mr G** – It's not your defiance that I seek, but your futility.

**Me** – I've got lots of that!

**Mr G** – Good. Once you're exhausted by the outer fascinations you will want to turn your attention to Me. It doesn't matter how or when, but eventually you will and 'now' is the best time to do so!

**Me** – Very apt.

**Mr G** *(peering at Me like a Wise White Owl)* – So in summary… Dextera!

> *Re: God and love.*
>
> *You are not going to win against me. You can try, and certainly there are many ways to ignore, refute, or disengage with me, but all those positions are to do with separation, which is the greatest illusion and pain of all.*
>
> *Eventually, you have to let go of everything that is old, limiting or out of balance and no longer serves the unconditional love of yourself and everything!*
>
> *Ultimately, it is all about connection and trust.*

**Me** – So my holding on was merely grist for my personal mill? Was I tilting at windmills again?

**Mr G** – You were stuck and needed to struggle with the last hurdle of self. That's when I loaded the powder keg and gave more power to your popcorn.

**Me** – Oh, is that why it bit back so unexpectedly?

**Mr G** – It tends to. Your auric irritations formed into a pearl, but you needed some agitation to help propel and release it. Now, as a minor point of interest for me, do you remember whether the popcorn was salty or sweet at the point of impact?

**Me** *(shaking his head and putting a finger in his mouth to feel the aforementioned chomp on the Tooth of Truth)* – No, apart from the initial crunch I don't really recall. These days I don't have much memory of anything at all. *(self-deceived)* Too busy being in the 'now'.

**Mr G** – Ah! It's a pity you couldn't discern whether it was salty or sweet, it might've helped you in the final consideration of imbalances.

**Me** – It was worse than a gob-stopper though! I thought I'd bitten on a kernel, but it puffed up and engulfed me.

**Mr G** – I think you'll find your comforting consumerism and sitting on the sofa was nursing one of your parasites. Some have a tendency to feed off your thoughts and essence rather than your blood.

**Me** *(sighing)* – Another unnecessary 'precious' gone I suppose?

**Mr G** – Another wonderful, prised pearl for my collection you mean! They're never unnecessary. It's part of a divine process. All your accumulated irritations, impurities and parasites removed in one go. Caught between your whirling dervish and Tasmanian devil I've extricated quite a collection of yours from throughout the ages.

**Me** – You can't help having an addictive personality if you have one?

**Mr G** – True, you either have one or you don't. Of course, there are always those in denial *(peers at Me, scrutinising the inscrutable)* and those secretly harbouring the desire for one, but not all are beyond help.

**Me** *(jesting)* – Boring goes the life without temptation!

**Mr G** *(jousting back)* – I can always send you Inferno to practise with if you want?

**Me** – Hellish flame?

**Mr G** – I've got some great red-hot imps and biting devils if you still think Hell's the hippest place to be.

**Me** *(considering)* – Oh, that's kind. *(cheekily)* I'll have a think and get back to you on that one!

**Mr G** – Don't take too long. Others are waiting. Now, as a former Sunday school dropout you do remember how to be sure of Hell?

**Me** – Er, no? *(tapping head)* No memory, remember?

**Mr G** *(helpfully listing)* – Deceive yourself by pretending there is no such place; philosophically argue that it's a man-made construct by lesser mortals to entrap greater, freer minds; neglect to make preparation for Heaven; and of course my favourite… *(beaming)* Trying to get there by any other way than through me!

**Me** *(having lived his life through pop songs he liked)* – Hm! Really? Not my way, but thy way. Damn it!

**Mr G** – Woe betide! Life acts out everything and anything it needs from the 'consciousness' side of things through all the different interconnecting bodies and realms.

**Me** *(suddenly worried)* – What! But you are joking right? Your list… There is no eternal woe?

**Mr G** *(says nothing then bursts out laughing)* – Apart from the self-created… No! But you should have seen the look on your face.

**Me** *(un-amused)* – If you really want me to do something you only have to ask. Or lure me in. You know my temptations…

**Mr G** – Like?

**Me** – Food, wine, chocolate, sending me a whole heap of money…

**Mr G** – Tsk! Not that again.

**Me** – Or the cast of 'True Blood' or 'Spartacus'.

**Mr G** *(nudging Me with his elbow)* – Southern blood and some lust in the dust. A great dangler! Can't have too much of a good-bad thing, huh? It's understandable… But there's greater wisdom to what you have done and been through than you realise. A sort of satisfaction from earthly arousal that leads to greater spiritual flow. But I know you like surprises…

**Me** *(clueless)* – I'm just a pearl producer shucked to order I suppose!

**Mr G** *(laughs)* – You could always pray and meditate the parasites and beasts away.

**Me** – You've got to realise that they're there first!

**Mr G** – Precisely!

**Me** *(cleverly)* – I was relying on the fact that "to err is human; to forgive, divine"!

**Mr G** *(disinterested, turning the pages on Me's file)* – Were you now.

**Me** – You know: I err… You and everyone else have to forgive me, which makes you and them divine! It's quite a gift I'm giving.

**Mr G** *(considering, but not really listening)* – Hmm.

**Me** *(pulls up the blind and looks out of window enviously at a passing reclining cherub sunbathing)* – That way I'm doing everybody a favour!

**Mr G** *(unconvinced)* – Perhaps…

**Me** *(sighing, expecting the worst)* – More work I suppose?

**Mr G** – No. In actual fact less work, and more acceptance of life as 'it is' within the grand scheme of things.

**Me** *(surprised)* – Oh! So not what we think or hope or want it to be?

**Mr G** – Still wanting it to be other than it is?

**Me** *(begrudging)* – I suppose…

**Mr G** – That's your wishful thinking. I'll pop it down on your 'more practice needed' list. As for your resplendent pearls… I'm wearing them as a necklace to the Galactic Masquerade Ball I'm throwing.

**Me** – Charming!

**Mr G** – Pleasure, Treasure. By the way, did you get your Gaia invitation?

**Me** – Yes, thanks.

**Mr G** – See? Cinderella does get to go to the Ball. Talking of which, how are your "Mary, Mary quite contrary" energy of opposites going?

**Me** – What? My cockleshells having done it then wishing they hadn't, or my silver bells not doing it and wishing they had?

**Mr G** – Indeed!

**Me** – As for my internal hypocrisy where my many old selves act out their parts of colluding behaviour to betray one another, shift the goalposts and gang up to pin the blame on me - yeah, all going great!

**Mr G** *(laughing)* – Rest assured that your mass, or should I say 'Eden Mess', of truths and lies and your many warring tensions are slowly bringing you to a point of balance. Integrating peace will do the rest and stop the rot of any negativity from old selves seeping through.

**Me** – Oh, I see. I seem to have a lot of them to consider.

**Mr G** *(smiling)* – Those doorways certainly do keep opening for you regardless. Oppositions and tensions are there for you to enjoy and explore and all the answers reside in the heart. *(the Almighty Hand firmly taps Me's chest)* Both sides of course…

**Me** – Of course, they would.

**Mr G** – The two-hearts being the activity centres where the nature of consciousness and spectrum perceptions collide.

**Me** – Fusing our confusion into wholeness no doubt!

**Mr G** *(sagely)* – Once properly centred. Wise-love is the only answer I ever sought from humanity. For it to continue it has to change and vibrate with that realisation.

**Me** – Wise up, become more loving?

**Mr G** – Exactly.

**Me** – Sounds simple, yet…

**Mr G** – All the secrets are hidden within the treasure chest of the human breast so dig deep. That's all you need to know.

**Me** – I imagine that's why you specifically put them there in the first place! Still, you don't necessarily expect popcorn to bite back.

**Mr G** – You should try biting on a daemon!

**Me** *(helpfully)* – Couldn't you make their exoskeletons a bit less brittle? You know, a bit more soft-centred and chewy?

**Mr G** – Possibly, but I like an occasional crunch with a sticky end! The purple ones in a tin of Quality Street are still my favourite. *(regarding Me)* I could see your aura in a more purple wrapping.

**Me** *(disregarding Mr G)* – Personally I hate it when an un-popped kernel takes out a filling. And that extraction process of yours was a pop up-and-out in the other direction!

**Mr G** – Magical?

**Me** – Extraordinary, but still scary and quite uncomfortable.

**Mr G** – It was a life event. It's supposed to be! It's all about spirit-science and education.

**Me** – The want of it or our approach to it?

**Mr G** – The exploration of your inner divinity requires a process of reconsideration. As you explore the greater realms of spiritual intelligence and existence through your thoughts and feelings you have to be open and allow yourself to be led to new understanding.

**Me** – Most unlikely! And who's teaching such things?

**Mr G** – Spiritual teaching from the mind's perspective can seem a bit surgical. On a clinical light level it *is* corrective alignment as your encounter the finer light waves, whereas the heart's artistic, broad inclusive sweep of the celestial brush can involve and combine all the elements of valour, truth, enthusiasm, tolerance and beauty.

**Me** – The teacher as artist?

**Mr G** – To teach is to learn. When you live and operate from the heart all becomes possible. Nevertheless you still have to know when to engage with the enemy and understand the tactics of the divide.

**Me** – Hmmm! The ongoing war of consciousness.

**Mr G** – First and foremost you need to take on-board your own inner struggle. That's the main thing - that you're engaged with life. Yesterday's issues and leftover problems are always good for gossip, grievances and shredding…

**Me** – Or cat litter?

**Mr G** – I find that's more newspapers and nasty journalism.

**Me** – More moisture-absorbent, I suppose, and quite a few have gone down the pan recently.

**Mr G** – A few bad apples, greedy conglomerates, sleaze and hacks…

**Me** – Though not forgetting Tintin…

**Mr G** *(agreeing)* – Never forgetting the real investigators of truth. *(repeating)* But yesterday's issues and leftover problems are always good for gossip, grievances and shredding… Yet little else. It's all about allowing the problems and cares of the day to drop away.

**Me** – Feel it and deal with it, but don't go to bed angry?

**Mr G** – Indeed. As far as world issues go the stopping of war is the main thing for humanity to achieve, as well you know.

**Me** – What? Weaving together the experiences of conflict and war and the human spirit to transcend it? 'That book!'.

**Mr G** – Precisely! 'That book!' of yours indeed.

**Me** – It appeared as something fragmented, complex and daunting.

**Mr G** – Possibly a case of "these fragments I have shored against my ruins." Didn't you like it?

**Me** – Yes. Well, kind of. It was very ambitious, difficult and strange.

**Mr G** *(chuckling)* – Old fidget knickers in a 'dream-of-consciousness' art-exercise.

**Me** – Anyway, all those speeches just kept arriving.

**Mr G** – "A book like no other" and a book of huge achievement whichever way you choose to look at it.

**Me** – True, and there are very many ways of looking at it.

**Mr G** *(quoting slowly)* – "I will show you fear in a handful of dust".

**Me** *(serious)* – I had to face many a fear in so many handfuls of dust.

**Mr G** – True. Fear can hold you back, yet you found a way to muster it and used it as a type of fuel to propel you to the cosmic heart.

**Me** – Combustible-courage?

**Mr G** – Once you've reconnected to the universal source of unconditional love you can travel anywhere… including the extraterrestrial dimensions.

**Me** – Really? *(a rumbling sound emanates from around Me. Could be stomach, might be hip flask, possibly an alien spaceship reverberating past)*

**Mr G** *(graciously)* – Yes, but by the sound of your stomach rumbling it might be time for elevenses?

**Me** *(relieved)* – Thank you. I thought you'd never ask.

**Mr G** *(claps his hands)* – Tea, vicar!

*(the Almighty Hand slips into a white glove and magically starts pouring two cups of tea from out of an enchanted teapot upon a small pop-up cloud-table covered with a fine-lace misty tablecloth. Me cannot figure out if the cup is Waterford or one of the Royals - Dalton, Albert or Spode - so says nothing as real china however cloud is a step up from his usual elevenses Eeyore coffee-mug at home)*

**Mr G** – Now… The legacies of conflict and war lie in the history, healing and hope of mankind. If you do have a problem with someone then you should face him or her and have a friendly talk and try to resolve it in a listening, respectful, non-violent way.

**Me** – Are there mechanisms for that?

**Mr G** *(offering Me a plate full of assorted biscuits)* – Leaving doors open and not exiling people from your immediate family or community. Understanding and comprehending differing needs.

**Me** *(considering biscuits, but adding helpfully)* – A round table perhaps?

**Mr G** – Feedback mutual support and understanding.

**Me** *(taking three biscuits in an attempt to make a biscuit sandwich, but quickly places two on his saucer)* – "Jaw, jaw, jaw… not war, war, war".

**Mr G** *(assessing whether any understanding of conflict points have sunk in)* – Arguing out your differences and taking the long-term 'friendship' overview rather than overly focusing on particular incidents or acting upon any immediate violent reactions.

**Me** – And remembering that a problem shared is a problem halved! *(Me illustratively breaks a biscuit in half)* That's an example of good division! Particularly at coffee mornings with a free biscuit.

**Mr G** *(peering, but not ticking any of the boxes on Me's file)* – Indubitably.

**Me** *(uncomfortable in case it includes an action point for him)* – Wow! I hope these activists and peace makers are out there somewhere. *(Mr G is silent. Me tries to change the subject whilst dunking another biscuit)* Anyhow, I presumed this review is more about keeping myself up-to-date with supernatural patterns and trends rather than general world conflict management and resolution?

**Mr G** *(dangerous)* – Did you? And which you? I don't think our talk was bound by any predetermined prerequisites or conditions, particularly not by any limiting thoughts of yours.

**Me** *(trying to eat a soggy, collapsing biscuit)* – Oh! I just thought the conversational purpose was slipping a bit.

**Mr G** *(snorting derisively)* – Human-conceived purpose? How very funny! *(Mr G leans forward as the Almighty Hand pokes Me with his index finger in the side of his head)* More 'G-A-B-A' less jibber-jabber! That's what I say.

**Me** *(quickly)* – I thought you said being friendly was the main thing?

*(Mr G says nothing as he watches Me drop his biscuit in his tea. Ingeniously, Me tries to salvage the floating remains of his first biscuit with a second, chocolate-coated biscuit, which unfortunately begins to melt on the scoop and incline on the way to his mouth)*

**Me** *(struggling to balance the perilously soggy biscuits)* – Sorry. Are we mortals that puny and little to you? So small and squabbling?

**Mr G** *(watching curiously at the state of Me's dismal dunking drama)* – Well, both yes and no. More like brain food when the mind is right. Proportionally speaking, no bigger than that biscuit is scaled to you.

**Me** *(attempting a half-hearted joke)* – Occasionally suitable for dunking, but often ends up in a mess!

**Mr G** – Extraordinary. Quite a lavish spectacle at times…*(watches as yet another biscuit collapses)* …disheartening and disappointing at others.

**Me** *(stares into his tea-cup wondering if biscuit rescue by spoon is allowable)* – The neck-breakers and heart-takers of ill intent you mean?

**Mr G** – It all stems from the idea that you are still separate. Dextera!

> *You are all a part of an inter-connected, diverse species-of-consciousness, living within an advanced spiritual system that is primarily concerned with the evolution of love.*
>
> *So, love, its sharing and the valuing of those myriad relationships, however brief or seemingly inconsequential, is the most rewarding and important of achievements.*
>
> *Through love you can remember the self. Through love you can remember me.*
>
> *Through love and light you can achieve so many great things!*

**Mr G** – All that slaughtering, warmongering, and arguing leads to rivalry and violent conflict rather than peaceful resolution. Plus many hearts and minds have been misled by outmoded institutes and errant authority. Then, of course, there is the truly abhorrent nature of rape, mutilation and sexual trafficking when there is so much room for playful fun these days.

**Me** *(nodding)* – And not forgetting all the hate crimes.

**Mr G** – Basically, anything that does not take the long-term, compassionate loving view is now best removed and that begins with individual responsibility, not societal law.

**Me** *(dexterously scooping the floating remains with his teaspoon, Me slurps the biscuit soup)* – Simple really when you put it that way.

**Mr G** – Humanity should lose the hubris, reconnect to Nature and not let prevailing conditions cloud their true spiritual identity. But as you said... *(Mr G points his finger and dissolves Me's chair)* Perhaps I'm slipping.

*(Me slowly slides through his cloud-chair precariously balancing his teacup so as not to spill his tea or lose his remaining biscuit)*

**Me** *(nervously grinning)* – A bit like me in this cloud chair of yours.

**Mr G** *(reinforcing)* – Of ours. Everything's shared here... And do try to remember your silver lining.

*(Me tries to pull himself together by concentrating on bolstering his silver lining. Not knowing how to prioritise correctly, Me does not know what to do with the spoon, biscuit and cup of tea he is holding. Me sinks further through his chair)*

**Me** *(speaking hopefully)* – It certainly is all muffins and doughnuts by the dozen these days.

**Mr G** – Muffins and doughnuts indeed!

*(Mr G claps his hand and quickly dissolves the tea set, cups and biscuits. The Almighty Hand picks Me up by the scruff of his neck and plonks him back on his chair, vigorously and brusquely dusting away any remaining cloud-vapour)*

**Mr G** – Domini! Well, it seems that you're starting to love your insubordination a bit more, which means your fighting spirit is returning, and this particular knot of past pain is being dissolved.

**Me** *(suddenly realising)* – Oh! And all due to the power of our little conversation? I see what you've been doing.

**Mr G** *(smiling)* – The removal of mental ticks and emotional fleas over a cup of tea.

**Me** *(gratefully)* – Thanks for that.

**Mr G** – Easy to catch, hard to get rid of. You should try it some time.

**Me** *(brightly)* – I do the cats and I thought about doing that with a few people during the last set of dramas and attacks.

**Mr G** – But you didn't. Lack of follow through?

**Me** – Yes, but good idea though.

**Mr G** *(helpfully)* – Were you trying to remove their ticks and fleas before you'd removed your own?

**Me** – Oh, probably!

**Mr G** *(leadingly)* – So, oh-non-slipping conversational person, but not so silver lining cloud-proof, what should we talk about next?

**Me** *(slightly warily)* – Not sure. I didn't call for this review. I just sort-of somehow turned up…

**Mr G** – Tugged up! Your soul was fed-up of constantly slipping through the review net.

**Me** *(honestly)* – Really? On Earth we're secretly pleased not to be under such scrutiny.

**Mr G** – I thought you were fed-up with being a knight-in-waiting?

**Me** *(reconsidering)* – That's true. It does feel like I've been waiting around a long while.

**Mr G** – Trust in Nature's timing. The interesting thing about this life of yours is the amount of stuff you get to do when you're older.

**Me** *(positively)* – Into the white in search of the beautiful.

**Mr G** – More opportunities for happiness, wisdom and growth then. However, since you are here, you'd better know that I don't make mistakes - only galactic-journeys and experiences.

**Me** – 'Relative occurrences'… you said.

**Mr G** – Social-science projects can be heated or cooled depending on the temperaments of Mother Nature and Gaia. And I can always abort any species-of-consciousness if they get too ugly.

**Me** *(slightly overwhelmed)* – Oh! At times I really have no idea what I'm doing here. Not only here, I mean, but here, there or anywhere.

**Mr G** – Well, tell me. What's life all about?

**Me** *(thinking)* – Um? Growing your self? Journeying and experiencing the various rites of passage? Discovering more aspects of love?

**Mr G** *(kindly)* – Yes, voyages of love is what you in the wonder-universe are all experiencing.

**Me** – I'm just an amateur in love with life, living on a wing and a prayer!

**Mr G** – The best kind of way for light travellers, so to speak.

*(As an experiment Mr G clicks his fingers under the table. In response there is a sudden whooshing noise caused by Me's unexpected expanding and unfolding of Light Wings. Me starts to float in an uncomfortable and irregular fashion)*

**Me** *(nervously)* – Sorry, I'm still trying to stabilise these energy wing-things.

**Mr G** – Remember to keep embracing all aspects of your humanity.

**Me** *(beginning to rotate upside down)* – What with all the world's quickening communication, cloud-storage and rapid interaction available in our present information age, I find I can't steady myself at all! *(Mr G smiles)* Please excuse me. My vertical lift and levitation keep muddling.

**Mr G** *(laughing royally)* – I can see. *(the Almighty Hand floats by prodding Me's stomach)* Your horizontal hold is not so good either!

**Me** – Charming!

**Mr G** – But seriously. I think they call it 'sensory overload'.

*(Hovering near the Cloud-Office ceiling Me inspects the beautiful shimmering silver lining. Holding his ankle, the Almighty Hand gently rotates Me the right way up like a balloon)*

**Me** – Thank you Hand. *(turning to look down at Mr G)* But what are you supposed to do with all the information? Is knowing half the battle? How do you manage?

**Mr G** *(nods to the Almighty Hand to return Me to his seat)* – That depends. Knowledge from books and knowledge from experience are entirely different things. Knowledge should be seen as information sharing and connection put to good purpose.

**Me** – The sharing of the vision rather than knowledge as power and ignorance being bliss?

**Mr G** – Exactly. Dextera! The magic white board please.

*(the Almighty Hand pulls down a white board and writes an illuminating list as Mr G dictates a round-up of astrological information)*

**Mr G** – Technically, knowing is one twelfth of the battle until you reach zero point and become free of the encaging static energy circle. The other eleven aspects as far as human beings are concerned are:

- being, as earthly activity exploring playful consciousness, not just doing

- having, the satisfaction of endeavours, not reductive materialism

- thinking, to acquire and generate knowledge and in turn to help achieve greater reasoning

- feeling, to develop the empathetic states and creative sensory perceptions
- willing and wanting, in order to achieve higher vision
- analysing, but not overly so - enough to understand the nature of calibration to bring about coherence
- balancing, to bring you into greater harmony with life
- desiring, to understand the nature of the many bodies and impulses toward life in order to integrate
- seeing, to bring you closer to wisdom
- using, to understand the beneficial roles you each act out in order to be helpful to others
- believing, to connect with the mystic realm of magic so you can have cosmic-interplay.

**Me** *(exhausted)* – Phew!

**Mr G** – They all need to be understood individually, then combined, synthesised and integrated to break free. Like at the old Solomon schools you used to attend.

**Me** – "C+ with a sense of regret!" I remember the report.

**Mr G** *(warmly)* – Too much of a good time back then too. Always something to distract your focus… Of course, you could simply trust in the knowledge of destiny. Then you wouldn't need to know about any of this.

**Me** – Oh, I wish I had known that in the first place. I could've saved myself a whole heap of unnecessary worry and figuring out!

**Mr G** *(smiling)* – Yes, a lot of people say that! Remember, consciousness is the reward reaped at the end not the beginning. But I know what you mean about information-overload these days. You can't keep up with the amount and speed of all the world wide web and Sun-information in these omni-shambles days of yours.

**Me** *(tartly)* – 'Ours'.

**Mr G** *(impressed, but only puts a silver star on Me's file this time)* – Quite right! Well done. You can only function according to your form and operational frequency. The 'now' was invented so you can keep current with the integrity of yourself in connection to Eternity. From there you can choose your interactions and relationships with others. Earth is a finishing school of the heart, not the mind.

**Me** – And Venus for the gaseous forms of love?

**Mr G** – And other planets similarly for other forms of existence. Remember, the mind is a gift from the heart. Consciousness is affected by inner and outer events, both seismic and small, like ripples in a pond.

**Me** – I do dislike too many ripples on the pond, particularly when they collide. It disturbs my tranquillity.

**Mr G** – Takes you out of your comfort zone you mean! The disturbance, distortion, and displacement you sometimes feel are part of the nature of energy exchange, but you do need to enter the 'profound silence' to understand it.

**Me** – Yeah, yeah. I've always found the silence to be very un-silent.

**Mr G** – Not the mysterious dark stuff. *(slowly, deliberately)* You alone suspended deep within the spirit of Mother Nature. *(hinting)* I think you'll find it's a very personal and introspective final journey.

**Me** *(not realising what is yet to come)* – It seems very busy in there... All those spooks and souls trying to help and have a word.

**Mr G** – Indeed! But getting back to your question. You deal with an omni-shambles as you would a normal shambles.

**Me** – What? Like eating an elephant one teaspoon at a time?

**Mr G** – Precisely! I tend to find things generally lean toward the unexpected...

**Me** – You mean a lot of things go tits-up!

**Mr G** – Remember, at the end of the day...

**Me** *(querying)* – Yours or mine?

**Mr G** *(reminding gently)* – 'Ours'... You're nothing more than Mother Nature's soft social-science project, which I have given the chance to experience and understand the immortality of your soul-selves and the infinity of the eternal universe.

**Me** – That's very generous of you. Thank you.

**Mr G** – No question about it! So even more reason for love, good human organization and compassionate interaction during unstable times. *(Me is caught looking out the window at a passing cloud in the shape of a bounding puppy-hound, 'So cute!')*

**Mr G** *(clearing his throat)* – H-hm!

**Me** – Sorry, I was listening, but that cloud looked so adorable. Anyhow... what are you supposed to do with all the information spiralling around the galactic system?

**Mr G** *(unimpressed and not being drawn)* – Why? What would you do with it?

**Me** *(apologetic)* – I'm not sure that I'm the right person to ask.

**Mr G** – Try! I thought you wanted to be a king or at least God-for-the-day?

**Me** *(guessing as he starts one of his infamous caught-out rambles)* – Well, I suppose you could try filtering it.

**Mr G** *(licking his lips)* – Digest it?

**Me** *(struggling)* – Act upon it? Er… do something useful with it?

**Mr G** *(getting impatient)* – Most importantly, share it! Then interact and play with it. Classify and order it if you really have to.

**Me** – Put it in its rightful place and resonate with it?

**Mr G** – Investigate it. Test it. Explore it. Be expressive with it. Run with it. Be at peace with it. Forget it.

**Me** – Oh! I like the sound of that last one.

**Mr G** *(explaining importantly)* – I meant move on from it. Once it's over, it's gone. One of your world's constants is change, so appreciate it. The cosmic universe's main constants are joy and love as serviced by the galactic geishas you call angels. The radial-Sun energy is very busy at the moment and the Moon having waned over the last solstice is now creation-waxing toward the summer solstice to bring in the next genesis of consciousness.

**Me** *(not seeing, but agreeing)* – I see…

*(suddenly, just as things were going smoothly, a green energy ball suspiciously like a Green Fairy explodes from out of Me's rumbling hip flask. Spotting Mr G, the Green Fairy flies quickly out of the window to wait in a nearby cloud. An*

*incriminating emerald green vapour trail hangs in the Cloud-Office back to Me's hip flask)*

**Me** *(light-heartedly trying to cover up the minor incursion)* – Oops! I mean whee! How pretty… *(Mr G looks bemused, wondering where the Green Fairy might have come from)* There's goes my muse "General Disarray".

**Mr G** *(suddenly comprehending, but looking suitably unimpressed)* – Is that *your* Green Fairy that's just flown out of the window?

**Me** *(taking a quick nip before putting the stopper back on his hip flask)* – She's such a cad! *(Me quickly reverts back to the previous topic of conversation)* I expect when you're omni-at-one with it all it's probably easier to understand.

**Mr G** *(sighs, shaking his head despairingly)* – Ultimately, until your duality stops warring, you cannot find peace.

**Me** – I know, I'm currently dealing with those two.

**Mr G** – You mean Buddha and Bacchus?

**Me** – Whilst trying to weld together my personal, double-bladed, axe-carrying warrior Viking with the purity of my Franciscan nun!

**Mr G** – So you don't know whether to fornicate or pray?

**Me** – You know me. Usually on the quiet side, but get me drunk and my wag comes out!

**Mr G** – There's always the middle ground.

**Me** – What? Sex and monastic adventure as a visceral meditation on love?

**Mr G** – Or just lust with the appropriate benediction.

**Me** – Better than yearning I suppose.

**Mr G** – Or wondering? Perhaps you need to let your nun out and keep your Viking indoors for a while. *(tapping file, cheerfully)* But they're both doing you a great service.

**Me** – I know if I try to choose one over the other I'm doomed.

**Mr G** *(smiles)* – Ah, the ultimate synthesis! Still thinking it's a trap?

**Me** *(prickly)* – Amongst other things.

**Mr G** *(broad grin)* – According to your star chart you have a lot of oppositional tensions to play with. *(the Almighty Hand pulls out a helpful 3-dimensional astrological globe, which Mr G spins and peers at as it transforms into Me's holographic birth-chart)* Your ongoing struggle between beauty, reality and imperfections means there's a lot of friction to create fiction! *(Mr G guffaws)* Don't resist - try to enjoy them more. Churning always produces good things. *(Mr G beams and Me is reminded of pure sunshine that melts away all former shadows)*

**Me** *(enchanted and somewhat hypnotised)* – I must say, you do have the loveliest of smiles. So if anyone's going to laugh at me it's probably best that it's you!

**Mr G** – Thank you. I have an in-built sweet smile, one the people of your world experience as seraph-serotonin when you're raised up this high.

**Me** – Oh! Like…?

**Mr G** – Like acacia honey or brown sugar to you.

**Me** – As long as it's not saccharine. I do try to avoid the synthetics.

**Mr G** – Remember, it's the bioflavonoid smile that stays. The clue of opposites is to at least try to understand them with good-humour. Like a dialogue. Be-friend them.

**Me** *(considering)* – Sometimes it just seems that they are... That I am... Oh, that it is all so overwhelming and seemingly impossible!

**Mr G** *(agreeing)* – I like those times the most. It's the experiencing of the impossible situations that enable the impossible to happen. How else would you generate friendship, love and other soul-miracles? And like all best bits, I always leave them until last. Particularly the rear guard army leaders.

**Me** – Is that me?

**Mr G** – Yes, that's you. KB 2.

**Me** – Oh! I see.

**Mr G** – KB CBE 1 was vanguard. Combined with the current overshadowing by the predominate feminine hierarchy of your time, the start of the new age is emerging in a very lovely way. You and they, and not forgetting the other patron saints of British music, are all really coming along rather nicely.

**Me** – Thanks.

**Mr G** – Try to ensure that your cream colour doesn't get soured and if it does don't forget to release and repair it! Off cream looks and smells terrible.

**Me** – Charming!

**Mr G** – Whereas on cream means you get to enjoy the 'fat-of-the-land'.

**Me** – I know, but trying to find cream peace, particularly in times of instability and transition, is difficult.

**Mr G** – Don't think I don't care, because I do… Deeply. You need to know that, but I'm not going to personally intervene and fight the evils of social injustice that you create. You do understand that?

**Me** *(shrugging his shoulders)* – I suppose.

**Mr G** – That's humankind's karmic rubbish to dispose of. Remember, it's you who inherit the Earth. It's you that keeps returning in the re-birthing stream of consciousness. It's you who needs to sort out the situations and take care of the Earth. Gaia is doing her patient best and she's been through her own dimensional upheavals recently.

**Me** *(scratching his head)* – That makes sense.

**Mr G** – My job is to look after her and you lot from my side. The corruption of the last astrological age was your en masse responsibility. She's been releasing the energy back through you to own and transmute.

**Me** *(conceding)* – Oh! It was all rather intense and depleting at times.

**Mr G** – It was, but that's okay - the Winter exhaust cycle is now over. Many of you, in order to survive, turned towards comforting habits and gratifying evasions. Now that the new Moon-phases are upon you it's time to re-integrate the original impulse to incarnate at this time and enjoy the cosmic energy release.

**Me** *(helpfully)* – Oh… I see.

**Mr G** – Do you?

**Me** *(honestly)* – I'm trying to. You mean habits will be prised from us like a comforting toy is taken away from a screaming, kicking child?

**Mr G** – Ultimately, giving up the impulses of humanity's collective bad horse will boil down to lone, individual, ethical conscious choice. But you need to be motivated by the will to change for the better for that is what the universe is currently undergoing.

**Me** – So we'd better wise up to the change because the change toward better is upon us.

**Mr G** – Indeed! The time for humanity's en-masse reconsideration is here.

**Me** – Just in time for the great humanitarian age of Aquarius.

**Mr G** – Yes. You can tip it in the right direction if you all help out. The galactic dynamic is currently energetically changing and re-charging all over the place. Humanity needs to reconsider its progress in the light of new consciousness and compassion. The war of consciousness and old social-religious fragmentation is upon you, but you are not helpless.

**Me** – Phew! I'm exhausted at the thought, but not more hate crimes or genocide… I can't bear it.

**Mr G** – Soul purge can be punishing and exacting as well as cleansing. Some phoenix-fire still remains on the ground.

**Me** – I suppose being the all and everything keeps you pretty busy?

**Mr G** – Super-Nature has quite a good dynamic system in place once you've got the hang of it. Fortunately for humanity there are many talented souls incarnated at present doing an awful lot of good work. You know… *(peering at Me)* Because of the mess and that God-awful muck-up.

**Me** – Okay! I get your point. We're 'on the brink' again and we've screwed up on more than one occasion in the past. No need to relish quite so much the 'I told you so'.

**Mr G** – Humanity has been warned several times before. As a species you cannot keep on destroying Nature and hurting higher incarnating souls sent to help. To continue living and doing without applied sustainable thinking and loving... I don't think so! *(Mr G swivels around in his chair to look out upon a bursting Rose-Star super-nova)* Not now. *(Me takes a sneaky snifter of snuff)* Not without consequences. *(Mr G turns his chair back around to face Me)*

**Me** – Believe me! Ignorance is bliss...

**Mr G** – *Was* bliss...

**Me** – And I thought we had all time to consider these things?

**Mr G** – Nothing is wasted to the journeying soul. Nothing is fake to the truth and integrity of your eternal self. No dragon sought and chased after is without its magic, but as you know, there are many different types of dragon.

**Me** *(recalling Wyverns, Deep Sea and, of course, the infamous Soup Dragon)* – And all can be for our own good?

**Mr G** – If turned to Gaia's advantage. Then the spiritual life will win out in the end.

**Me** – It has to?

**Mr G** – The system is designed to... Soul-survival. Humanity needs to balance itself within the bigger picture. However, even Eternity needs to push on a bit every now and then. Unfolding plans, crunch time, apocalyptic tides... That kind of thing.

**Me** – Come Hell or high cosmic water?

**Mr G** – Mother Nature could drown you all, freeze or boil over. And the Universe can pack itself away whenever it wishes. *(cheerfully)* These kind of seeming troublesome things in humanity's history are nothing but radiant opportunities.

**Me** – Seems a bit steep.

**Mr G** – Although on that matter, I do have a message from the Moon here somewhere for you, *(rummages through file)* but I can't seem to find it… *(the Almighty Hand starts searching in earnest lifting and uncovering many unfiled pieces of paper in his attempt)*

**Me** *(not particularly bothered and wondering when he can leave)* – I'm sure it'll turn up. These things often have a mind of their own! I wonder if it's concerning our little chat at the Moon party?

**Mr G** – Maybe. Right. So… *(pause)* How's it going?

**Me** – What! This review? I like a good meander as much as the next river, but are You doing the reviewing or me? I'm a bit confused…

**Mr G** – It's that entwining, non-separation thing again. It happens to energy streams when you're in the higher altitudes.

**Me** – Yes, but your meander is more Mekong than Thames!

**Mr G** – As long as we're not both in 'de Nile!' *(laughs heartily)*

**Me** *(sighs)* – And I suspect that you're hoping that I catch myself on the next bend?

**Mr G** *(chuckling)* – Only metaphysically speaking.

**Me** *(half-smiling)* – Of course!

**Mr G** *(composing himself)* – I've covered most of the areas I wanted to talk about. I see from your notes that you're growing to appreciate the isolation and the silence a bit more.

**Me** – True, I like being in Nature in pursuit of silent and sacred spaces and different types of contemplation.

**Mr G** *(ticking a green box with a green pen)* – That's good. Take to the Parks and build up your walking meditation practice a bit more.

**Me** – I like meditating as long as it's not too dull or orthodox. But I want… No, need… and might I press the 'urgency' of this request upon you, somewhere more natural to live.

**Mr G** – I get your drift. Somewhere that would help your telepathic telephone line to the divine and reduce some of the static and interference you sometimes experience. Remember, you are encompassed within me as much as all deities and I reside innately within the breast-of-all-humans.

**Me** – Sorry, but where's the disco and jazz-hands in any of this?

**Mr G** *(realising Me is getting restless and drifting)* – Okay, so how about a few million and you choose? Does that help?

*(Mr G flashes a subliminal dance routine with accompanying harp and disco-strings before Me's eyes whilst a series of number sequences runs quickly through the cloud's lining)*

**Me** *(suddenly perking up)* – Er! Oh! Sort of. What was that? Was that a clue? It was a bit too fast and what with everything else going on it's quite a lot to take on board!

**Mr G** – Exactly. Universal energy as concurrent input and output. You have to be zippy.

**Me** *(hoping he has not missed something materially important)* – Er! More food for thought or something I should be acting upon?

**Mr G** – Ah, spiritual opportunities! A quick last grab of life, before the degradation and decay sets in. *(puts on a dazzling light display)* Photon pile-up. Proton dispersal. *(mini star-bursts everywhere)* That kind of thing. All that delicious energy being dispersed and transformed.

**Me** *(bedazzled by all the sparkles and glitter)* – Wow!

**Mr G** – Energy as sustenance and food.

**Me** – Er… I heard that when a planet goes AWOL their magnetic and gravitational field get redistributed and swallowed up by those planetary systems surrounding them whilst the planet itself gets pulverised to dust? *(Mr G waves his hands and creates a panoramic sonovision of an orbiting planet wobbling and then exploding)*

**Mr G** – Yes, it can be unfortunate. Let's hope the Earth doesn't go the same way and end up in the asteroid belt with the previous planet that failed to make the evolutionary jump.

**Me** – Gulp! Let's hope not. The Earth is very beautiful.

**Mr G** – She is, but the laws of spirit are the laws of physics. You experience them on the biological end so be careful of the usurpers. Be grateful I'm not a Parallax or a Galactus come to devour!

**Me** – Good! I was beginning to worry that you might be hungry now it's almost lunchtime.

**Mr G** *(looking at his wrist sundial)* – You're right. It is nearly lunchtime and I do fancy a small mortal… *(light snort)* Sorry, I meant morsel.

**Me** – Hmmm! Perhaps a spot of lunch all round would be best.

**Mr G** – Just kidding! Where's your sense of humour? Remember, I am creator, sustainer and destroyer all in one. I tend to work through my break times. If I bring my own sandwiches it means I can pop home a bit early. You know, Mrs G and the G-kids. Between you and me they can be quite a handful.

**Me** – Very energetic and demanding I'm sure.

**Mr G** – The galactic aeons are just the beginning of their formative teenage years! You don't really know what it's like until you have kids of your own. And about that? Would you like to know?

**Me** – It keeps coming back, but perhaps best kept a secret. Feasibly when the time and the money are right.

**Mr G** – You mean love?

**Me** – Indeed! Love, time and money. Children are a big commitment, consideration and expense. Us struggling aspiring artists may be free and happy, but we are presently very poor and can hardly keep a roof over our heads!

**Mr G** *(attentively)* – Depends on who's incarnating of course.

**Me** *(agreeing)* – Yeah, there's all of that to consider too.

**Mr G** *(as though doing Me a favour)* – Now, talking of disruption, destruction and general chaos and ruination, would you like to see the back of me?

**Me** – Er! Do you mean view you from the back, end the review or for you to go and leave me alone entirely? That might be pretty awesome in some respects, a bit inconvenient if you have more information for me, and horribly abandoning respectively.

**Mr G** *(roguish)* – I'm not that mean. It's only that you've always viewed me from the front, had glimpses of the expanding universe, the flickering light points, and the galactic portals. I was offering you a sneak peek at my back. A chance to see what's hidden behind the scenes, so to speak.

**Me** – Um… Well… Has anyone done that before and survived?

**Mr G** – I don't remember. Out of sight, out of mind. I push them off, but I can't always wait around to watch their journey and return.

**Me** *(considering the kindness of the offer)* – I mean, you revealing to me the sacred anatomy of yourself and the universe was all very well…

**Mr G** – Well, as much as your limited mortal vision and mind could grasp before it blew.

**Me** – That's all very fine and dandy…

**Mr G** – Shiny?

**Me** – Beautiful, but seeing you from the back?

**Mr G** – Well?

**Me** – I'm not so sure. All those tenth dimensional chakras moving in gold 6-D, holographic, kaleidoscopic rotation? Also, I thought the back of you was where you placed and ate all the leftover races and unnecessary nations that had become atrocities before your eyes?

**Mr G** – Those abominable inter-species, half-breeds, orcs and wicked giants had to be recycled somewhere. Some of early Gaia creations got a bit ugly and full of themselves. So I rejected their offerings and scrapped some of the more monstrous episodes.

**Me** – A bit like I scrapped some of my early lives when I was first trying to get the hang of reincarnation?

**Mr G** *(remembering)* – Oh so long ago! Harmonisation isn't so easy on your side of the cloud. It's a soft science, often imprecise and experimental, where you draw your own conclusions on shifting perspectives, altering attitudes and conceptions that take you back to the place-in-the-stars where you were first conceived. Once you've got the basic principles you can start living in harmony with Nature, Gaia and the good galactic universe.

**Me** – Ah, yes! At-one-ment.

**Mr G** – Perhaps here I can hint at your upcoming harmonisation work. Don't get caught up in harmonising people and things. Be part of the star symphony you already are and emanate from there. Star craft is an ancient art where the convergence of the split feminine and masculine achieves holistic unity through acceptance and peace.

**Me** – I'm more of an inspirational kind of romantic, idealistic, post-modern mishmash of doom, hope and humanity!

**Mr G** – Right now you can have the earthly satisfaction of being where you are supposed to be with the right people. You have got your timing right which is a big plus. Congratulations! *(ticks a box shaped like the T.A.R.D.I.S.)*

**Me** – Thanks, I think.

**Mr G** – You're perfectly welcome. Trust yourself and your soul urges a bit more. You see, rummaging around your dreams and broken ideals can be useful. Spend your time being helpful and have a wonderful lifespan with lots of different phases, cycles, encounters and achievements.

**Me** – Like "always look on the bright side of life"?

**Mr G** – Exactly! You're all the same. All uniquely individual.

**Me** *(spiritedly)* – "I'm not!"

**Mr G** *(laughs)* – Especially the contrary ones of your particular primate sub-genus!

**Me** – Right…

**Mr G** *(smiling)* – Progression. That's what you're here for. To fully realise yourself, whoever that might be. But most important is the tap… *(Mr G thinks about doing a spectacular Top-Hat-and-Cane routine as both Fred Astaire and Ginger Rogers to prove he can out dance them, forward, backward and in heels, but decides against it)* …I mean the chat. Don't forget to chat to people along The Way. 'Hello' is the best icebreaker, unless you're visiting the silence of course. Then it can be very annoying and distracting, particularly when emitting from the more garrulous ones.

**Me** *(bemused)* – The chattering monkeys and eternal babble. Yes, the Buddha mentioned those, but thanks for re-iterating.

**Mr G** – Very important in teaching. *(peering at Me)* Particularly the remedial.

**Me** – But a bit boring to educated audiences.

**Mr G** – Quite! So, how about that view of Me from the back?

**Me** – Thanks, but I think I'll pass. Given my sudden inclination to swirls, star-bursts and energy vortices I don't want to end up being sucked into one of your annihilation chakras by mistake!

**Mr G** – I'd put you a safe distance of course.

**Me** – Of course, but orbiting black holes or death stars, however much on the golden side, is not really my thing.

**Mr G** – Where's your love of sky-high sci-fi and drama?

**Me** – I'm more of a social-cultural-observer-from-the-sofa-kind-of-guy than space-action hero nowadays.

**Mr G** – And to think you never used to have a television.

**Me** *(shrugs)* – I know. Just been getting more human like you said.

**Mr G** *(winking)* – But boundaries understood if still a bit hazy. Willing sacrificial energy morsels are so hard to find these days.

**Me** – Really! I'm glad to hear that. Blood sacrifices aren't really part of the new energy down here.

**Mr G** – Okay, we'll leave the 'back view' for the moment, but you can't put off the inevitable.

**Me** – Sorry, is it avoidance again?

**Mr G** – Usually best to go there and push on through.

**Me** – Sounds a bit painful!

**Mr G** – Not for one such as you.

**Me** *(surprised)* – Oh…

**Mr G** – Because of your flexibility.

**Me** *(perplexed)* – Right! Er, so?

**Mr G** – Remember the triangles? *(Mr G creates a 3D folding model that swivels into an array of geometric triangles and cosmological star-shapes with a satisfying 'ping' sound)* With those you can always re-orbit at leisure.

**Me** *(bothered, bewitched, bemused)* – Not that one again! No! I don't get the triangles, *(truly not getting the new star-art-craft implications being shown)* but thanks for the demonstration. *(pause as Mr G hands Me a geometric star-construction model. Mr G waits. Me guesses wildly)* Is it the Pleiades?

**Mr G** – No.

**Me** – Oh! *(instantly giving in, Me places the triangular-star configuration model back on Mr G's desk)* Thanks anyway, but can't I just watch 'The Sky at Night' and you overshadow it?

**Mr G** – No. *(slowly)* So… *(pause)*

**Me** – So…?

**Mr G** – About your review? Anything else to consider?

**Me** – Me? About my life?

**Mr G** – Yes.

**Me** *(slightly stunned, but trying to gather himself together)* – Um… You know when we die and have to review the whole thing…

**Mr G** – *Choose to* review in your well-earned love-wisdom at the end of days. But you're right, everyone does.

**Me** – Okay, 'choose to' review the whole thing…

**Mr G** – In the magnetic lake of recorded-reflection before going off to the halls of healing or the library of learning. *(chortles)* That's if you're lucky to escape the imprisonment of your own self-defined Heaven-or-Hell in-between life-system that is!

**Me** – Oh! Is it self-imposed?

**Mr G** – Who else is judging you but you? Yet I will act out anything you might wish to experience. Heaven or Hell… *(smiles)*

**Me** – Well, it's going to be pretty terrible isn't it? It's been such a gloopy spaghetti mess.

**Mr G** – You mean your rich, full and rather tasty life?

**Me** – Yes, but it's just been so ridiculous at times.

**Mr G** – True, your Mediterranean muddle, struggle and personal coping mechanism-of-change have all been stretched along The Way.

It's all about testing your reactions and responses. You do remember the difference between those two?

**Me** *(struggling to answer)* – Er? The difference between our conditioning and choice?

**Mr G** – Well, your learned responses, instinctive reactions and your environmentally affected, adaptive gene-action are the sum total of your enhanced life's activity response. The struggle is to be fully in the operative 'now' in connection to Eternity and the life force. *(jokingly)* To 'free will,' or not to 'free will,' that is the question?

**Me** *(joshing back)* – I prefer my Shakespeare freed!

**Mr G** – Then the nobler mind will *suffer* until it takes arms.

**Me** – Humph, it would! But oh, "the slings and arrows of my outrageous 'mis'-fortune"!

**Mr G** *(smiling)* – And 'mis'-quoting! Perhaps from here on in you could try…

**Me** – Oh! I know, I know. Try and be a bit more mindful.

**Mr G** *(gently)* – No, I was going to say you could try being less hard on yourself and develop a greater sense of humour.

**Me** *(pleasantly surprised)* – Oh! Really?

**Mr G** – Believe me, you all look pretty funny from where I reside.

**Me** – Oh! What? From your great, big, comfy cloud-sofa-throne in the sky, you mean?

**Mr G** – The quantum eyeball does like to watch down upon people from the 'window of the world' from time to time. And humour is one of my more forgotten qualities.

**Me** *(acerbic)* – Yes, I know. Very funny, ha ha! All our plans, for example. That old chestnut.

**Mr G** *(self-satisfied)* – Well, I did make you and make no mistake that's pretty funny in itself.

**Me** – I'm glad you're so readily amused!

**Mr G** – You must admit that the human race… It is pretty entertaining on the whole - are you not?

**Me** – I suppose we were just a last minute divine whim?

**Mr G** – Well, if I'm to be fair, more of a Darwinian-divine-comedy, evolution, extinction-vacuum replacement, Big Bang, Nature kind of thing. Nature made you. I created Nature. Yet consciousness inhabited the geo-sphere long before you lot came along.

**Me** *(baffled)* – The rock people?

**Mr G** *(laughing)* – Everything replicates even minerals. The outward born came from the intermingling cosmic comet carbon races. Spirit and soul were born from the light-of-consciousness. Humanity was an afterthought suggested by one of the light-bearing Star Angels. Spirit resides in the place between maths and physics in the computational frequencies that currently confound. The back-and-forth interaction is the experience you call life existences.

**Me** *(utterly bewildered)* – Oh…

**Mr G** – There was a space so Nature kindly fitted you lot in. Well… splurging Nature did it in tandem with surging Supernature, but a light-survival soul-retrieval scheme had to be introduced first.

**Me** – Very generous of you.

**Mr G** – Now, now. You do really need to unnecessarily suffer to get the whole joke.

**Me** – Thanks, again!

**Mr G** – Everyone has an inbuilt joy-capacitor, which they need to activate. Certain societies have nurtured this more than others. You've certainly created some great civilisations in the past and on the whole this one isn't too bad…

**Me** – For some…

**Mr G** – However, I spent a lot of time on getting the planets and stars right. It's quite a craft. Perhaps you would like to come back as a planet or a star and keep a regulatory eye on them for me?

**Me** – I don't think I have the patience.

**Mr G** *(smiling)* – 'Yet!' It's just waiting to be extracted.

**Me** *(ignoring Mr G, but not wanting to encourage any more long-suffering)* – If I have to come back I was thinking of spending some time as a tree.

**Mr G** – Useful then?

**Me** *(musing)* – "Deep in the heart of the Hundred Acre Wood". It might help me with serenity.

**Mr G** – I think your future fantasy plans are more a harking back to childhood and a wistful reminiscence of past tree lives.

**Me** – Yes, I did love the orchards and the big old walnut tree overlooking the small farm.

**Mr G** – Lots in your active, outdoor childhood to be grateful for and a reminder of the much forgotten element and way of wood. Yet you are no longer the sapling, but the great oak tree itself.

**Me** *(absorbed and distant)* – True, too true.

*(affected by Me's childhood reflection, Mr G suddenly becomes introspective, pensive and withdrawn. Whole early-forming galaxies and constellations whip up and explode about him turning to cosmic dust. Black holes start grinding star-clusters into energy ribbons. The Almighty Hand gets out a dustpan and brush)*

**Mr G** – Ah! The exploration of gravitational regret and nostalgia.

**Me** *(seizing the opportunity for an old joke)* – It's not what it used to be! Boom! Boom!

*(lost in the echoing sound of 'kabooming' exploding worlds, Mr G does not respond and grows distant. Me watches as Mr G drifts off into a momentary cataleptic state whilst pondering on the ever-expanding and collapsing multi-verse's all-and-everything. Mr G releases a loud sigh, then catches his breath whilst giving out a slight 'Ah ha!' sound as though he is conducting a surprise rather than a sunrise. In response, the Cloud-Office shimmers and flickers, quickly blinking off-then-on again creating a ghostly spectral-rift in the time-space continuum. Afterwards, everything seems the same, but the fabric of the universe feels different)*

**Me** *(concerned)* – Are you all right?

**Mr G** *(rousing)* – Oops! Did I drop off? I hope we didn't disappear?

*(shaken, Me pats himself down to make sure he, the hip flask, snuff pouch and Post-it notes are all still present and correct)*

**Me** *(concerned)* – Are you all right? Was that a senior moment or something more serious?

**Mr G** – More of a consciousness portal-drift between naps. Sorry about that. It's an occasional slip I sometimes have between dream and the alternating greater reality. It's like a cosmic reboot, I still get the occasional unexpected surge, but I think that was just a slight bubble-bump between the multi-verses.

*(the Almighty Hand brings a glass of water with effervescing star gems sparkling and dissolving within. Mr G necks back the soluble cosmic dust and holds onto his liver. 'That's better.' Coming to, Mr G re-orientates himself and picks up Me's file which is now looking rather thin and empty)*

**Mr G** – More importantly though… How's your present going?

**Me** – To be honest, I'm a little dazed and confused.

**Mr G** – You always were. A certain amount of confusion can sometimes be helpful. Stupidity should be like an eager dog learning new tricks snapping at the heels of wisdom. However, whilst enthusiasm is helpful, over-worrying and pessimism are not.

**Me** – I know, I know, but I still get the occasional self-doubt day.

**Mr G** – Some of those hazy days of eradicating vagueness that you like are part of an old impressionistic approach toward love and life. Like sparkling light on water, or when squinting at a field of sunflowers and poppies, or looking at a face through a forest of fingers, it sometimes helps you get a different version of light and a new angle on events. Forgetfulness is a type of memory loss and gain given over to the greater magnetic force of forgiveness.

**Me** – And if I've been a bit of an Eeyore of late, I do apologise.

**Mr G** – It's understandable when you've had the stuffing knocked out of you, but a tendency to droop in the neck means your general demeanour becomes a bit characterized.

**Me** – I know, gloom and doom. Rain clouds! Thistles! Soggy chocolate! That kind of thing.

**Mr G** – I get the picture, but don't forget the pretty, pink ribbon tied around your tail! And remember, "he who sits on a thistle shall rise again". You've been waiting around so long you've been staring at the ground counting the clouds' shadows and forgetting their silver linings. Adverse weather conditions began to prevail. That's why you needed the new electricity. *(smiling)* Generally, old souls can be a bit on the grumpy and sulky side, more to refer to and rationalise, but you've tapped into your inner resources and are now resonating well.

**Me** – Sometimes I get despondent so I had to dig deep.

**Mr G** – Your energy reserves were greater than most, and now you are a new welcomed source of optimism and universal energy, which is nice.

**Me** *(hesitantly enquiring)* – For others or me?

**Mr G** – Does it matter? Just enjoy. Optimism is considered the best kind of unfair advantage life has to offer. That and precious Sun-energy. If you could see the holographic light seeds and star formations from where I stand you might reconsider your outlook.

**Me** – Will it hurt? That kind of reassessment might be a bit big for my brain to comprehend at this point. Another mind-fuse blow out isn't really what I need at this point.

**Mr G** – You're more elastic than that, but okay. Another time. Perhaps when you decide to orbit the back of me.

**Me** *(boldly)* – Right. Now, about this money thing. I thought pocket prosperity was something you readily provided for everyone? So c'mon! Show me your wallet and not one stuffed with pterodactyl moths and tetradrams! If you believe in me then invest in me.

**Mr G** *(amused)* – I let you know which slots to play.

**Me** – Oh! Thanks, but even that was a trap.

**Mr G** *(smiling)* – You mean all roads lead to God. As you unwind you have to retrace the trail you originally took when you first left me.

**Me** – But we never left?

**Mr G** – Precisely! An interesting illusion.

**Me** *(pleading)* – But I need money…

**Mr G** – Tsk! I've already discussed this with you. You're rich in difficult experience. That should be worth a bob or two.

**Me** – Okay, enough said. Take money out of the system. For richer or poorer… Is that the gist?

**Mr G** – Why? Are you still stuck in survival mode counting the pennies and pounds and debating deservedness and privilege?

**Me** *(inwardly groaning afraid of another action point)* – No, but it's hard to let go of money worries when you have so little of it!

**Mr G** – Focus on abundance rather than diminishing financial return and buffers. That should sort it out.

**Me** *(still unclear)* – Right…?

**Mr G** – Good. Otherwise it becomes a stuck force in your subconscious, which in turn blocks the prosperity provision of all. *(smiling)* And you wouldn't want to do that now, would you?

**Me** *(resignedly)* – Of course not! I'll see what I can do.

**Mr G** – Perhaps see it as a pleasant 'prosperity' action-point that you'd like to work on.

**Me** – That sounds better. I certainly will.

**Mr G** – And I look forward to seeing the results. When there's truly nothing left you really will need a miracle. Remember what your grandmother said?

**Me** *(fondly remembering)* – "Your life will turn on a sixpence."

**Mr G** – Exactly, but as I said, you are a millionaire in the making.

**Me** *(agitated)* – Am I? Did you? Did I forget to write down the winning lottery numbers?

**Mr G** – Oh! Didn't you catch the flashing number sequence earlier? Your memory. Should we set it as one of your performance targets?

**Me** – Is that one of those SMART things? You know - specific, measurable, attainable, realistic and timely?

**Mr G** – Why? Am I not all those things?

**Me** – Er… I don't really know. Are you quantifiable in that way? I experience you more as emotional qualities.

**Mr G** – Yes, you do, don't you? Feelings and oh-so-slow thoughts, which isn't really me at all. More of a 'you' thing.

**Me** – Oh, sorry. What I meant is, will it hurt, hinder or help doing those kinds of analysis things?

**Mr G** – What happened to the unexpected twist with happy endings and that famous sense of 'fun and adventure' of yours? Have I ever let you down?

**Me** *(carefully)* – Noooo…

**Mr G** – Even the difficult bits?

**Me** *(slowly considering)* – Well, no. In the end all has turned out well.

**Mr G** *(smiling, briskly)* – Yes, it usually does.

**Me** *(muttering)* – Purely a matter of surviving and getting there, that's all.

**Mr G** *(ignoring Me)* – Says here, *(tapping file)* beginnings and endings you like, but less fond of the middle 'processing' bits. Even when the tragedy has served a releasing and rejuvenating purpose?

**Me** – That's true.

**Mr G** *(reading notes)* – Also says here that you're super-sensitive to stress and often feel bewildered?

**Me** – I'm not so good at dealing with minor irritations or containing frustrations and general vexations to very good plans.

**Mr G** – Enough already of your moans and groans on the paper-cuts of life! Do you really want me to supply all the safeguards and answers? *(Me is tempted to say, 'Yes', but wisely stays silent)* Life happens. That's the point. Just because you judge some experiences as good or bad doesn't mean it's not all useful.

**Me** – I know, I know.

**Mr G** – All that 'strange fruit' growing on your branches didn't get there by itself. Why else would I be shaking your tree and beating your branches with a stick?

**Me** *(puzzled)* – You want my fruit?

**Mr G** – Eating fruit is eating the sex of a plant, which as a process required a third party to intervene to achieve its full-blossoming and ripening.

**Me** *(quizzically)* – The bee's knees? The rain's fall? The Sun's shine?

**Mr G** *(smiling brightly)* – Sometimes you get a chance to think about what you're going to do. Other times you have to get on with it and trust your intuitions and instincts. Whilst on rare occasions you might sometimes be the recipient of an incoming divine gold buzzing, cross-pollinating honey-bee of higher forces!

**Me** *(not knowing whether to be pleased or not)* – Oh!

**Mr G** – The onus here today is on your own self-evaluation with a few useful pointers from me as necessary. Now, o-bemoaning-one in a seemingly endless sea-of-troubles, bottom line! Would you like me to recall you so you can start the whole process again or not?

**Me** – What? Of course not, but I get your point! And if you don't mind me saying, you're getting a bit tetchy. I didn't think you were allowed to be like that?

**Mr G** *(setting the record straight)* – Remember, I am! Consequently, I can be however, whoever and whatever I want to be.

**Me** – But mainly love?

**Mr G** – Yes, mainly love. But remember to add 'and' or 'with' to the love-word if it helps.

**Me** *(tentative)* – Let go 'with' love? Love 'and' anger? Truth 'with' love.

**Mr G** – Good examples. *(ticks three boxes)* So?

**Me** – So… Tempting as your offer is to give up the ghost, come home early and start again, I'd rather not go just now.

**Mr G** – If it's reassurances you're after, I can remind you that I helped create the world, I shall help sustain it and I will help destroy it.

**Me** – Very helpful, but not at all reassuring. You must really like your job to make statements like that?

**Mr G** – Be under no illusion. For your species, I am vengeance and suffering to those who turn away from me in as much as I am love and peace to those who walk toward me. Nature and Super Nature will avenge. They have to, for they were designed to. Ultimately, it's all about balance and planetary regulation *(Mr G puts on a display demonstrating how galactic dragons and cosmic serpents hold the galaxies together and bring about the homeostasis of planets and nations)*

**Me** *(boggled)* – Thanks! So gravity as a force is alive?

**Mr G** *(smiling)* – Certainly! Dragons' tails act like anchors whilst serpents stretch and work as expanding coils, but I like to keep them as pets.

**Me** – And whilst I am extremely grateful for the path of light on which I find myself treading, sometimes the physics is all a bit too much.

**Mr G** – I'm pleased to hear it, but brown-nosing won't change anything. Likewise, *(referring to file)* I've noticed a bit too much self-recrimination in your life encounters recently.

**Me** – Well, perhaps a bit hard on myself as previously mentioned.

**Mr G** – Whereas you are not on others. Suggests a bit of an imbalance to me. But on the whole…

**Me** *(joking, but with diminishing return)* – Not 'in' the hole? I do have a tendency toward tripping and falling into them. Usually the same one.

**Mr G** *(kindly, but disinterestedly)* – I see. Was it self-dug?

**Me** – I know, too stunning for words! Luckily for me, my head's just about screwed on and my inner idiot always knows what time it is.

**Mr G** *(playing along)* – And pray, what time is that?

**Me** – Stupid o'clock, silly! Sometimes I'm so dumb, but I get there in the end - usually in the nick of time to save the day. *(Me does a Super Ted impression)*

**Mr G** *(laughing)* – Dumb, disinterested or disorganised?

**Me** – The usual lack of interest and lots of resistance.

**Mr G** – They're all quite usual in rainbow experiences. You are only human whatever other complexes you might have. In some areas you have extra-ordinary insight and wisdom, but in other areas you have blind spots and fear points.

**Me** – You mean jeopardising weaknesses?

**Mr G** – You're a specialised force so you do have rather large chunks of astrological data missing from your chart.

**Me** *(forthright)* – You mean stupid, absent-minded and in some respects under-developed. Some things I just don't get!

**Mr G** *(gently)* – Perhaps a bit Looney Tunes at times. You're not so fond of other people's nonsense, but beginning to enjoy your own, which at least is now the right way round. So… *(wanting to tick a box, grinning)* Is that 'daft bugger' or 'silly old sod'?

**Me** – Even you don't know whether to be angry or loving with me!

**Mr G** – Indeed, quite the challenge… With you it's more a case of one, two, buckle my shoe.

**Me** – You mean, one step forwards, two steps back?

**Mr G** *(smiling)* – Too much water off the old duck's back, but you're a better life warrior-dancer than that.

**Me** – Really?

**Mr G** – Your approach to life and its circumstances could be considered as being like a needle-and-thread. You were experiencing recent events as the loop of a thread in a backstitch within an otherwise rich progressive tapestry. Your physical body is the point of metal contact engaging with physical matter and experience whilst the streaming energy ribbons and threads flow about and behind you.

**Me** – Back to being blunt or sharp again?

**Mr G** – Remember, soft and weak overcome hard and strong. There is much more going on behind the scenes than you will ever know. Yet you find you cannot always grasp or hold onto the true nature of life as it constantly evaporates about you. But apart from being a bit backwards in coming forwards, you're turning into quite a nice person... Badly hidden crimes, mild-mannered misdemeanours, white lies and transgressions aside, that is.

**Me** *(perking up)* – Really? Is that good?

**Mr G** – Yes. Well, better than being bad if you're talking dualistically!

**Me** *(can't believe his luck)* – Am I off the hook?

**Mr G** *(guilelessly)* – Why? Had you put yourself on one?

**Me** *(confused)* – Maybe?

**Mr G** – Did it help?

**Me** *(puzzled)* – Not sure.

**Mr G** – It all depends as to whether or not you see me as a benevolent or a malevolent force. Dextera!

> *On one level, and until your spiritual breakthrough, GOD - the Galactic Ordering Dynamic - simply reflects you and your internal guilt, crime-and-punishment system.*
>
> *Likewise, the universe echoes whichever imposed religious-social code you are viewing the cosmos through if your conditioned self is still prevalent.*
>
> *Being good and doing the right thing, or rather being heart-centred and not mind-centred, is the best approach for the planet and all concerned right now.*
>
> *Ultimately, love and truth combined into peace is all there is.*

**Mr G** – Unfortunately, the heart is taking a beating. Look at Tibet. Personally I would suggest a little more self-encouragement and faith in your approach to future projects. Talking of which, there are quite a few coming up so I suggest you get cracking, catch up with yourself and get your plate clean.

**Me** *(unenthusiastically)* – Oh, not more work!

**Mr G** – Trim the sails and clear the decks so to speak.

**Me** *(muttering)* – Out of the frying pan into the fire. I was hoping for a vacation.

**Mr G** – You've got quite a lot of rather interesting work stacking up in front of you, that's all.

**Me** – Oh…

**Mr G** – That perked you up a bit.

**Me** – Fun projects?

**Mr G** – Yes, it's a big job. 5-stars coming right at ya.

**Me** *(resignedly)* – Make it 7-stars and I'm in. Bring it on.

**Mr G** – That's the spirit. Broke, not broken. Needs a heart exploding with love and goodness, not pusillanimity.

**Me** – Better than dancing on graves and all that cross-examination, I suppose. Do I have to re-visit the past?

**Mr G** – No, not in this instance. Although if you do have to re-visit the past you shouldn't be afraid to. As long as you've grieved and forgiven you can move forward. This is more about your approach to the future. Just remember that in silence and immobility, those on this side of the cloud can help you a whole lot quicker. Still, as long as you're letting the spirit in…

**Me** – All sounds a bit Zen. The grass grows… The rain falls… Thy will be done! That kind of thing.

**Mr G** *(distracted)* – Now, what I do need to talk to you about before you go is this note from the Moon…

**Me** – Yes, she's been very helpful in my etheric night sky gazing practice lately. It's quite hard for us Sun signs to go her way. *(lyrically)* "When the Lady's Moon is new, kiss the hand to her times two."

**Mr G** *(rhyming back)* – "When the Moon rides at her peak then your heart's desire seek."

*(Mr G and Me both smile, when the Almighty Hand suddenly uncovers the note from the Moon amongst a clutter of files, leaves and drifting paper, and intervenes)*

**Mr G** – Thank you, Domini. *(reading note)* Now, it says here, that when you were at the Full Moon Beach Island party, you tried listening in, but were a bit reluctant to start with.

**Me** – Yes, er… Well, it was all very distracting and I didn't really feel inclined to listen about past relations and exes.

**Mr G** – No, apparently not, but you found it useful when you did?

**Me** – Yes, the Moon was full of wisdom and compassion as ever.

**Mr G** *(making note on Me's file)* – What did you learn?

**Me** *(reflectively)* – That on looking back, I was to cherish the memories of experience, to be thankful - even the difficult ones and those with imperfect endings.

**Mr G** – In part they made you who you are and likewise you them. Perhaps more regular reflective practice and a little more looking at things from other people's perspectives? Otherwise, your Moon report was excellent.

**Me** – Yes, she's good for the heart and soul in that way.

**Mr G** – And not forgetting the necessary madness of the Moon mind and the terror of the night sky?

**Me** *(honestly)* – I wasn't initially so good at all that. A bit frightening.

**Mr G** *(continues reading note verbatim)* – Says here, 'Your tutelage was an interesting struggle in growth and development, but ultimately you began to understand the necessary holism and unity of the grand design to work towards your deepening integration of your light strands and the spiritually-encapsulated self'.

**Me** *(scratching head in a puzzled manner)* – Oh, sounds promising so far!

**Mr G** *(continuing)* – Yes. 'Nothing left now except for your total immersion and absorption into the final fabric rays of cosmic life'.

**Me** *(unsure)* – Oh! Is that a pleasant experience?

**Mr G** – Depends on your ability to synchronize with the energies of the harmonic convergence. Your Jupiter might be a bit stuck.

**Me** – Remind me again. Is that a me-thing or a you-thing?

**Mr G** – A little bit of both. Remember, we're not separate.

**Me** *(hitting his head)* – Boing! Of course, silly me.

**Mr G** *(reading from file and laughing)* – There is one big event still to come, a shared spiritual vision kind of thing, and several smaller wonderful occasions. Plus quite a few lovely surprise experiences you'll be pleased to know.

**Me** – Thanks, most helpful if not terribly enlightening! *(distant thunder roll as the Almighty Hand trembles a wobble-board with a soft timpani mallet)*

**Mr G** *(eagerly)* – What was that? You'd like more ways of lightning?

**Me** *(un-amused)* – You're deliberately mishearing. Anyway lightning rarely strikes twice.

**Mr G** *(smiling)* – Not impossible, but once struck, twice bifurcated and bitten!

**Me** *(confused)* – I thought that was snakes?

**Mr G** – Plenty of those around at the moment too. Now, tell me one thing… Do people still tend to see God as a person?

**Me** – I imagine each species tends to project their own image on to you, that's all.

**Mr G** – Good. As long as they know that I'm not actually a person and that in truth I am a…

**Me** *(interjecting)* – Synchronized, organized, dynamic, galactic, unified, extra-ordinary, universal loving energy system. Yes, I think they all know that.

**Mr G** *(places another gold star on Me's file whilst the Almighty Hand does a generous thumbs up)* – With the God-head being full of new forming, tachyon, multi-dimensional qi-energy?

**Me** – That undivided, frothing, white energy stuff, you mean?

**Mr G** – Yes. Because if they still think I'm a guy in a cloud with an office in the sky… That would be pretty ridiculous!

**Me** *(agreeing, but wanting to leave)* – Absolutely ridiculous! Anyway, can we get back to manifesting and me?

**Mr G** – I provide for the sparrows don't I? All in all, you *are* a tiny bit funny in making monetary demands on me - rather like someone biting the hand that feeds them? *(feeling financially frustrated, irritated and restricted, Me purses his lips, sits on his hands and says nothing)* No, not even a little bit funny? *(ignoring Mr G, Me looks out of the window defiantly)* Remember, spirit is impersonal. How else could the streaming of the quantum field work?

**Me** *(struggling to boldly re-engage)* – With less entanglement if we had a clue how it worked properly and how we functioned within it!

**Mr G** – Precisely, keep up the good guess work.

**Me** – Thanks, I think they call it science!

**Mr G** – Cute, is it a growing art?

**Me** – Very funny. Anyway, I thought science was a branch of old alchemical magic?

**Mr G** – It is. It's only in recent times that it seems to have become rather reductionist. At least most of the ancient meta-physicists knew karma was a cause-and-effect Newtonian principle caused by undissolved light links. Ultimately there is no shame, yet whereas wrongdoing creates karma it is unforgiveness that maintains it.

**Me** – Karma, but that's for spiritual people, right?

**Mr G** – Still seeing karma as good deed cookies placed in a cookie jar?

**Me** – Too right, and I'm looking forward to a complete blow out with my inner cookie monster after all this and scoff the lot!

**Mr G** – As long as you know that the components you borrow from the elemental universe for your soul's earthly journey have to be paid back untarnished. In and of themselves they are non-corruptible, but if you corrupt them you are personally responsible.

**Me** – So, be free, harm none and do what you will. I just believe in your compassion and forgiveness… and a clip round the ear if I deserve one. *(the Almighty Hand hovers near Me's head hopefully)* It's all in the observers' hearts and mind I suppose?

**Mr G** *(smiling fondly, but shooing the Almighty Hand away)* – In the current seeming war-of-consciousness people's choices will either put them on the right or wrong side of mankind's history. Any new karmic bonds and links will unfold from there.

**Me** – As a kind of elemental justice? But you've got to believe it before you can see it?

**Mr G** – Yes and no. The light fabric exists without you believing or seeing it. However, the outlook of the observer moves the energy field and affects the quantum world where you and many other forms of existence all co-exist. Some scientists tend to forget the telepathic interplay and inter-connected nature of consciousness. Yet, it is belief that allows you to harness the electro-magnetic principles of magic - scientist or artist. *(pause)*

**Me** *(innocently, but cleverly)* – So...

**Mr G** – Is it that time again? Ah! I see what you're doing there. Managing our little conversation. Turning the 'so' around. Remember, you're in a good position, but make sure you look after yourself. Don't get lazy and don't eat too much bread or too many chips otherwise you'll develop 'angel wing'.

**Me** – What's that?

**Mr G** – It's a flight problem suffered by angels and swans. It results in stunted deformed growth and weak energy feathers.

**Me** – Fallout feathers no good as quills then?

**Mr G** – No, your quips will be stunted too.

**Me** *(sadly)* – So no more chips with curry sauce, onion gravy, pickled onions or extra cheese?

**Mr G** – Well, never say never... But if your wings get out of balance keep re-attuning, otherwise it might stop you from flying so high.

**Me** – I do like my food.

**Mr G** *(reading from file)* – Indeed! Your file self-assessment says that you 'maintain a sensible stomach, practical shoes and a regular mind!' But I must say with a tendency to flap.

**Me** – I get a bit 'over anxious' and that, mixed with my ability to go around in circles, isn't always great.

**Mr G** – You're more 'over easy' than anything else. *(Mr G laughs unto himself and makes a mental note, 'It's the little things that still get me')* Your anxiety reveals a lack of trust and creates most of your problems. So don't do it. Remember, "Cast all your cares upon me".

**Me** *(enthusiastically)* – Ah, my cares and wears of the world. You're most welcome to them.

**Mr G** – Or rather know when you are leading from anxiety, re-align yourself to the inspiration of the source and operate from there.

**Me** – So less distress, more success?

**Mr G** – "Pick yourself up. Dust yourself down. Start all over again." A sort of new planetary swing time. Rise each day afresh and remember… "Don't worry. Be Happy." The universe provides.

**Me** – Is that another me thing?

**Mr G** – It certainly is! Who else is there? You seem to have forgotten that you are the solution you seek.

**Me** – Oh! I thought it might be a mutual trust 'us' thing and that you could help out a bit more.

**Mr G** *(directly)* – I'm *always* helping. Looking after you is my job. Unfortunately for you my job is now becoming your job.

**Me** – I thought you had proper sky angels for that?

**Mr G** *(sighs)* – Trust in your wings and natural providence as you would the life Force. One wing is Mother-God; the other wing is Father-God. The golden-clasp holds the green emerald and links the two energy circuits together in the centre of your chest. *(the Almighty Hand polishes Me's Light Wing harness until it gleams)* Remember the space-suit conversation?

**Me** *(brightly, but having forgotten)* – Oh yeah!

**Mr G** *(flicking to the end of Me's report)* – Now, I do need to put you down for some kind of life aspiration. If you can't make a decision between space cadet, peace warrior or wizard, how about we settle for one of the 'realised' type of lives?

**Me** – Sounds a bit challenging and a bit… You know… Possibly a bit too wholesome for me? How about a 'surf 'n' turf', quick-slow, spicy-life combo aspiration?

**Mr G** – Can you handle it without complaining?

**Me** – Of course! As long as I can remain in disguise.

**Mr G** – No, you can't remain covert. The size of your wings will make it harder for you to slip under the radar now. And we haven't really discussed name and costume options yet.

**Me** *(considering)* – What do lounging poet-pirate-kings wear these days?

**Mr G** – How about a beard and a 1920's suit? Or a Louis XV frilly shirt?

**Me** – Vintage! They sound nice, but not a bit specific or a tad too old-fashioned?

**Mr G** – You old-fashioned? Don't make me laugh. What do you want? Gown, staff… Burning bush?

**Me** *(miffed)* – I rather like special effects, but should I sport the beard of wisdom? Or how about a Tintin quiff with a shiny, happy face?

**Mr G** – Well, if you stop compartmentalising yourself you'll find that you do have a flair for the theatrical. So why not balance and combine the lot and have fun with it.

**Me** – Oh, okay. I wonder if Neptune would lend me his trident for that outdoor, sea-blown look? He would look good as a figurehead.

**Mr G** *(continuing oblivious)* – And did you want a name?

**Me** – Okay, go on. What is it or should I guess? Oh! Oh! I've got one. Let me tell you…

*(pause, then together)*

**Me** – 'Squirrel Nutkin!'

**Mr G** – 'Arch-Mage!'

*(uncomfortable pause)*

**Me** – Oh! Is that snap?

**Mr G** – No, mine is trumps.

**Me** – Cool. I like the sound of yours, but I'd settle for being a 'Starship Trooper'.

**Mr G** – I'd like to say ditto, but on second thoughts I think yours might be more realistic.

**Me** – Does it involve disco?

**Mr G** *(teasingly)* – Might do.

**Me** – Then perhaps 'Funky Silver Disco Fox' would be a good name.

**Mr G** *(unimpressed)* – Hm! Along with a fluffy radio soundtrack to sublimate your Father Christmas fantasy?

**Me** *(shrugs)* – I can see that you're not keen. Does it mean more fun?

**Mr G** – Possibly. So… *(turning back to the file wanting to tick a box)* What type of life should I put you down for then?

**Me** – I don't know. How about an ordinary, happy and fulfilled one? If I'm hesitant to commit it's because I'm not sure of my options or what I'm signing up to. I don't want to restrict the possibilities.

**Mr G** – Fair enough, but that probably relates to your comment written here on the bottom of your last feedback form. I can't quite read your writing…

**Me** – I know. My notes-to-self are just as indecipherable!

**Mr G** – Something about initiation and you being 'sacrifice adverse'? I do understand that many an ending to some of your previous incarnations have been on the more violent and martyr side.

**Me** *(remembering a particularly painful, inverted crucifixion)* – They hurt.

**Mr G** – Understandable then, that the 'wounding' aspect should be so prevalent. Remember, the deeper the wound the greater the payback healing and earthly repair.

**Me** – That's okay, I'm just not going to choose that way in the future. But it wasn't me who corrupted the last age.

**Mr G** *(slightly exasperated)* – You're all in it together! If you have any genuine positive improvements to the galactic Earth heart-time system then please let me know. Meanwhile, once you reach the 95% pass mark then re-incarnation is only for those wanting to help… a life of service beyond self.

**Me** *(concerned)* – Oh, that percentage pass mark seems rather high.

**Mr G** – It's based on your reconciled feather-of-truth heart-scale score.

**Me** – Oh! Love of self, God or others?

**Mr G** – You're not separate remember.

**Me** – Duh! See, I'm that stupid.

**Mr G** – Neither God-realisation or self-realisation come easy.

**Me** *(puzzled)* – And is it 'self' or 'God' that I'm currently working on?

**Mr G** – Classic! You've realised God already otherwise you couldn't be here. Self is more difficult. Always more to come to terms with.

**Me** – Good job there's no exam board or grade inflation to worry about!

**Mr G** – No, but we do have the most wonderful standards of love.

**Me** – Hopefully not too exacting! And please don't mention that 'perfection' word. Really not useful.

**Mr G** – You mean the love of imperfection, surely? In the final consideration when all burns to ashes and the phoenix rises, 'practically perfect' will do.

**Me** – And you mean joy, right? Service is such an old-fashioned word.

**Mr G** – I'm glad to hear you say that, but it's been awhile since your last incarnation. *(tapping file and reading notes: 1929 last breath. Reborn 1964)* So, 35 years out of it. That's why it's taken you a bit longer than usual to fully wake up.

**Me** – The Rip Van Winkle effect. I was warned about it.

**Mr G** – It's an unusual amount of time to take out between lives, although it can be anywhere between a few minutes and 100 years maximum. After that it's too difficult to acclimatise to planetary change unless you're a master. 35 years is still quite a long time and that's why your memory and ability for languages was affected. But 'in the spirit of things' you're at your happiest when helping others.

**Me** – Apparently!

**Mr G** – You all have to get off the reincarnation roundabout at some point. Plenty of other things to do, but sometimes spirit misses not being in flesh and pops down even if not in a full human life.

**Me** – I see… I find my life is more bins, bills and shopping bags than anything else these days!

**Mr G** – You are here to realise yourself in consciousness terms, but it is 'beingness' and not 'business' that you should be banking on! Yet you humans have made it so hard for yourselves to achieve the most important thing amidst your human ambition and 'doingness'.

**Me** – What's that?

**Mr G** – Awareness of 'uninterruptedconsciousness' - the continuing dance of birth and death where the process between lives is like the space between words.

**Me** – Like breathing.

**Mr G** – Can you imagine?

**Me** – What? Being a translucent spirit running around trying to capture the essence of each day remembering both sides of the veil? *(Mr G writes something on file whilst mumbling, 'Unsure if Me's remarks are an aspiration or an illusion of grandeur. Either way, he's still away with the fairies!')*

**Mr G** *(smiling, helpful)* – You're not Glinda the Good or Petal the Washing-up Fairy, however caught up in a magical bubble or over house-worked you might at times feel.

**Me** – Hm! Are you sure? Everyone else seems to think I am.

**Mr G** – Other than it being a good use of your OCD are you still being nicer than you actually are? Perhaps it's time to pin up an honesty rota and stop pretending to be such a good fairy.

**Me** – What! Point out that I do everything whilst doing everything and nobody listening?

**Mr G** *(sighs)* – Sounds familiar. Everyone passes through the cosmic veil automatically, but most don't remember. Amnesia between lives is there to protect you until you are ready to piece it all together, enjoying the cosmos through eternal change and awakening personal involvement.

**Me** – So inner adventure will be the new 'going out'?

**Mr G** – So much time and space to explore. Make it all about the light and love and you'll have amazing adventures. Explore the joy. Unlock the mysteries of the wonder-verse. Let the old associations go and the gathered samsaras unwind.

**Me** – Let life learn you, so to speak.

**Mr G** – Exactly! Travel. Unravel…

**Me** – Oh the unravelling! So… Is there anything else I need to be considering?

**Mr G** – Yes. Remember that painting-poem reminder I sent you?

**Me** *(uncertain)* – Which one?

**Mr G** – "Know thyself and thy wings of flight".

**Me** – That was over twenty-five years ago.

**Mr G** – My, how seeming-time flies. Well did you?

**Me** – What?

**Mr G** – Remember "thy wings of flight?"

**Me** – No, not until recently when it was wrapped up in experience and I had to apply it.

**Mr G** – Re-apply it on a grander scheme. That's how most people learn, when they're thrown out the nest and forced to fly! So stop undervaluing your experiences and be a little bit more grateful and understanding of your current situation and its timing.

**Me** – Oh, okay.

**Mr G** – The correct oracle quote is "Man, know thyself in true proportion." Only now in current conditions can you assess this properly as the lunar-time ratios begin to take full effect. The previously perceived historical timeline of apparent human-tragedy is a distortion.

**Me** – So less bellicose moaning and groaning, and more action adventure?

**Mr G** – Well, non-action… And by that I don't mean watching TV whilst sitting on the sofa practising telekinesis!

**Me** *(dejectedly)* – Okay.

**Mr G** – Or mithering, which isn't really a super-power!

**Me** – I don't know. I think it's right up there with maudlin and stifling!

**Mr G** – Sogginess and stiff upper lips? No thanks. *(Does Miss Piggy impression - 'Hi-ya!')* Perhaps more hair-tossing and karate-chopping would be appropriate!

**Me** *(smiling, musing)* – Hm! Back to the power of impossible. You know, you really *are* rather good at some of these impressions.

**Mr G** *(does an impression of a grumbling Muttley)* – You bet I am! "Rashin', fashin', 'teeth gnashing', dastardly Rick Rastardly!" *(laughs)*

My own additional wording of course! Anyway, I suggest you get out and about a bit more now that you're feeling more up to it.

**Me** – Life's been intense and complex.

**Mr G** – You mean you're complex? There's a knife for that. It's called simplicity.

**Me** *(taking a pinch of snuff)* – I'm only complex because you're complex and remember, "simple pleasures… are the last refuge of the complex".

**Mr G** – But would you have it any other way? Timing is everything this side of the cloud uncertainty curtain and you've been called up. You have become synchronicity. It's quite a gift. Got that?

**Me** – Got it.

**Mr G** – Good, now remember. If you're going to lead, lead from the front and remember to listen so everyone has a valued voice. And as a leader practise what you preach.

**Me** – So don't preach? *(raising arms and bowing)* All hail the great White Bunny-Rabbit of silence!

**Mr G** *(laughing)* – That should end any world hypocrisy and answer the question of free will. Say nothing and let people figure it out for themselves. *(suddenly, the Almighty Hand sounds a long, trembling rolling note on a gong)* Right, your time is up!

**Me** *(aghast)* – What?

**Mr G** – Sorry, I didn't mean your personal time is up, but the meeting has come to its end. Off you go. My next appointment is about to arrive and I have lunch to fit in first.

**Me** *(somewhat relieved)* – Oh, who's that?

**Mr G** – One of the old Greek gods. A bit overdue. Needs a circuit rewiring. Still has a storm temper on him. I'd scarper if I were you.

**Me** – Thanks for the heads up, but can I ask you something?

**Mr G** – What's that?

**Me** – I've been carrying this thread of light attached to you and this Cloud-Office for a very long time. Can I let go of it now?

**Mr G** – Sure, why not? You got here in the end and I'm a voice in your head now. The thread was part of my telescopic, light probe-o-scope. Everyone has one so I can keep tabs on you all. Wouldn't want you getting lost between worlds and incarnations now would I?

**Me** – Phew! Thank you. It's a relief to let go.

**Mr G** – Keep exercising your wings, and I better mention that you might experience a sensation of free fall on the return home.

**Me** – I hope I fall looking like a Chagall angel with a flower bouquet.

**Mr G** – How very bridal! Journeying back down from the Cloud Nine altitudes can make you feel a bit distant from people at first.

**Me** – A bit separated and lost? Another round of not fitting in.

**Mr G** *(smiling reassuringly)* – See you sometime soon?

**Me** – Perhaps in another million lives or so.

**Mr G** – Give or take a few. Feel free to pop in for a cup of tea.

**Me** *(playfully)* – I'll certainly remember you the next time I'm on the beg!

**Mr G** *(smiling)* – You always do...

**Me** *(pointedly)* – I'm only ever on the scrounge from you when I'm on the thin end of the wedge down here!

**Mr G** – Yes, that's the problem. I don't hear from you otherwise. Remember to treat your fleas, ticks and parasites?

**Me** *(smiling)* – Good habits?

**Mr G** – Bad habits!

**Me** *(trying it on with comedic charm one last time)* – Nun habits?

**Mr G** *(seeing where this is going in the lame double-acts states)* – White habits?

**Me** – What habits?

**Mr G** – And not forgetting…

**Me** – The magical…

**Mr G** – Most mysterious…

**Mr G** – Ever appearing…

**Me** – Yet disappearing…

**Mr G** – Wonderfully white…

**Me** – Bugsy with bite…

**Mr G** – Ghostly delight…

**Me** – Delightfully bright…

**Mr G** – Moon Bunny…

**Me** – That rascally Habit-W'abbit!

**Mr G** – The inhabitation by the impish lunar Were-Hare!

**Both** *(together)* – Phew!

**Mr G** – That was exhausting, but we got there in the end. Remember, habits have a habit of hitting the wall at some point.

**Me** – Poor rabbit!

**Mr G** – It could've been worse. You could have been possessed by a Were-Bear.

**Me** – Tell me about it! I know all about those. There's one at home!

**Mr G** – I know.

**Me** *(caught off-guard)* – Oh, how's that?

**Mr G** – Who do you think put it there?

**Me** *(flummoxed)* – You certainly do move in mysterious ways.

**Mr G** *(knowingly)* – Perhaps that could explain some of the recent grisly episodes and Ming-the-Merciless incidents?

**Me** – Oh, yes!

**Mr G** – Trouble and opportunity - same face, different outfits. Both double-dealing "cross-dressers".

**Me** – It's all very irrational.

**Mr G** – So… *(pause)*

**Both** *(together)* – So, one final thing before I go…

*(Mr G and Me smile simultaneously)*

**Mr G** *(politely)* – Go on, you first.

**Me** – About mantras? Is it true that if you manage to remember to chant your mantra on your deathbed you don't have to come back?

**Mr G** – Well…

**Me** – And what happens if you don't have one?

**Mr G** – Why? Were you thinking that chanting "Um diddle diddle diddle um diddle ay" on your deathbed will free you from returning?

**Me** – Yes, sort of. Well, more up-tempo than "tiddly pom, tiddly pom" I suppose if you're going to be like that about it. Most of us are just ordinary folk trying to get by, that's all. It's a bit annoying if the TM-ers get to skip the exam.

**Mr G** – It's a 50/50 chance with that particular one. Of course, most

TM-ers won't remember their mantras at death as it's snatched away at the last gasp.

**Me** – Really?

**Mr G** *(laughing)* – No, the cosmos isn't some mean-machine, however unsorted your idea of the universe is! It's the same for everyone and that depends on whether you've achieved moksha. Some souls are ascending, some descending, some transcending, whilst others like yourself are trying to get to the alchemical centre of the cosmic heart which is more of an occult, mystic journey.

**Me** *(baffled)* – But what happens if you don't have a mantra?

**Mr G** – My preferred deathbed options other than the comments about the sausage, not being afraid of death but not wanting to be there, and changing the wallpaper are: 'Awesome!', 'That was fun!', 'What's next?' 'Fancy another quick flit?' or simply 'Thank God!'

**Me** – Or 'Duh! Now I remember'.

**Mr G** – Stunning! Getting to see the light at the end of the tunnel as the death-train of life runs you over. Back to your blinking funny-bunny being caught in the headlights again!

**Me** – Okay. So, your turn. What did you want to ask?

**Mr G** – Could you give me some feedback on our review? I need it to show the Big Boss.

**Me** *(puzzled)* – I'm confused.

**Mr G** *(sincerely)* – Yes you are.

**Me** – Sorry, I thought you were the Big Cheese?

**Mr G** – Well, I'm not the 'Baby Cheese' if that's what you were alluding to. No, it's for the other one in the final quality assurance division - the ultimate head-of-the-good-and-bad soul department. *(Me shows no sign of comprehending)* Customer satisfaction, targets, complaints, spirit returns and maceration. Audits, yields, prosperity provision, lightening seeds. In-between lives commitment, allocation of Heaven and Hell, destiny's remits and providence's chits.

**Me** *(shaking head)* – Sorry, I still don't get you.

**Mr G** – The glorious Great Emanatory. The big light-bulb in the sky from whom we all proceed and owe our existence! *(Me looks blank as the Almighty Hand helpfully points upwards)* The Mr G as God Transcendent, the Godhead. Not *me* Mr G that you're experiencing as God Immanent. *(Me still fails to comprehend)* The nature of radiant reality as opposed to the one experienced and realised through the nature of *your* limited human personal reality.

**Me** *(struggling)* – Er…?

**Mr G** *(exasperated)* – *The* ultimate cloud you-and-me of us now in which all clouds exist, not *your* narrow construct of a cloud!

**Me** – Okay, simmer down. Even in this raised cloud-state I can't perceive and conceive the all and everything however much you go on about it. But like what? How can I help?

**Mr G** *(long sigh, focusing on the out breath to contain himself)* – Right, I need some anecdotal feedback. A juicy sound bite of some kind.

**Me** *(showing off his bird-speak)* – How about an assimilated screecher or a little rattling variant?

**Mr G** – I do like it when people take the time to speak bird to me, but do you have any useful comments?

**Me** *(thinking, then brightly)* – Oh, I know. What about, "It was educational and enlightening, ironic, yet fun". How's that?

**Mr G** *(impressed)* – Perfect.

**Me** – So, any final word for me? I'm not getting too good or too big for my flying-boots?

**Mr G** – What! With all that juicy vengeful goddess office stuff. *(nudging)* I'm hardly choking on your virtuosity. Now, one final, *final*, tiny, incy-wincy thing from you…

**Me** – Only if you tell me one final thing.

**Mr G** – Go on. I do find last minute, tit-for-tat deals with me fascinating.

**Me** – Do I get my hair back on the other side?

**Mr G** – What? Yes, of course you get your hair back.

**Me** – Promise?

**Mr G** – Promise.

**Me** – Good, because you've got a diminishing job if you're sitting around counting the receding hairs on my head! And what about sex?

**Mr G** – Yes, there's sex, but perhaps not in the way you presently understand it.

**Me** – Fair enough. So, go on then. What's your final, *final*, tiny, incy-wincy thing?

**Mr G** – You like a challenge.

**Me** – No, not really. I thought we'd covered that.

**Mr G** – Come on. That's not the spiritual warrior I know and love. So, one further request and favour?

**Me** – Well, it all depends what it is. Remember the easy, peaceful life-thing. Casual superhero if I have to at a push.

**Mr G** – I thought you liked saving the universe?

**Me** *(proudly)* – I do, but as long as nobody knows about it.

**Mr G** – But you're still trying to do it single-handedly.

**Me** – Tell me about it - up the hill backwards in stilettos and flip-flops!

**Mr G** – Genius! *(placing a generous tick nowhere in particular on Me's file, but wanting the interview to be over)*

**Me** – I know, but Daisy usually pulls it off! I suppose that's where you might come in handy, just don't take too long about it.

**Mr G** – Well… *(long pause whilst Mr G writes concluding notes on Me's file - Annual Review, update 2013; final assessment: 'Client shows a well-developed sense of play, if little else. Struggles with balancing desire, irrationality, wisdom and reason. Room for all round improvement; particularly for courage, faith and responsibility. Continue to stretch aura to fit around the outer edges of his personal star cluster. Mutually agreed that client is not the sharpest knife in the drawer. Still has problems tying shoelaces, specifically the right one, but knows the importance of double bows on dancing shoes. Client is slowly remembering what he has forgotten along The Way, but generally poor memory skills. Good at recycling and notions of greening the planet, with a developing sense of involvement in eco-activism and engaging in social change. Gaia was pleased that her invitation had been accepted. A 'very good' Moon report showed a well-developed sense of kindness, when not being impatient or too long-suffering. Strangely given to poetry and posy. Can turn a good phrase when required, but generally restless and can be fractious. Strong biological knowledge shown, with a good grasp of therapy and* *spiritual science, when not directly applied to the quantum field of physics and light theory. Rather a Luddite in relation to the new fandangled. Regarding ongoing alchemy: some excellent understanding shown in places of personal experience, but lacks finer understanding to be a miracle magician just yet. Quite efficient once started, but often lacks enterprise. Well-integrated 'aspect conflict' after much 'shadow work'. A few leftover 'moans and groans' were well honed and polished whilst producing his latest pearl for the Galactic Ball. Shows valour and strength when pressed, but unimpressive otherwise, with an inclination to watching too much TV and eating too much popcorn in the name of research and general consumerism. Useless at shopping and not particularly good with left hand reversal skills. Hearing impediment means client has the deteriorated hearing of a 60-year-old, so I must remember to shout louder to get his attention next time. Money, disco and chocolate seem good lures and incentives. Overall mark: 98.2% - pass. Client has accepted 5-star mission, but still does not fully understand its implications or role of space-suit. As client remains undecided whether he is imprudent or wise, a grade of 'king of fools' is to be awarded with a growing sense of wizard wonder, activity and achievement noted. Crown to follow. Whilst client has not fully understood the nature of geometric patterns and triangles, he has begun to radiate somewhat usefully as a universal star plug-in. However, in rummaging around the Olde Ying-Yang Curiosity Shop of his mind, the client is becoming a more interesting masterpiece of consciousness, rather like a grand wardrobe or impressive antique left in the attic. He now needs to dust himself off to fully realise and achieve his potential, through greater appreciation and acceptance of all the worlds, whilst working towards greater harmony of his many aspects. I look forward to seeing and hearing the results. It should not be too long now, but who knows when you are scatter-brained and have so much time and so little money on your hands)* There… all done. Now, how would you like to receive your Storm Report?

**Me** *(still trying to read and decipher Mr G's scribbled hieroglyphs and comments upside down, unsure)* – I have to choose? What are my options?

**Mr G** – Raven, albatross or dove?

**Me** *(deliberating)* – Oh… I'm inclined toward the dove - the other two sound a bit perturbing. *(Mr G stares at Me in a disconcerting manner. Me quickly adds…)* Although I'm sure all of them are pretty spectacular and delightful in their own way. Is the report tied to their leg or do they carry it in their beak?

**Mr G** – Usually word of mouth so you get to practise bird, but I can write it down on a piece of sky parchment and tie it to a twig so you won't mishear.

**Me** *(genuinely)* – Thanks, that would be helpful. *(still worried about what each type of bird indicates)* And what's the difference between the birds and their individual cawing and twittering?

**Mr G** – Depends on where you'll be living at the time, of course. City, sea or country.

**Me** *(relaxing)* – Oh, of course! Silly me. Well, that's a relief.

**Mr G** *(fatherly)* – There's a lot of universal support and love for you to let in on this next job so I'm sending in another couple of knights to help.

**Me** – Thanks. Does it involve upholding the truth or raising up my newly sharpened sword?

**Mr G** – Yes.

**Me** – Then I'm not so keen.

**Mr G** *(peering at Me's hip flask)* – Now, you do know that you have been harbouring a fugitive Green Fairy?

**Me** *(innocently)* – Really?

**Mr G** – Intriguing. You do know that her name's Ting…

**Me** – Yes, Tinker-Ting - the most elusive of fifth fairies. *(Ting flies in and sits on the window sill behind Mr G's shoulder waving at Me)* I've been chasing her for months!

**Mr G** – She's on the Nowhere Land's 'most wanted' list.

**Me** – Missing or AWOL? *(Ting allows the Almighty Hand to scoop her up. She then perches pertly on his index finger swinging her legs, crossed at the ankles, knees pressed together in a lady-like manner)*

**Mr G** *(peering intently)* – Well, she certainly is a law unto herself.

**Me** *(tapping his hip flask)* – This particular special brew is her own concoction. It's a bit volatile, but the occasional nip does wonders.

**Mr G** *(bemused, shaking his head)* – I'm sure it does, but that's her in her liquid and gaseous forms. In her solid state she's harder to find, and whilst everything looks cosier through her emerald-haze, you both have to go home at some point.

**Me** *(Ting flaps her tinkling wings and flies around the room. She settles boldly back onto Me's right shoulder and winks at Me)* – Oh! So does that make you the great and powerful Wizard of Oz to my Peter Pan?

**Mr G** – No, that's just more of your confused fantasy. Ensure you let her fly freely or else she'll turn into a Toxic Fairy and nobody wants one of those.

**Me** – I don't know. If she does, I could put her with the Om-Zombies and the Daleks of Love I seem to be collecting.

**Mr G** – Indeed! Meanwhile, keep trying to calm your agitated states. The next job up should be fun. *(emphatically)* So don't stress.

**Me** – Thanks. *(placing finger in ear and wiggling)* Roger that.

**Mr G** *(shouting)* – Over and out!

**Me** *(grinning)* – Least I know where to find you.

**Mr G** *(repeating)* – At least you know where to find me now.

**Me** *(slight sense of dis-engagement)* – Here, there and everywhere, right?

**Mr G** *(grinning back)* – Welcome to Cloud Nowhere Land. Remember, as a permanent resident there is nowhere to go, no escaping the real universe of love, and originating true consciousness exists outside of time and space - the joy is in the adventure and inter-play.

**Me** – Thanks, it certainly is a divine puzzle and spiritual paradigm you operate. *(ribbing)* You'll probably be expecting me to show initiative next!

*(as Me speaks, the Almighty Hand swirls around the Cloud-Office polishing the remaining thinning surfaces of the cloud which become clean and bright as sparkling crystal. The cloud-lining shines through in a dazzling display of multi-silvers that begin to glow. Mr G starts reciting a mantra, 'Om mani padme hum, Om mani padme hum'. For those people lucky enough to be looking up into the big sky from the ground, the white, outer aspect of the Cloud-Office looks like a bejewelled lotus. For a brief moment everything becomes clearer as though a lens has been wiped, adjusted and brought into focus and Me is at last looking out onto a clear day. Suddenly, different shades of crazy and solitude start appearing through the remaining wispy fabric and wrap around Me like lead. Instantly becoming heavier, Me feels a downward tug back toward the ground)*

**Mr G** – I don't know. I think you've been quite enterprising at times. But why? Are you still waiting for some sign from above?

**Me** *(getting increasingly nervous as the Cloud-Office begins to evaporate)* – Ha ha. Indeed! By the way? Do these Cloud Nines appear often?

**Mr G** – Only when required. Part of the all and everything to help overcome any reluctance or leftover residue holding you back. They disappear just as quickly as they are formed. Magic by its nature naturally evaporates.

**Me** – Cheers! But where and when will the next one be?

**Mr G** – Not 'here' or 'there', but around the rainbow bend, somewhere over your shoulder when the Sun meets the right kind of opportunistic cloud. If you still want to drink your troubles away there's a bar I can recommend - the 'One-Way Saloon'. We can drop you off if you like?

**Me** *(perplexed)* – Cheers! Why not?

**Mr G** *(beguiling)* – Why not indeed!

**Me** – Now, go on, spit it out. What's your final thing? I know you want the last word…

*(long uncomfortable pause as the last remnants of the silver lining of the Cloud Nine Office dissolve. Me slips through the cloud-walls momentarily forgetting he has Light Wings and how to use them)*

**Mr G** – Stop struggling. The flight of the free is all in the wings and the taking off, but don't forget as you descend to double loop the rainbow hoop before threading the eye of the needle with your Sopwith Camel manoeuvre I've seen you practising…

**Me** *(beginning to free-fall)* – Was that the flying squirrel trampoline position you were teaching me at the gym?

**Mr G** – Yes, that's right.

**Me** *(doubtful)* – I'm not sure I've perfected that manoeuvre yet!

**Mr G** *(smiling)* – Straight is the gate, but spinning and dizzying the trajectory! Oh, and mind the dust-planks and rain-splinters of the cloud ceilings and floors during your descent. Try to enjoy the ride.

**Me** *(falling backwards)* – Okay, thanks for the reminder. *(in a farewell gesture of good will, the Almighty Hand tugs at Me's Light Wings and pulls them out like an unfurling parachute)*

**Me** – Thanks Hand.

**Mr G** – Oh! And keep on winging your way into the almighty-algorithm. Your audience is out there somewhere.

**Me** – Okay, I'll try. Cheers.

**Mr G** – Keep following the golden goose…

**Me** *(falling further and faster now, the Post-it notes peel and flutter away in the wind. Ting helpfully scrabbles to grab what she can, but some disappear into the distance)* – Can I ask? Is this you leading me on another merry dance?

**Mr G** *(smiling like the blazing Sun)* – Maybe… *(checking)* You do like those, don't you?

**Me** *(holding on to his hip flask, snuff pouch and the remaining few Post-it notes as he begins to turn face forward in a nosedive, fast heading towards a Mexican Cactus Desert below)* – True, I do. Was that it?

**Mr G** *(somewhere in the diminishing distance now far, far away)* – No, of course not… Prove me.

**Me** – Is that the end?

*Indistinctly, far away from Nowhere Land, the voice of Mr G laughs,*
*'You wish…'*

*Falling, Me enquires, 'Do conversations with God ever end?'*

*The faintest of echoes… 'Only if you stop listening.'*

*Pondering, distracted, Me hits the desert ground with a dull thud.*

*Tinker-Ting gracefully transforms into a large green chameleon and sets a*
*purposeful course to a near, far-off point – a white, shimmering building in the*
*distance.*

*Me follows her into the sweltering Agave desert.*

# 3. MEZCAL - 'CON GUSANO'

a bar-scene dialogue

Scene:

Sunset at the 'One-Way Saloon'

— soon to be knocked down and made into a 'Buddha-Bar'

— somewhere near a Cactus Desert, down Mexico Way

Characters:

A once famous Sleepy Mexican Mouse,

Sam — an American-Buddhist barman,

Everyman — a drifting English Dapper Dan,

A magical Mexican Mezcal Worm floating in a bottle of Mezcal

on top of the bar.

*Saloon doors swing open...*

**Sleepy Mouse** *(sleeping in the corner beside a golden spittoon)*: Zzzz'd...

**Sam – the friendly barman**: Howdy strange traveller. Thanks for swinging on by.

**Everyman**: Hi there. Hello. Hola!

**Worm**: Welcome El Gringo! Welcome signor.

**Sam – the greeting barman**: Welcome to the 'One-Way Saloon'.

**Worm** *(backflips excitedly in a circle)*: Welcome to the 'Wunder-Bar'.

**Sam – the informative barman**: The home of good food...

**Everyman** *(snake hips a salsa move)*: Yet not the home of mojitos!

**Worm** *(affronted)*: But no less a place of good cheer and good beer.

**Sam – the precise barman**: And good atmosphere.

**Worm**: Yet do not seek the Cuban Highballs here! We seasoned souls prefer things a bit drier.

**Everyman** *(looking about)*: Is there anybody else around?

**Sam – the ignoring barman**: In this bar we help the travelling light.

**Worm** *(confirming)*: The alone, dull and oh-so-bright.

**Sam – the continuing barman**: The homeless and the hopeless all find an opportune drink here. Welcome Mister...?

**Everyman** *(bowing)*: My name is Dapper Dan, Mister Everyman, but you can call me Sir or Dan.

**Worm**: Welcome Signor Everyman. El Inglés?

**Everyman** *(using the very little Spanish he knows)*: Sí, I am.

**Worm**: Your barman is Sam and we both welcome you to the day you hit the wall.

**Everyman** *(puzzled)*: Sorry, didn't quite catch that. Your accent. The fluid in the bottle. My hearing. What's that you say?

**Worm** *(speaking up)*: I said, welcome El Compañero! Welcome to the day you hit the wall. Do you comprende now?

**Sam – the advising barman**: Don't mind him, Sir. He means the bar is undergoing construction. Last day before the Sun sets on the 'One-Way Saloon' and the start of the 'Buddha-Bar' makeover.

**Everyman**: Oh, I see.

**Worm** *(enquiringly)*: Do you Signor? Do you?

**Sam – the investigative barman**: So, Dan, what's your poison?

**Worm**: Your Dutch courage?

**Everyman**: My holy water? I'll have whatever the Worm's having… and one for the Worm, why not! *(peering into the bottle)* You look like a curious fellow.

**Worm** *(sizing Dan Everyman up and down)*: Gracias Signor, you are generous to consider me. To render you pot-valiant in the sequestering of your services…

**Everyman**: Sorry?

**Sam – the helpful barman** *(tapping a picture of an Angel holding guns hanging on the wall)*: Desperados – Wanted! Dead or alive.

**Worm**: Let us make it… Tequila Surprise!

**Everyman**: Do you mean Tequila Sunrise?

**Worm**: No Signor, I do not.

**Sam – the confirming barman**: He sure does not.

**Everyman** *(shrugging his shoulders)*: Then Tequila Surprise all round!

**Sam – the fiscal barman**: One jug of 'cheap-round' coming right up.

**Everyman**: Why does he say that?

**Worm**: Look around, Signor. Apart from the cheap liquor and beer, the sand on your shoes and we three strange buccaneers, there is no one else here.

**Sleepy Mouse**: Zzzz'd...

**Everyman** *(espying the Sleepy Mouse)*: Four?

**Worm**: Sí, four including the infamous mouse, but best forget him.

**Sam – the acknowledging barman**: Here in this low-life town even the notoriously quick are semi-retired and sleeping.

**Worm**: Signor! You do not wish to wake him for he is busy dreaming of former glory and his service, though always speedy, is last minute and comes at a price.

**Everyman**: Really! What does he do?

**Sam – the whispering barman**: He usually saves the day, Sir.

**Everyman**: And how much does he cost?

**Worm**: What price your soul, Signor? What price your soul?

**Sam – the astute barman**: The Skeleton Man has already been to collect the other Dancing Spirits.

**Worm**: So no Mariachi band and dancing for you tonight, Signor.

**Everyman** *(disappointed)*: Oh. Now, how about that drink? *(big-heartedly to Sam)* And one for yourself, of course.

**Sam – the abstaining barman**: Thanks. I don't drink, but I'll take a splash of the old, sparkling agua mineral if you don't mind. Two Tequila Surprises it is.

**Everyman**: So, what's the surprise bit?

**Worm**: ¡Hijole! Fire and rain, Signor. Fire and rain! Chipi chipi! On this the Mother of all days!

**Sam – the elucidating barman**: In case you don't know it's the Mexican Day-of-the-Dead.

**Everyman** *(doing a bolero impression)*: Olé! It would be.

**Worm** *(unimpressed)*: Cute Signor! Cute!

**Everyman to Sam – the listening barman**: Is he always like this?

**Sam – the eye-rolling, shoulder-shrugging barman**: Only to the special ones… the warriors, the sandal-wearers, those lost and lone travellers.

**Everyman**: The marching armies or the weary and weak?

**Sam – the clarifying barman**: Souls with broken hearts and dusty feet.

**Worm**: All those stranded, standing naked amidst their Cactus Desert who call upon Jesus… Whilst not forgetting his beautiful bride and her terrible torment.

**Everyman**: That's true. I too have recently felt the troubles of the bereft and damned.

**Sam – the expounding barman**: And not overlooking the friendless, forsaken and half-forgotten.

**Everyman**: The down-and-out in need of some help?

**Sam – the inclusive barman**: The sick and the feeble. Plus, of course, *(peering at Dan)* all the wounding of the self-inflicted.

**Worm**: Sí, all those who hang loose without fear of the noose!

**Everyman**: Any of us who have faced hard truths?

**Sam – the insightful barman**: Those troubling truths both uncomfortable and inconvenient.

**Worm**: Signor Dan, we have seen them all sat there on your stool worshipping at our strange altar.

**Everyman** *(wriggling as though the bar-stool is still warm from previous customers)*: Really?

**Sam – the riposting barman**: How do you think we made it here ourselves to the 'Fellowship-of-the-Tankard-and-Brim'? *(Sam lifts up his bottle of sparkling water and clinks it against the Worm's Mezcal bottle)*

**Worm**: Saludos!

**Sam – the water-sipping barman**: Straight up!

**Everyman**: Cheers! *(Dan downs his drink in one)* Same again, Sam. Now, at a guess *(looking at the Worm)* you were stuffed in, crawled in or dropped in. As for you *(regarding Sam, the blond, blue-eyed, adorable barman)*… Haven't a clue.

**Sam – the Tequila pouring, personal detail revealing barman**: In my rather resplendent youth, you might say I was pampered in all the trappings of wealth and a true follower of the bumper and skin.

**Everyman**: Do you mean the frantic and frenetic or the over-indulged?

**Sam – the recalling barman**: Ah, the disregarded spoils of my former luxurious life.

**Worm**: The uncontrollable cravings of all our inner youths.

**Everyman** *(slightly defiant)*: My inner youth and my middle-aged man!

**Worm**: Sí, Signor. The World grows up differently now. Are you not now the wicked letch as once you were the nubile wench?

**Everyman**: Enjoying Life's opportunities? You bet!

**Worm**: And not forgetting the changing desires yet to come of your diminishing dotage.

**Everyman** *(joking)*: My dotty-age?

**Worm**: Your senility or your serenity, Signor? Your embracing strength or your diminishing weakness?

**Sam – the smiling barman**: We are sincerely other parts of you simply further along The Way.

**Worm**: Sí. As you can see… *(swimming around playfully)* Some of us are truly immersed in the nature of Teotl.

**Everyman**: Really? *(laughing, self-amused)* But not the tea-total!

**Worm** *(sighing)*: Signor, all those with the wiggling itch seek out the expedient scratch and, like you, all those following the inclination of their urges pass through here eventually.

**Sam – the addending barman**: Even those who fear they might have missed the boat.

**Everyman** *(taking a slurp of Tequila)*: So, there's always hope?

**Sam – the illustrative barman** *(twists open a cocktail-umbrella and floats it upside down across the jug of Tequila, then looks across and points over at the Sleeping Mouse)*: Both for the Speedy…

**Sleepy Mouse** *(momentarily waking up, sleepily yawns)*: Don't siesta, let's fiesta. *(then turns over and falls asleep again)* Zzzz'd…

**Sam – the sentence-completing barman** *(measuring up Dan Everyman with a plastic cherry skewer)*: …and the Slowpoke.

**Everyman** *(suddenly recollecting)*: Golly! Now I remember. Isn't that…?

**Worm**: Ssh, Signor! Here in this bar we mention no names.

**Sam – the treasure-keeping barman**: Sir, any bottom-of-the-glass revelations, foaming tall-truths or glugged swilled-stories told here by passing strangers are shared secrets sunk to the bottom of the cask.

**Worm**: So do not ask.

**Everyman**: And is that list of troubles you mentioned really me?

**Worm**: Is it, Amigo? Is it? A poco Signor. Please help me out here. Everyman by name, Everyman's vice by nature.

**Sam – the 'Desperado' poster-tapping barman**: And by that he means to know yourself and the nature of what ails and afflicts you.

**Everyman** *(enthusiastically)*: In which case I've been well and truly lumbered! Another drink.

**Sam – the good-natured barman**: Mister Dan, I suspect the Worm espies something in the back of your eyes.

**Everyman** *(surprised)*: Really?

**Sam – the enquiring barman**: Are you recovering from some recent dereliction or perhaps you're a fugitive from some internal storm?

**Everyman** *(warily)*: I have recently been dislodged from comfort.

**Worm**: Sí, Signor. I sense you have a new light in your eyes, a fresh fire in your loins and a growing hunger in your belly.

**Everyman**: A different kind of longing and yearning?

**Sam – the checking barman**: Have you been having fun and messing about along The Way?

**Everyman**: I merrily roll along to my own sweet song if that's what you mean. Most was pleasure, although in wretched times I might've had some more desperate kinds of madness and mindless fun.

**Worm**: Sí, but do you not rise from the gutter with a renewed desire for the Stars and the Sun, Mi Amigo?

**Sam – the learned barman**: And if you don't mind me saying, you do have the look of one with the left-over heat of the Burning Heart still smouldering upon you.

**Everyman**: Really! You can tell?

**Worm**: Sí, Signor. You still carry the remnants of the shedding snake and the phoenix scorching.

**Everyman** *(brushing himself down)*: Ashes? Dust? Sand and skin?

**Worm**: Signor, you are like the Mexican Skeleton Man, lingering as pale smoke adrift in the moonlight, and a long way from home.

**Everyman** *(put out)*: Oh!

**Worm**: Yet I can still sense your searching, still feel your heart-ache, still touch and taste your suffering from the tumbling-down.

**Everyman** *(nodding his head)*: I hear what you're saying.

**Worm**: Do you, Signor? *(peering intently at Dan through the bottle)* I recognise you, for yours are the squiffy-view and the cock-eyed insight, but do you not recognise me?

**Everyman** *(peering back)*: Er?

**Worm**: In certain respects we are not so dissimilar.

**Everyman**: Really?

**Worm**: Truly, Signor, but why do the smokes still swirl about you? Why continue to employ the anaesthetics and fogs?

**Everyman** *(slightly baffled)*: Are you sure? If anyone's living in the permanent swirl of a saturated solution it looks like you!

**Worm** *(offended)*: Believe me Signor, I speak true. Look at the leftover impurities, the cloud fluff-and-stuff and all the cumulous sky-high vapours hanging about you.

**Sam – the pleasantly corroborating barman**: Yes Siree! You only have to look.

**Worm**: Amigo, even though I swim at the bottom of a bottle suspended in a warm-world of amber liquor, know that everything permeates to this spot.

**Everyman**: What do you mean?

**Worm**: All downward spirals and self-defeating cycles lead here. All punctured dreams and spectrums of life are open to me through my entrapped prisms of air, glass and firewater. Floating this way, I see what you don't see and what you don't want to see.

**Everyman** *(flippant)*: Are you a Mexican Worm or some kind of psychic gypsy?

**Worm** *(tapping his nose with his tail)*: Signor, I have a sensitive, discerning nose that will sniff into any man's business and a curious crystal bottle from which to gaze. How else could I tell?

**Everyman** *(peering around the bottle, trying to be clever)*: Eyes in the back of your head?

**Worm**: Signor! You are visiting me. Leave your rhetoric and insults at the door. I cannot leave the bottle or the bar. What can I do?

**Everyman** *(cheekily)*: Float? Hope? Joke?

**Worm**: Believe me, my lenticular, three-dimensional eyes are both blessing and curse! Trinocular in their range finding, they might add a certain depth perception and a more beautiful vision, but what am I to do with my seemingly skew-whiff wisdom and amber-view?

**Everyman**: Call you Cassandra?

**Worm**: Signor, like you, the snakes once cleaned my ears, but still you do not listen. What can I do except peer back at those who peer in to greet me and tell them what I see?

**Everyman**: Stop looking? Stop offering unsolicited truths? *(Dan swirls the Mezcal bottle, which turns the Worm floating upside down)* Bottoms up! Another drink please, Sam.

**Worm** *(affronted)*: You Mad-dogs and Englishmen! Don't you know, Signor, "Para todo mal, mezcal, y para todo bien también".

**Sam – the settling barman**: That's right. That's how the saying goes.

**Everyman** *(not understanding the phrase, but trying to be clever)*: Qué?

**Worm**: Signor! I seek only to help and expand your horizons. Your petty addictions are everywhere and obvious to anyone with an eye to behold. As above, so below... so goes Teotl.

**Sam – the scrutinising barman**: Before and behind...

**Worm**: All your old patterns and misguided behaviours, your habituations and little hedonic hits.

**Sam – the fortifying barman**: The pursuit of secret highs, the escape from worrying lows and, of course, all your guilty pleasures.

**Everyman**: Hey, leave my gratifications out of it!

**Worm**: They all leave a smoky trail of destruction behind you. You forget already that love is wiser than wisdom...

**Sam – the truth-seeking barman**: Which is mighty wise!

**Worm**: And love more mighty than power…

**Sam – the agreeable barman**: Which is mighty powerful!

**Worm**: Signor! I seek only to bring you to a deeper understanding of yourself. These things might seemingly suit you…

**Sam – the sagacious barman**: Temptation sure is tailored that way.

**Worm**: Specifically for you.

**Sam – the selecting barman**: And chosen by you.

**Worm**: Yet by a former you! What happened to the survivor who made it through the desert wilderness of 'which and whatever'?

**Everyman**: Steady on! That's all a bit much. It's personal.

**Sam – the respectful barman**: It always is.

**Worm**: The eye and heart of love burn afresh, but the old, thirsty throat and parched tongue still look for yesterday's saliva. Then lick, slam, suck! You're on a weekend bender in search of some…

**Everyman** *(rapidly interrupting)*: I say!

**Worm**: Luck, Signor, luck! Why else do you post your car keys back to yourself and not know where the hell you are?

**Sam – the jangling, car-key collecting barman**: Or get the barman to.

**Everyman** *(checking his pockets)*: Hey, are those mine? How did you get them?

**Sam – the adorable barman**: In search of the last, big bad-a-boom blow out. Anything for the release of a final high of fun. Yes Siree!

**Worm**: But Signor, there's always the more with you!

**Everyman**: Perhaps a little something to ease the pain or further excite the senses, but who wouldn't?

**Sam – the meditative barman**: Nirvana or oblivion?

**Worm**: Or were you really searching for a new way of living? The desire not to get out of it… *(the Worm astutely allows a reflective pause)*

**Everyman** *(considering)*: But to get back in? I see what you're saying, but what's that got to do with me?

**Worm** *(hitting the bottom of the bottle with his tail)*: Then bang! You fall off the wagon and you're back on a roll… but it's an old roll of desire and dice.

**Sleepy Mouse** *(yawning, stretching)*: Did someone say 'de fire of mice'?

**Worm** *(ignoring the mouse)*: Now look what a roll of Fate's dice has brought you? *(Dan looks blank)* Me, Signor! Mexican me and Sam, the American-Buddhist, but most importantly the Sleepy Mouse and you…

**Everyman** *(pointing to the mouse)*: Why him? Why me?

**Worm**: Because, Dapper Dan, it is you who are sitting alone on a barstool in the 'One-Way Saloon' so very far from home.

**Sam – the affirming barman**: That's true.

**Worm**: The heat of the burning Sun still throbs upon your newly shed skin, the desert sand still sticks to the bottom of your well-heeled shoes, the cactus prick of your fall from Cloud Nine bliss still stings. Did you fall so very far? Did you forget your wings?

**Sam – the provocative barman** *(nudging and winking at Everyman)*: There's a wish as well as a lipstick kiss still lingering upon your collar.

**Everyman** *(rubbing at a stain on his shirt and collar)*: Whoa! Steady on. What I get up to in my own free time is my own damn business!

**Worm**: Sí Signor, but sitting there on that stool… Well… For a little while you are mine. You are not here for no reason. So why not take Opportunity's chance to look into my bottle?

**Everyman**: Why? Are you some kind of hypnotising amber-genie?

**Worm** *(offended)*: Para Nada, Signor! I am no bruja, but gather your courage, look deep and tell me what you dare to see?

**Everyman** *(peering into the amber depths)*: What are those ghostly flecks and specks floating around you?

**Worm**: Signor, they are what is known as your 'junk', your DNA activators, your stranded bits waiting to be reclaimed, salvaged, rescued… They are the gathered daemons and demigods swimming in your Teotl deep.

**Everyman** *(scrutinising, tapping the bottle)*: Why are they so far out to sea?

**Worm**: Signor, they swim around you just as you swim in the greater bottle of alchemy without knowing it. They are would-be friends and enemies… past roommates of fire, desire and deadly addictions.

**Everyman** *(splutters, spraying his 'yes-no-but-maybe' repudiations and drink all over the bar)*: What!

**Worm**: ¿Eres loco de remate¿ *(Sam – the obliging, satirising barman circles his finger by the side of his head to clarify the Worm's meaning to Dan)* Signor, you ignore them at your peril.

**Everyman** *(dismissive)*: Whatever.

**Worm**: Do not pretend, Signor! Why leave them adrift when you know you need to gather yourself up? The time has come for the final hustle… A chance to double-or-quit your former satisfactions and dissatisfactions.

**Everyman**: What kind of insane Worm are you?

**Worm**: Why Amigo, don't you know? You stumble in here from the World of Distortion and still not know the Agave where you are!

**Everyman**: Are you the Tequila Sunrise Worm by any chance?

**Worm** *(blushing)*: Signor! You guess well, but incorrectly.

**Everyman**: Then what manner of Worm are you?

**Worm**: Do you not recognise me, Signor? I am the Worm of all your cares… and the Worm of all your troubles and woes. Does that not make me the wisest-Worm in all the world?

**Everyman**: Are you one of Ayahuasca's Shaman escaped from the jungle?

**Worm** *(reflective)*: More one state of your being…

**Sam – the philosophical barman**: Perhaps the state of 'One Being'?

**Worm**: I am that judged as mistaken and felt as regret. I am the Fool's reproach to the unwise approach. I am the medicine that you must take as antidote to make you a confident and newborn king.

**Everyman**: Really?

**Worm**: Amigo, when all your previous virtues and vices have been sufficiently mulled over and swallowed, then I am that left at the bottom of the bottle upon which you must think, and sink, and drink.

**Everyman**: The draff and the dregs?

**Sam – the drink-terminologically appreciative barman**: "Sur lie…"

**Everyman** *(confused)*: Who are you calling Shirley?

**Sam the sentence completing barman**: …but the savouring, not the glugging.

**Everyman**: Then you must be the Bacchus Magic-of-Mexico! The Mezcal Spirit 'con gusano' of whom we have all been warned.

**Worm**: ¡Hijue puta¡ You do well to identify me, Signor. That might serve you, but do not think that it will save you.

**Everyman**: Why? Do I need saving from your low-grade liquor and outlook on life?

**Worm** *(taking a little slurp from the Mezcal liquid inside his bottle)*: At 106% proof? Only from yourself, Signor. Only from the imprisoning-environment of your conditioned self. Why else would you be sitting here alone with me?

**Everyman** *(facetiously)*: Me? I was just passing by enjoying the view.

**Worm**: Signor, you are like tumbleweed that thinks it drifts to its own desire, but truly it is the wind that whistles your tune.

**Everyman**: Really?

**Worm**: Yet there is always purpose, however rootless and blown about you might feel. All your life I have been swilling and distilling right by your side, Mi Amigo, awaiting the appropriate fermenting moment.

**Sam – the agreeing barman**: Never more than a barstool away.

**Worm**: And have I ever forsaken you, my friend?

**Everyman** *(shrugs)*: I don't feel very distant, disorientated or forsook! Anything I did was purely for stress relief, pleasurable excitation, and exploration of moments of outrageous fun.

**Worm**: Sí Signor, but what about the last bits, the lost bits, the residual shadow and remaining shame? I can see from what is floating within my bottle that you have many friends, Amigo, but not all of them continue to serve you.

**Everyman**: I see.

**Worm**: Some are the helpful friends of everyone in need of a supporting crutch. They prop us up whilst we are limping, but Signor! You limp no more so need them not.

**Everyman**: What, the lot?

**Worm**: Sí, Signor. Not one of them.

**Everyman**: Not even the last jot?

**Worm**: Particularly not the last peculiar comforting bedfellow. That is like an addiction to umbrellas after the storm clouds and the rain-of-pain have passed.

**Sam – the interpreting barman**: Or a craving for nicotine patches.

**Everyman** (*nodding*): True, but so much self-medication goes on.

**Worm**: Medicate or meditate? Your Life offers resistance to the unwished-for withdrawal-of-the-old and to the hitherto unknown expansion-of-the-new.

**Everyman**: That's true, I suppose.

**Worm**: Sí. Status quos shatter, but brave new worlds are formed. Mi Amigo, it is time for you to kick the crutch.

**Sam – the shaker-shaking barman**: Disable the ritual.

**Worm**: Break the spell.

**Sam – the purifying barman**: Clear the toxins.

**Worm**: Rid the small.

**Sam – the encouraging barman**: Become beautiful.

**Worm**: Become who you truly are.

**Everyman**: It's difficult. The World's a glamorous stage and we all operate on the addictions of our age.

**Worm**: Signor, whilst the world is full of toxic states…

**Everyman** *(interjecting)*: Don't tell me, I know. I've danced with her and dined with him… Been with them both. *(remembering fondly)* Oh, the long bedroom nights of soul, the rolled-down socks and stockings, the lusty grin of shame and dusty lascivious sin!

**Sam – the chipping-in barman**: If you don't mind me asking, Dan, was it love or just a good time that you were after?

**Worm**: Sí, frivolous fun or a serious sex-fest?

**Everyman**: Was I gung-ho and cavalier? Perhaps. The frolics might've got entwined and confused, but I was only ever trying to be a model lover, eradicating the embarrassment from sex whilst seizing a moment of passion.

**Worm**: Perhaps, but did Casanova have so much sex in the dark?

**Everyman**: There were candles! It was romantic not hidden.

**Worm**: And not forgetting all the farmyard fun in the afternoon Sun.

**Sam – the interloping barman**: Yup! That's where most of us were first begun.

**Everyman**: It was a lark! All that dancing and making-out in the park.

**Worm**: Signor, if that is true, what is this leftover mantle-of-habit you wear that exhausts you so? Are these old patterns merely expressions and defences of an uninhabited toxic fortress? Inner conflicts or cravings? Crumbling securities or an over-fondness of your former split self? They're all so pernicious.

**Everyman** *(suddenly feeling overwhelmed)*: Help, god damn it! I needed something to hold onto. Something in life that didn't slip through my fingers like gravy.

**Worm**: Signor! There's no getting away with it or from it! You cannot escape the process of change. Happiness and wisdom demands it.

**Sam – the precise barman**: Not even with your quick-fit kitten-slippers and cha-cha chocolate-heels.

**Everyman** *(looking at his feet)*: You mean my trickster sneakers?

**Worm**: Sí, your smooth manoeuvres.

**Everyman** *(clicking his heels)*: I never did find the ruby slippers.

**Sam – the finger-shushing barman**: Still using silence and stealth to raid the fridge and the larder shelf?

**Everyman**: You mean my secret, midnight lemonade drinker?

**Sam – the understanding barman**: Your would-be sleeper and sneaky banana thief.

**Everyman**: Was I so hopelessly unaware?

**Worm**: No more hiding, Signor. No more dodging, ducking and diving. It is time for a new start.

**Sam – the elucidatory barman**: A fresh slate.

**Worm**: Universal spring cleaning time.

**Sam – the advocating barman** *(staring intently at Dan whilst emptying his cocktail shakers)*: You know, pour away your poison, take a stand, square up, say 'No thank you' and be a man.

**Everyman** *(despairing)*: I see.

**Worm**: Signor, forget your old wants and attend to your new needs.

**Everyman** *(desperate)*: What about the withdrawal and loss of control?

**Worm**: Replace it with something more loving to yourself.

**Everyman** *(trying to be clever)*: How about another drink then? *(pause. As there is no response from Sam – the bottle-decanting barman, Everyman pours himself another slug from the Tequila Jug whilst mumbling incoherently)*

**Worm**: More mutterings of your wretched state, Signor?

**Everyman** *(self-pitying)*: What's it to you? *(slams a Tequila shot)*

**Worm**: Signor, go tell your liver your Life's down the river, but do not waste my time!

**Everyman**: Another drink. Another kink. What of it? Doesn't make me mad, bad or sick?

**Worm**: No Amigo, just another caught up in the joy and pain of unaware doing.

**Everyman**: Believe me, I knew what I was doing.

**Worm**: Does that make it better, Signor?

**Sam – the intimating barman**: Was it your Viking practising disregard?

**Worm**: Or was your Nun inwardly soft, yet somehow repressed and outwardly hard?

**Sam – the inquisitive barman**: And your High Sex-Magic Priestess?

**Everyman**: She certainly was the wayward best.

**Worm**: Signor, you mean an out-of-balance beast!

**Sam – the extrapolating barman**: And your Nailer? Your Jailor? Your Soldier and Sailor? Your Fighter and Writer? Who could be better or worse or blinder? Yes Sir! You sure knew how to have a good time.

**Everyman** *(defiant)*: Oh, those aspects! Nothing to do with me.

**Worm**: Signor, this is not about guilt, but Teotl healing and Agave growth. See it as a new flourishing... a new bloom of self-love.

**Everyman**: Oh! So, what are you going to do? Legalise my desires? Regulate all our highs and lows?

**Sam – the once more poster-tapping, appreciative barman**: Mister Dan, Temperance is no moral watch-guard. Any suppression and oppression you felt were part of society's old prohibitionist ways.

**Everyman**: Was I simply liberating myself?

**Sam – the sage barman**: Each to their earthly own in the finding of the fullness of themselves, but enough, Mister Dan, or too much?

**Everyman** *(considering)*: In my world there's never enough and you can't have too much, but I see amateurs fall by the wayside.

**Worm**: Signor, there are many ways with many rooms, but winged help is always at hand for those who choose and for those who continue to use and abuse.

**Sam – the captivating barman**: For the foolish and the wise, Prudence usually intercedes somewhere along the line.

**Everyman**: Hey! Is this some kind of intervention?

**Sam – the supportive barman**: Perhaps more of a compassionate education.

**Worm**: Recovery is like an Angel with guns - a teacher of tough love and sober boundaries.

**Sam – the balancing barman**: However long or short the hours and days you can stick to them.

**Everyman** *(confused)*: Your guns you mean? *(looking at the poster)* Or hers?

**Sam – the forcefully moderate barman**: Moderation not enforcement, whilst nonetheless always the affection.

**Worm** *(looking up at the Angel poster lovingly)*: Sí, listen to Temperance for is she not beautiful?

**Everyman** *(looking at the poster and reconsidering)*: Never met her.

**Worm**: Signor, she is the Angel of truth, enthusiasm, tolerance and beauty. How could you not wish to be with her?

**Everyman** *(shrugs)*: Not really my type.

**Sam – the Temperance comprehending barman**: She who soothes as she pours calm waters upon all of your warring dualities.

**Everyman**: Certainly sounds impressive. Impossible, but impressive.

**Worm**: Signor, as she washes in the dew of morning she brushes her wings against dawn skies. Simultaneously standing still, she hovers and soars and that is how the honey waters of the Agave arise.

**Sam – the poetic barman**: She sure is the glad of day at sunrise.

**Everyman**: Whereas we are well met, suitable fellows drinking at sunset.

**Sam – the guiding barman**: Dan Everyman, listen to the wisdom of the Worm. Give yourself everything you need to release in a positive way. Another drink?

**Everyman** *(regardless)*: Yes, please. Thanks Sam.

**Worm**: Signor, draw forth fresh waters. The world is full of everybody else's toxic truth and Time's former, tragic, linear history.

**Sam – the socially aware barman**: It sure did get contaminated.

**Worm**: Sí, corrupted.

**Sam – the explicating barman**: Full of cupidity and profit…

**Worm**: Power and pollution…

**Sam – the rounding off barman**: Exhaust and addictions.

**Everyman**: The snuff, the puff, the drag… I see.

**Worm**: Signor Dan. Old desires mushroomed under the noxious hit of the leftover power stations, the concrete installations, the in-and-out exhalations of the depletion cycle. Yet…

**Sam – the second-guessing barman**: For the privileged and fortunate few…

**Worm**: Some people still found the money for wine and a fine time.

**Sam – the not particularly cashing-in barman**: Ching! Ching! Yes Siree! *(rubbing his fingers together to illustrate)* Success! The sweetest perfume of all our desires.

**Everyman**: Intoxicating! Purchase and procurement… Did they benefit us not?

**Sam – the happy, small-town, merchant barman** *(polishing a glass and watching it shine)*: Some of the sellers of cars, drugs and drinks in bars certainly did cash in.

**Everyman**: Retail cravings, longings for stocks-'n'-things, or general racketeering?

**Worm**: Signor, do you question the World's rampant materialism or your own careless consuming involvement?

**Sam – the ideological questioning barman**: Don't tell me - it was just tarnation incarnation into capitalism.

**Everyman**: The shopping channels and instant online purchasing?

**Worm**: Sí, Signor. The over indulgence of any one of the senses. Why the allure of so many fancy shops and stores, food, fun and fur?

**Sam – the pondering barman**: Ah! All the modern upholstered spiritual inconveniences.

**Everyman**: The worship of shoes, the trading of jewellery, the collectable accessories. Possession as gain is not a sin, is it?

**Sam – the nodding barman**: To have and to hug, to hog and to hold.

**Worm**: Sí, yet without compassion it all gets so ferociously close to the bone. Where was the World-sharing?

**Sam – the reiterative barman**: Not forgetting the smorgasbord-of-plenty, the in-your-face food programmes and the mountains of waste.

**Everyman** *(reflecting on past feasts and stuffing)*: Oh, all the foraging, the filling and the farmers' markets!

**Sam – the escalating barman**: The gluttony of greed, not the breed.

**Everyman**: The scoff and nosh. The roast hog. *(staring intently into the bottle as he reaches in with a cocktail stick to stab at the Worm)* You know, it's the early rising true gourmand who gets first peck at the worm!

**Worm** *(sinking lower to the bottom of the bottle to avoid being caught)*: Signor, you leave me alone. I warn you. I am not so easily consumed and you are no early bird. In fact you are the last scrap left on the plate. So Amigo, beware the Worm that turns and don't be late.

**Sam – the expanding barman**: Ah! All the waddling fat ducks and greedy pigs.

**Everyman**: The fish and chips. The deep-fried saveloys.

**Worm**: Signor, have you been toying with the sausages again?

**Everyman** *(punning, dismissive)*: The 'Wurst' was certainly the best if that's what you mean! Food and sex are appetites to explore and exploit, not afflictions! The eat-as-much-as-you-want buffet, the spit-roasts and midnight kebabs, but give me a break. What was I supposed to do with all the mulled wine and my much-deserved glugging of a glass of good time?

**Worm**: Sí, but then came the compulsion and gorging.

**Sam – the listing barman**: The bottles of brandy.

**Worm**: The chilli cocoa.

**Everyman**: The tubs of ice cream. The chocolate fountain.

**Worm**: Sí, the binging on popcorn and the candyfloss mountain! Temptation and ignorance as false-comforters.

**Sam – the colluding barman**: The delving fat cat. The 'just-one-more' dunked biscuit in front of the TV and then never moving.

**Everyman**: It's true, but I needed to relax and unwind. They were difficult times.

**Sam – the explicit barman**: The hours lying-in-the-bath listening to the radio, a bottle of wine and consuming all the chocoladorro!

**Worm**: Sí, never for a moment should you forget the love of the chocoladorro, but the whole box, Signor? The whole box?

**Everyman** *(nodding)*: It's true. Chocolate excess is a personal weakness. I just can't stop. Can I have a cigarillo, please Sam?

**Sam – the ad-relating barman** *(lighting up a cigarillo)*: Was it another flaky, non-reflective moment, Dan? Another tuck and suck too far without regarding the consequences?

**Everyman**: Oh! The snacks and sweets, the takeout and takeaways. *(bringing it on, listing)* The Lucifer biscuits. The stinking bishops. The Devil's own ginger! The sticky fingers. The red velvet slice.

**Sam – the patisserie passionate barman**: All those patisserie girls with their fancy pants and whirls and swirls.

**Worm**: The savoury and sweet?

**Everyman**: Oh! The buns and cake. Why cook and bake when you can order and over-eat?

**Worm**: Sí, the stuffed disregarding the starved, but habits and dependencies become detrimental to your health and wealth.

**Everyman**: Old, bursting, indefensible positions?

**Sam – the word-engorging barman**: Yup! All the over-clogged, custard arteries that push against the restraints of the gastric band.

**Everyman** *(running his fingers around his belt and waistline)*: My belt?

**Worm**: Your yelp.

**Everyman**: My trousers let out!

**Sam – the trim, drink-mixing barman**: The ungainly alterations. All the feel good factors of deservedness, but then your reward of style and flair mixes infernally with your pain and despair.

**Worm**: Sí, which in turn leads to all the drinking, injecting, pill-popping, shopaholic, pleasure seeking, thrilling spiral down.

**Everyman**: But oh-so much fun! Those were the days.

**Worm**: Extending your credit or enslaving yourself?

**Everyman**: My stupid fund?

**Sam – the quantifying barman**: The consumer or the consumed? A taste for spending can help you lose your head as well as your wits, your waistline and your wealth.

**Everyman** *(sighing)*: A fool's misfortune indeed.

**Worm**: Loco, Signor! Loco!

**Everyman**: All my dreams of the slim-fit, narrow-hip. Yet always the last cream cake… The last iced bun.

**Worm**: Sí, Signor. Was it not the cherry on top that burst the fat man's stomach!

**Sam – the pretending-to-explode barman**: What a blast from the past!

**Everyman** *(reminiscing)*: I always left the best to last.

**Sam – the assenting barman**: That's true.

**Worm** *(wisely)*: And now that tasty morsel is you.

**Sam – the affectionate barman**: Fruit ripe for the shaking and picking.

**Everyman** *(oblivious, but considering)*: So much and so many unnecessary sweet things, I suppose.

**Worm**: Sí, all those donut crimes and custard-creams?

**Everyman**: My happy-shags? Were they simply sugar-sins?

**Sam – the asking barman** *(aside to the Worm)*: By that does he mean his over-indulgence and wayward proclivities?

**Worm** *(getting carried away as he swirls joyously in his bottle)*: Sí Signor, but was it sugar, sex or love that you needed?

**Everyman**: Ah! All the candy boys and girls. I only ever wanted to be where the birds and bees were swirling and buzzing... free, and dipped in honey of course!

**Worm**: Sí, all the warm, smooth sweeteners.

**Everyman** *(smarmily)*: The glass chink and coffee-cup clink where desires and eyes and footsies all link, but I very rarely tried it on. Mind you, I didn't have to!

**Worm**: Signor, you mean the stir, the whirr, and the purr. La muchacha! Muchacha! La mujer fatal, la mujer objeto, la mujer pública?

**Sam – the augmenting barman**: By that he means the women.

**Everyman**: I understand. I was a rock 'n' roll bride myself once.

**Worm**: Sí, cheeky Cholula hot sauce indeed! You had a quick-chick, rock-'n'-roll, old-styled soul. All the women...

**Everyman**: So fast and loose.

**Worm**: And of course the men!

**Everyman**: Ah! The wonderful world of pleasure and men.

**Worm**: Those who 'lo aceptó como un hombre'.

**Everyman**: Is he talking about the joys of the body again?

**Worm** *(flipping himself around in giddying circles)*: Sí, Signor. The lust, the musk, the powders and dust, the over-employment of your magnetised loins.

**Everyman**: You mean the celebratory sex?

**Sam – the reminding barman**: But not dishonouring the quickies and bone-breakers!

**Worm** *(warming-up and wiggling)*: Sí, fast love. The indiscriminate. The uncontainable. The lust in the dust.

**Sam – the eliciting barman**: And not forgetting the prophylactic passion and pre-arranged degradation.

**Everyman**: The temporary lovers?

**Worm** *(over-excited)*: Sí, the oh-so many ways of sexual pleasure and ecstasy.

**Sam – the ongoing barman**: The secret assignations? Were they one of the 'Ten Thousand of Fabulous Things'?

**Worm**: The hip-rendezvous.

**Everyman**: I was only releasing my inhibitions.

**Worm**: Freeing the spirit or feeding the worm in your spirit?

**Everyman**: I was creating my own brand of mayhem and mischief!

**Sam – the configuring barman**: Was it a personal style?

**Worm**: So very messy and libidinoso?

**Everyman** *(carelessly)*: I might have been wild, but I was no Jekyll and Hyde.

**Worm**: What was confining you? What made you continue?

**Everyman**: Not sure. I was just searching for a good time.

**Worm** *(tapping his own head with his tail)*: Think, Mi Amigo. Think!

**Everyman** *(automatically taking a sip of something handed to him by Sam – the ever-attendant barman)*: Was it society's customs?

**Sam – the sobering barman** *(nodding towards the worm and taking Dan's drink away)*: He said 'think, my friend', not drink. Your answers, not your questions.

**Worm**: Was it your judgements or lack of any discernment?

**Sam – the tendering barman**: Personal expectations, imbalances or other people's restrictions?

**Worm**: Regulations and outmoded laws?

**Everyman**: My 'shoulds' and 'should nots'? Who knows where they came from, but I have no rues and regrets. I merely wanted to explore the more.

**Worm**: No minor shames or leftover embarrassments?

**Everyman** *(unabashed)*: No, it was fun! Are you two ganging up on me?

**Worm** *(daring)*: Signor, we are your friends. So why not put all of your swank out on parade for consideration in the sharing?

**Everyman** *(defiant)*: By Jove, I will. Starting with love under Juno's peacocks aided, of course, by the friction of Thor's bridging, thunderous-thighs.

**Sam – the announcing barman**: You sure do like your muscles tight and ripped.

**Worm**: Holy guacamole, Signor! Now you mix your gods, your metaphors and your drink. Don't you see the paradise that surrounds you?

**Everyman** *(looking around blankly before spotting the detailed male-female, vida laguna, yellow-aqua-marine, fertility paradise-paintings covering the walls)*: No, I hadn't, but how very intricate and beautiful.

**Sam – the reliable barman**: No peeking-booths here, Sir, only timely sunset soul-releases.

**Worm**: Signor, in this bar we simply reconsider the balancing of all your energies including the masculine and feminine ones.

**Everyman** *(espying multitudes of interlinked coupling)*: By Jupiter's cock!

**Sam – the prophylactic proffering barman** *(in an aside to the Worm)*: I suggest we give Dan the Man a packet of Blue Zeus so he can remove the Roman within immediately!

**Everyman** *(overhearing)*: How very posh and considerate!

**Sam – the remembering barman**: The selective moods of Eros sure do deserve all of your loving tantric-touch.

**Everyman**: Does he mean the seeking of God through the joys of sex and the cock? Why not!

**Worm**: Signor!

**Everyman** *(baring all)*: Oh, the lovely ladies and the tousled-hair young men. The tufted, bearded youths. The satyrs and fauns.

**Sam – the suddenly Latin-speaking barman**: The *in flagrante delicto…*

**Worm**: The exploration of the body for the very first time.

**Sam – the idiomatic barman**: The "making hay when the Sun did shine!"

**Everyman**: Oh! The explorations and excavations.

**Worm**: Did you have your fill?

**Everyman**: I did like my oats!

**Sam – the endorsing barman**: No two ways about it.

**Worm**: Sí Signor, but the hunting down of all your hormones?

**Sam – the colourful barman**: The chasing and probing of so many crazy pheromones?

**Everyman**: So many mantras, moans and groans. It was fantastic!

**Worm**: And not forgetting the homemade videos!

**Sam – the question-asking barman**: Was it fair-trade? You know… all the delayed exposure?

**Everyman**: You mean the hours of fun, film and gratification as sexual education?

**Worm**: Tell me, Signor. Did you find or forget yourself?

**Everyman**: I had no morals to question. I took the diverse and different as it arrived. I'd do a little slide-and-glide and give any straight gate or narrow path a grinning wide berth.

**Worm**: Ah, Life's crooked line!

**Everyman**: I was there to dare, not judge or care.

**Worm**: Sí, Everyman's handy excuse and justification.

**Sam – the reasoning barman**: Still, one man's meat might be another man's poison…

**Everyman**: Are you talking disparagingly about my shenanigans?

**Worm**: More about not taking positions.

**Everyman**: Don't talk about those! The regular, the irregular, the highly improbably. Plus my Valentine favourites - the reversed cowboy, the kangaroo cowgirl and the simply messed up!

**Worm**: Sí, all the freedoms of the yantra, tantra…

**Sam – the informed barman**: And all of the karma sutra if they didn't suit ya!

**Worm**: Sí, the apocalyptic kissing as though there were no more tomorrows and no last-minute goodbyes.

**Everyman**: I lived for the moment. I lived for the day.

**Sam – the thigh-slapping barman**: *Carpe diem yeehaw!* Yet even the bucking broncos sometimes get saddled.

**Everyman** *(manoeuvring his hips)*: I was never going to be cornered by any of the dealmakers or heart breakers!

**Worm**: Sí Signor, you picked, you plucked, you seized, you…

**Everyman** *(interjecting)*: Why? What are you saying? Is it time for a change?

**Worm** *(leaning forward to peer through the side of the bottle)*: You tell me, Signor? Were your previous encounters and positions gainly or ungainly? Do they become uncomfortable in the reconsideration?

**Everyman** *(thrusting his hips suggestively)*: If the shoe fit, I wore it!

**Worm**: Signor, please! No need to be so rude or crude.

**Everyman**: What? I was talking about the costumes from the back of the wardrobe. The dressing up, bad weather, leather sex. The furry outfits. The kilts, pelts and highland flings! *(Dan dances a jig)* The romance and the fetish Kit-Kat club swing. The frolicking nights of descents from poles and climbing from ceilings. Amazing! *(grinning)* I had no shame, though I know others wished I did.

**Sam – the ribbing barman**: The great-big, beautiful, bendy Suprendo!

**Everyman**: How did you know?

**Sam – the confessing barman**: I saw that show!

**Everyman**: It was the performing gypsy-cowboy me!

**Worm**: Sí, but then there's all the 'après l'amour' to consider.

**Everyman**: The pleasure. The awkwardness. The downright weird.

**Worm**: The fumbling moments and throwing away of phone numbers? The post-coital cigarettes? The texts never sent?

**Sam – the melodic barman**: "You were gone without leaving, yet left them believing."

**Everyman**: Oh, any necessary pleasantries to make the passing desire all right.

**Worm**: Sí, depending on your mood and attitude.

**Sam – the wondering barman**: Was it hunger's craving fly-by-night?

**Everyman**: The gracious excuse, the occasional follow-up drink, going-nowhere, yet always polite.

**Sam – the barista barman**: The unprocessed kopi luak.

**Worm**: The organic Bolivian.

**Sam – the knowledgeable barman**: The Columbian agustin.

**Worm**: The Nicaraguan illusion.

**Everyman**: True! So many slugs, dregs and cups of coffee.

**Sam – the erudite barman**: Not forgetting the beautiful Brazilian and the gorgeous Guatemalan.

**Worm**: Not chasing the soup-dragon, but riding the daemon's back?

**Everyman**: Ah yes, all the satisfaction of the freshly squeezed!

**Sam – the lemon-pressing, lime-crushing, pineapple-squeezing barman**: The juicy erotica of all the fruits' sex.

**Worm**: The grapes clutched and crushed from the Bacchus-vine.

**Everyman**: So many worshipping glugs of glorious wine!

**Worm**: Si! How the thirsty throat swigs, Signor.

**Sam – the ratifying barman**: The taste and enjoyment is all in the sensitivity of the gulp and the savouring of the swallow.

**Worm**: The fruit juices.

**Everyman**: The amber nectar.

**Sam – the ever-wise barman**: All the world loves a drink

**Everyman**: But you don't drink?

**Sam – the non-sequitur barman** *(juggling his cocktail shakers)*: I might be a vegetarian, but I know how to make a living!

**Everyman** *(resignedly)*: Just like funeral directors.

**Sam – the rational barman**: Yup! We certainly are all going to die, so there's profit for some in those universal truths!

**Worm** *(lights up a small, but thick Cuban cigar stub and starts blowing smoke-rings in the amber liquid of his bottle)*: Sí, and other such Life certainties.

**Sam – the joshing barman**: In banal-finalities…

**Everyman**: Like mustard fortunes left on the plate?

**Sam – the practical barman**: It ain't what you use; it's what you lose and break.

**Everyman**: Or waste and leave behind! *(fascinated, Dan watches the Worm swim through the smoke rings)*

**Sam – the consolidating barman**: Do you mean repair or replacing? Or the owning and facing? My advice…

**Everyman** *(entranced, distracted by the Worm's antics)*: And do you always give advice, Sam?

**Sam – the towel-snapping barman**: Yes, Mister Dan, but only the worst kind… good!

**Everyman** *(being hit by Sam's towel)*: Ouch! Go on… I'm listening.

**Sam – the suddenly serious, counselling barman**: Don't get stuck on the intoxicants, but don't get too encumbered with abstinence if you can help it!

**Everyman** *(trying to steady himself as well as the turn of the dizzying conversation and the spinning of the Worm who has been performing a whole circus-routine of aqua-acrobatics)*: Whoa there! Everybody take it easy and take a break. Give me some space... Is that it, Sam? Is that your advice?

**Worm** *(circling the evaporating smoke-rings more slowly)*: It's true, Signor. Be merry, not mortified. A little bit sober... a little bit not. *(balancing himself on a smoke-rubber-ring on the last of the reverberating Mezcal ripples)* How else can you investigate the altered states of yourself?

**Sam – the suddenly singing barman**: "A little bit country..."

**Everyman** *(joining in karaoke style)*: "And a little bit rock-'n'-roll."

**Worm**: And never intervene.

**Sam – the intervening barman**: Unless, of course, you have to.

**Worm**: In Mexico, we never forget the roar of the sip.

**Sam – the aggrandising barman**: The exuberant shout.

**Everyman**: The power of the sniff, the snort and the nip let out?

**Worm**: Signor! I am talking about the snuff, not the snout.

**Everyman** *(to Sam)*: Is he talking about truffles?

**Worm**: Not only the food, the booze and the medicine bottle, but the prolonged tease, the rub without release. The crack, the wrap, the arousal without flow.

**Sam – the encompassing barman**: Yet still we watch the people and their pain come and go.

**Worm**: Sí, some ride the surf of a very different wave.

**Everyman**: The lost or the brave?

**Worm**: The deadening click, the poisonous lick, the swipe and wipe.

**Everyman**: The click, the lick, the swipe and wipe? Is he referring to my gaming addiction, a generation's excited pill-popping, or those addicted to some kind of slamming euphoria?

**Worm**: Signor. Irrespective of the opium or the desire, the generations X and Y soared sky-high trying to catch Peter Pan. They fly when they can, only to rub wings with the Tinker-Bell generation.

**Everyman**: Sounds like fun if you forget the regret.

**Worm**: Yet the World and everybody in it is in such a terrible state of flux and flutter.

**Everyman** (*confused*): The horses? The dogs? The drinking and gambling or the Stars viewed from the gutter?

**Worm**: Does it matter? Generational mistakes being learnt on the brink or the surge and purge of Nature in Hopi catch-up?

**Sam – the life-affirming barman**: In the end, Mother Ayahuasca learns us all well!

**Worm**: If we let her.

**Sam – the warning barman**: So best respect her.

**Everyman**: Who is she? Have I met her?

**Worm**: Signor! Nobody knows better than the Spirit of Nature, whatever we might choose to call her. Ayahuasca is our true Birth Mother.

**Sam – the explaining barman**: Hers is the spirit of life that accommodates our personal growth and spiritual change.

**Worm**: Sí, her way is fertile… not the futile old search of human ambition for satisfaction that leads to so much current dissatisfaction.

**Sam – the recapping barman**: And not the relentless pursuit of pleasure and money for material gain.

**Worm**: Everyone needs to be embraced by Ayahuasca's bounteous new love, not fed by the leftover exhaust cycle and the way of addictions and ashtrays!

**Everyman**: The pleasure and pain of all our old desires?

**Worm**: Sí Signor, the fires of your previous days. The stubbed-out ashes and remains of all your burnt-out yesterdays.

**Everyman**: I only wanted what we all want - affection.

**Sam – the shrewd barman**: A little love and some attention?

**Everyman**: Until the boredom, the division and Life's separation.

**Worm**: Sí, solace often seeks something or someone else to replace the missing, but these were Opportunity's gaps.

**Everyman**: There were no lower or higher choices to be made only replacements for the ongoing losses.

**Worm**: Amigo, were you imprisoned by habits, or did you abandon your responsibilities?

**Everyman**: I was just one of the many holding it together. Events got overwhelming.

**Sam – the ice-stabbing barman** (*cracking the ice in his ice-bucket with an ice-pick*): Excepting those over-indulged rich who were underwhelmed until the iceberg hit!

**Everyman**: People cope without hope in so many ways, but I managed to keep climbing back on the horse.

**Worm**: But those disaffected days are no longer here for you, Signor. You are different now. New days are beckoning.

**Sam – the reassuring barman**: He's right! The rays are new reckoning.

**Worm**: Signor, were those pleasurable pursuits purely distractions from the daily discord and stress?

**Everyman** *(reflecting)*: I suppose. Somehow the distractions always seemed more interesting to the flesh.

**Worm**: More beguiling, perhaps, but were they more important?

**Everyman** *(shrugging his shoulders)*: Sometimes, but that's life I suppose. And there's nothing quite like temptation and instant gratification to get you through!

**Sam – the incorporating barman**: Singular or en masse?

**Worm**: Signor, you cannot keep spending more than you can afford.

**Sam – the judicious barman**: Giving out that which you don't have.

**Worm**: Otherwise your addictions will wear you out, however seemingly functional or secretly dysfunctional they are.

**Everyman**: You mean my louche ways?

**Sam – the deciphering barman**: Dapper Dan the Dandy Man always in pursuit of the next exotic holiday.

**Everyman** *(agreeing)*: I felt the need to escape and get away.

**Worm**: Escape from yourself? But what to do with all your baggage?

**Sam – the gregarious barman**: One man's trash sure is another man's treasure! Rich pickings for those who know.

**Worm**: Sí, but how could you abandon yourself?

**Everyman**: It was not too difficult. I tried to leave it all behind.

**Worm**: The rugged adventurer voyaging abroad?

**Everyman**: A wandering traveller out to see the poverty and riches of the world.

**Worm**: Sí Signor. Did you ever find the elusive Bohemia?

**Everyman**: The Promised Land? My chocolate factory? 'Anywhere' was my golden ticket out of there. I had to keep moving on. These days my dreams of a Pleasure Dome are all gone. Wishful thinking and security blankets I suppose?

**Worm**: Signor, it is the confusing mix of awakening dream and broken reality, but beware the Easy Street that leads to being trapped on Pleasure Island.

**Sam – the humorous barman**: For that makes jack-asses out of us all!

**Everyman**: I was innocent.

**Worm**: Sí Signor, somewhat innocent, somewhat naïve, yet always in search of gratifying experience.

**Everyman**: I needed to escape from the converging clouds and the darkening storm. Dissatisfaction drove me on. Did I grow too old, too bold, too self-satisfied? Have I become a pompous ass?

**Worm**: Amigo, whether grandiose or bellicose now, a young man's search for Excalibur can sometimes get way-laid and over-gilded.

**Everyman**: Was I bedazzled by bling? In my enthusiasm and exuberance did I grow replete, yet continue on in reckless abandonment?

**Sam – the interrogative barman**: Do you mean your recent recline and decline?

**Everyman** (*reminiscing*): Only ever the humanising…

**Worm**: But so much over-spending and indulging? Do you not know that way of misery, Signor?

**Everyman**: There were so many resplendent and hideous states of shame to consider and explore! What could I do?

**Worm**: Sí, always another permission and boundary to be wiped from the floor.

**Sam – the clock-observing barman**: Another drink? It's happy hour. Last ever orders!

**Everyman**: Is it Pimm's-o-clock?

**Sam – the stirring barman**: It's always cocktail o'clock somewhere.

**Worm**: So, how about it? Double or quits?

**Everyman** *(wildly)*: Anything's better than unhappy hour! How about slammers and shooters all round?

**Sam – the cocktail menu-reading barman**: Ok, what's your mood, gentleman? Zombies or Slings? A Cactus Banger or a Señorita's Orgasm?

**Everyman** *(drolly)*: Anything! Don't give me a choice. Can't you see I'm just a permanently grateful, half-bombed lime-biter?

**Worm**: Ah! The refuge of alcohol.

**Everyman**: The most social, yet boring of drugs, but not tonight!

**Sam – the listing barman**: A Psycho Tsunami or a Speedy Gonzales?

**Sleepy Mouse** *(slowly stretching and yawning)*: Did I hear my name called in vain? *(turns over and falls back to sleep again muttering)* …Amigo Dan? Hurry up. Do you need my illustrious services or not?

**Sam – the still helpfully listing barman**: How about a Face Off or an Adios Amigo?

**Everyman**: I don't like the sound of those last two!

**Sam – the quick-on-the-uptake barman**: Thought so. A bit too sobering. How about another Tequila Surprise then?

**Everyman** *(looking at the Worm)*: Whoa, no thanks! Not after the outpouring the last one inspired.

**Sam – the culturally enquiring barman**: Or how about a genuine old-fashioned?

**Everyman**: What? You serve G&T?

**Sam – the misquoting barman**: You know what they say. If it ruined your Mother it's good enough for anyone in here!

**Worm**: And think of change as being the tonic, Signor.

**Everyman**: How very Sagittarian! Not fond of change myself. How about a Vietnamese Vodka extra spicy?

**Sam – the international barman**: Remind me, Dan. Is that with or without the dash of scorpion sting? Perhaps a cactus spike for your Martini olive? And shaken, I presume, not overly stirred?

**Everyman** *(ridiculously inspired)*: How about a Snake Bite?

**Worm** *(exasperated)*: Scurrilous, Signor, you mix the grain with the grape!

**Everyman**: Is that a mistake?

**Worm**: Frog spit! Black death! That is a lunatic's soup, Signor! You grow grotesque. Do not disrespect the snake… *(emphatically bearing his fangs)* for the Worm with teeth turns and bites back.

**Everyman**: So, the over-the-top, self-imploding Molotov cocktail solutions…

**Worm** *(shaking his head)*: Will end up with nothing but the mop, Signor. Nothing but the mop.

**Everyman** *(laughing, refusing to take it seriously)*: Sounds positively pepto-blissmic!

**Worm**: What about rehabilitation and the recall of the defiant?

**Everyman**: What! Rehab is for quitters.

**Worm**: Even the great big rehab in the sky? *(Everyman says nothing)* A sobering thought, is it not Signor? But I do not think you want to see God so soon.

**Everyman**: We all come round again.

**Worm**: Sí, but best tackle the problem now without compounding it.

**Everyman**: Is it a 'bitter' pill?

**Sam – the revising barman**: See it as a 'better' pill.

**Worm**: It strikes me, Amigo, that you are not always so suitably sober for a casual stranger in a faraway bar.

**Everyman** *(taking another drink)*: What d'ya mean? I'm perfectly sober and aware enough to know it's your round or have you hit me with the hypnotics and the Rohypnol already?

**Sam – the carousing barman**: "Just one more madeira, my dear!"

**Worm**: Signor, I'll be gentle with you if you'll be gentle with me. You can see I live all alone in a world without coinage. Can you imagine such a world where no such corruption exists?

**Everyman**: Hardly!

**Worm**: I rely simply on the kindness of passing bar-strangers and the goodness of travellers high-on-the-seek such as yourself.

**Everyman** *(leaning on the bar with his elbow)*: Don't we all!

**Worm**: Signor! Your state of freedom is what so many desperately want and fight for. Independence is what every youngster truly desires. Look at all the limited love you have struggled to release over the years to get to where you are now.

**Everyman** *(perplexed)*: My exes?

**Worm**: Reflections of yourself and your approach to life, Signor. Look at the greater love that has since encompassed you.

**Everyman**: My currents?

**Worm**: Look around and see where Life has led you.

**Everyman** *(confused)*: Where? Here?

**Worm**: Your present potential is rapidly becoming exponential, is it not? And not from any earthly pleasure… *(gazing up and down at Dan)* but look at the uninspiring state of you!

**Everyman**: But I'm not in the Land of Plenty yet. I thought I was on the road to the Emerald City? I thought I was to get to Oz?

**Worm**: Only the 'oz' in sozzled, Signor. The yellow-bricked path was not made of golden bars, the emerald-heart is not some gem-filled safe or faraway city, the rainbow-mind is not some form of diamond mine for greed's desperate grasping!

**Everyman** *(staring into the Worm's bottle, pointing and cackling)*: Of course not! It's all about the little people you meet on the way!

**Worm**: El Gringo, desist. Your neuro-transmitters grow twisted!

**Everyman** *(lifts up the bottle to eye-height to stare accusingly at the Worm)*: Oh, so now you're a scientist as well as a pickled orator!

**Worm**: Sí Signor, that's true. Here in Mexico we all own our mad scientist, but tell me this… How goes your current life purpose?

**Sam – the ever-helpful barman** *(guiding Everyman back to his bar-stool and helping him to sit down)*: Spectacular, ordinary, cabaret or circus?

**Everyman** *(defeated)*: O Wise Worm tell me, for I fear I have become disenchanted. Is there a central solution to all of this? Some unknown greater magic yet to come?

**Worm**: Mellow your soul, Signor, and trust in Teotl. Soothe your previous sunrises and sunsets and wait patiently with love. Why do we all do it to ourselves, Hombre? Why do we make it so hard?

**Everyman**: I don't know. To get in. To get out. To face up to our personal sorrows and all the World's carnival of horrors.

**Worm**: Sí, I understand. Man's inhumanity is always at hand, but what about your pride, Signor? Your own importance?

**Everyman**: My recent despair and impotence, you mean?

**Worm**: Ah! The fading hits and glories of all your inebriations and golden glows.

**Sam – the scientific barman**: Those endorphins and that dopamine sure do kick us around the town.

**Everyman**: The teenage kicks and salutary celebrations? I had no cautionary tale to prevail.

**Worm**: Sí, merely the pursuit of your adrenaline habits, but still you must find a way to walk tall.

**Everyman** *(reminiscing)*: The happy releases and hours of fun chasing the butterflies of desire into the Sun.

**Sam – the non-flying barman**: Couldn't get much higher!

**Everyman**: The power, the enhancement, the factor attractors…

**Worm**: The nails and lashes.

**Everyman** *(flashing his cuticles)*: The slick tips. The getting away with it.

**Sam – the playful barman**: Oh! Vicious you.

**Everyman**: Tails, nails, lips and bits - everything!

**Sam – the film-alluding barman**: Were they "jungle red"?

**Worm**: All part of the social 'remove and rectify' beauty regimes.

**Everyman**: The out-of-office pursuits and the internet recruits. The brilliance treatments…

**Worm**: Is that not like God's own true 'renovation and regeneration programme' - the Hydra-flex package?

**Everyman**: Funny, I've been fighting those for ages!

**Worm**: The wrinkles?

**Everyman**: The mistakes.

**Worm**: There you are erroneous, Signor. There are no blunders or blemishes in Ayahuasca's greater acceptance.

**Everyman**: Just blurred experiences and slurred beauty to inform you along the way?

**Worm** *(reminding)*: By that you mean a chance to change?

**Everyman** *(raising a glass)*: To my future development!

**Worm**: Sí, to growing up. We'd all drink to that!

**Everyman** *(looking at himself)*: To boudoir chic. 'Instant perfection' and 'lasting correction'. Well, that's what the labels promised and said.

**Worm**: Sí, to all the convenient products of the dermatological demographic, but Everyman deserves a second chance.

**Everyman**: Even Dapper Dan, the wandering man?

**Worm**: Sí Signor, even him. *(warmly)* Perhaps especially him!

**Sam – the straight-talking barman**: But you are the only one accountable to yourself.

**Worm**: Sí, your life is between you, your God and the eternal spirits. But let me tell you as one who lives in a pickled world of spirit… The spirits, Signor, sometimes love us more than we do ourselves and sometimes they come to claim. *(Sam taps the Wanted Poster)*

**Everyman** *(rallying)*: Worm! I hear your wise words. I heed your sage counsel.

**Worm**: Signor, instead of changing your drug of choice why not transform your pleasure and pain?

**Sam – the sanctioning barman**: Don't forget… Your past and future can always change.

**Everyman**: O Wise Worm, pickled in spirit! What do I do? Where do I go from here?

**Worm**: Amigo, I have one final Mexican salute and blessing for you, so listen well…

**Sam – the leaning-forward-to-listen barman**: It's an oldie, but goodie!

**Everyman**: Go on.

**Worm**: Signor Dan. "May you be blessed like the Agave-desert century-plant. May a lightning bolt strike you, burn you, split open your heart and cook you in order to reveal the elixir of gods residing within."

**Everyman**: Thanks… I think.

**Sam – the beautiful, sparkling barman** *(looking out through the window)*: The Moon of Integrity sure shines bright tonight.

**Everyman**: Say it again Sam. Say it again.

**Sam – the blessed barman**: I think she's here to collect you.

**Everyman** *(looking up)*: Am I Moon-struck? But where do I go, Sam? O Worm! In this madness which way do I turn?

**Worm**: Signor, do you not have an exit strategy of your own?

**Everyman** *(beginning to panic)*: No, why? Do I need one? Is that what I'm doing… Exiting?

**Worm**: Sí Signor, but Everyman has an exit strategy. If you've not thought about it, then it will be the usual, default, universal, soul-factory setting.

**Everyman** *(slightly tearful)*: What! Sorry, not safe, squander everything, get it hopelessly wrong and then regret - crying pitifully over all the spilt milk?

**Worm**: Mercy unto yourself, Signor. Mercy. A grown man crying in a faraway bar in Mexico. This is not about false hope and desperation, Signor Dan.

**Everyman** *(stifling back tears)*: No? I thought it was trick-or-treat time?

**Worm**: That's nothing but your fear talking, Amigo, not the good plan. This is resurrection through destruction. Though you stand once more at sunset's last door, do not be afraid to look into the Night sky for the twilight Stars ignite just for you.

**Sam – the ushering barman** (*escorting Dan to the window whilst carrying the Worm's bottle and a shot glass*): Last call for the lost and forlorn.

**Everyman** (*pointing*): Is that the Evening Star, Sam? It looks lonesome.

**Sam – the randomly quoting barman**: "Once more unto the breach, dear friends, once more"…

**Everyman** (*beseeching*): Tell me Worm, how do I wangle my way out of this one?

**Worm**: As I said, El Compañero, ¡Hijole! Fire and rain! Fire and rain! There is no more digging in of heels, no room left to wiggle or out manoeuvre. Cunning cannot save you now and you cannot outsmart the heart. So when only courage will serve, best step into the cave and let Ayahuasca claim.

**Sam – the soon-to-be 'Buddha-Bar' barman** (*ringing the Saloon bell*): Last spiralling exit of self-defeat, self-deceit and pleasurable avoidance.

**Worm**: No more hiding from your future self, Signor. Do not ignore the dark behind the swinging door, but know there is no coming back this way.

**Sam – the echoing barman**: No coming back.

**Everyman** (*looking around the bar, fretful*): But I don't want to leave. I'm frightened.

**Worm**: Sí, Mi Amigo, no one ever does. No Man's mouse ever wants to meet Midnight's black cat or enter a gaping hole of dark mystery.

But if you don't leave 'now' on a high, you'll have to leave 'now' on a low.

**Everyman**: Which one is better?

**Worm**: Whichever one is most useful! It is different for everyone.

**Sam – the sympathetic barman**: That's right, Sir. The Sun is setting and the Moon creeps up so high time to skedaddle.

**Worm**: Sí Signor, look! See how the Second Star twinkles and shines.

**Sam – the beaming, beguiling barman**: She sure is beckoning pretty. All your happy and unhappy hours are over so finish up your final drink. *(Sam gives Dan a shot from the Worm's Mezcal bottle)* It's time for you to go.

**Worm**: Sí, it's time for all Banditos and Burrito-Heads to leave the 'One-Way Saloon' and dance the way of the Skeleton Man and his bright Bride Moon…

**Everyman** *(rapidly downs the smoky Mezcal drink and resignedly begins to leave)*: Phoaw! What was in that?

**Sam – the honest, calibrating barman** *(winking at the Worm)*: Just a little 'Larva Bitters' of Ayahuasca's Agave-mind-divine!

**Everyman** *(spluttering)*: Have I been Teotl Tango'd?

**Sam – the considerate, yet correcting barman**: Sir, though you'd look good in orange, consider yourself Grasshoppered.

**Everyman** *(confused)*: Into the green?

**Worm**: Sí, thoroughly Snowballed.

**Everyman** *(more confused)*: Into the white?

*(Sam high-fives the Worm in his Mezcal bottle)*

**Worm and Sam together** *(to Dan)*: Just a flutter-bye. *(to each other)*

We sure do get 'em!

**Everyman** *(reluctantly accepting defeat)*: So, which way do I go?

**Worm**: There is only one-way, Signor. You have no choice in the matter.

**Everyman**: I thought we always had choice?

**Sam – the arm-extending, gesturing, smiling barman**: So why don't you just sidle on out the backdoor and have yourself a great night. Or should I say… rest of life?

**Worm**: Sí Signor, step on through. It truly is a good night to die.

**Sam – the sky-gazing barman** *(looking up at the Crystal Moon)*: One of the best!

**Worm**: Look out for the dancing Skeleton Man, Signor Dan.

**Sam – the jigging barman**: You can't miss him. Bones a-dangling and jangling as though he might break. He's very black and white if you get my drift.

**Everyman** *(uncertain)*: Is this the right way? Those swinging doors? Where do they go?

**Sam – the truly enlightened barman**: Only one of us here knows where you are now heading. *(looks over at the Sleepy Mouse and nods his head)* As for us? We've never left the 'Last Gasp' bar.

**Everyman** *(anxiously)*: I thought it was the 'One-Way Saloon?'

**Sam – the lovely barman**: That's right. Last gasp, then only one way out before you find Ayahuasca, receive her gift and return to yourself.

**Everyman** *(scared)*: Will it hurt? Is it a Tunnel-of-Love or the last Exit-to-Hell?

**Worm**: We don't know, Signor. We suspect it all depends on what you've done and how you choose to respond.

**Sam – the ever-cheery barman**: You must admit it's a Rattler's tale!

**Everyman**: Is it a dangerous mouse trap?

**Sam – the modifying barman**: More of a sleepy mouse murder mystery.

**Everyman**: God damn it! Does the mouse-following man ever get away?

**Worm**: Signor Dan, you are never totally powerless whatever the seeming, insurmountable odds.

**Sam – the illuminating barman**: So best step forward now and have yourself a God-dang, wonderful life.

**Worm** *(shouting out to awaken and summon the infamous rescuing mouse)*: "¡Arriba! ¡Arriba! ¡Ándele! ¡Ándele!" *(turns quietly to Dan Everyman)* Go speedily, good Sir. ¡Â vamos! And pray Teotl saves the day.

**Everyman** *(walking through the swinging doors into the gathering shadows)*: Oh my! Is this the heart of darkness?

**Sam – the cautioning barman**: Watch your feet now, Sir.

*(the infamous Sleepy Mouse suddenly wakes up, double loops the Golden Spittoon then races Everyman through the saloon doors to guide him along The Way. Everyman stumbles, almost tripping over the Mouse)*

**Everyman**: Blasted mouse!

**Sleepy Mouse** *(disappearing into the dark distance)*: "¡Ándele! ¡Ándele! ¡Arriba! ¡Arriba! ¡Epa! ¡Epa! ¡Epa! Yeehaw!"

## 4. THE CAVE OF MYSTERY

The door of darkness opens. A mouse runs in. The door deadlocks behind. It is cold. No sunlit room is this. No sense yet of either love or bliss, but it is not as overwhelmingly hot in here, as in the arid, outside, cactus-desert air. Nor is it as dry and parched as the smoky ashes of my burnt-out Wilderness Days that I leave behind. Yet this compressing black cat-of-a-chakra, what does it guard? Fear becomes deadly halfway between the Alpha and Omega rooms. Am I in a cave at the bottom of Mount Doom? The entrance is hidden at the base of a well-known mountain, yet the fissure emerges somewhere at the sunlit-top. The only way forward is through the shadows and mysterious passageways. I must climb up, but what is it that I behold in this most dangerous of caves in my journeying?

This well-worn grotto is the abode of the rattler and the den of many a good snake. Did I follow a speeding sleepy mouse to this place? Am I here by mistake? Thus drawn, my slumbering hero strangely stirs and awakes. I follow a rough-hewn walkway through an open stretch of stone. How many Angels, Cowboys and Indians have been this way before? I do not know and cannot tell. By the scratches, names and drawings on the wall and floor I know that there have been many previous visitors and dwellers though, except for the mouse, I entered alone. How else can I experience my self other than through the testing of the laws-of-nature and spiritual reality? Still, I cannot comprehend the pure vastness of this particular shadow cave madness.

As I journey through the dark, my assumed previous identities and many roles become subsumed. In the closing chapter they gather around, but are diminished to the point of disappearing. Is this some holographic simulation of Plato's cave from which I clamber in order to escape, or is it a wizard's final resting place that I unwittingly investigate – some cryptic, etheric-glass, birdcage surrounding us in outer space? Plato climbed out long ago. Merlin is still here, residing in turrets and towers and walls of mysterious air. I am in his enchanted prison rotating within a cosmic cave-dark kingdom. Captured? Enraptured. Unfathomable. I do not know if I am sky-above or sea-below.

I behold darkness everywhere. A faint light illuminates the ghostly hollow like a spectral flare fired from on-board a ship into the distant cloud-draped air. I cannot perceive the source. Momentarily, it is as though I am far out at sea. If so, who is there to rescue me? The sometime luminous cave looks like a wave-carved cathedral, cavernous, with huge rocks and stones slammed together in some ancient giant tumult. Then unexpectedly from beneath – beware! A rearing shadow leviathan, from which I must escape and run, appears. Suddenly, like a little boy of wood and sticks I am inside an engulfing whale given over to goodness in the desperate search to find his father. Is he lost to me forever, or is he right by my side?

Oppressively, the darkness and light flicker, alternating between states of blindness and sight. The dark devours its own shadow until it comes to rest in the equilibrium of pitch black like midnight-oil in a lifted, tilted lamp finding a smoothing table. Washed up on such strange, stony shores I am unsure of my footing. I slide and fall against a slippery wall until I come to rest in a flinty lookout nest. I sit and watch and pray. Will I ever see the light of day? Trembling between two rocks I try to take my bearings, yet what rose-compass of the heart do I need to traverse such rocky shadow-seas as these?

Throughout the cave, filaments of finest spun silver pulse like synaptic strands of an electric web running onto a connecting network of strange plexuses. I am on the sacred ground of ghosts, skin-shedders and spiders. No unjust bones can pass this point or enter in. Only imagination and inner insight can give full flight now, but there is no guaranteed safe passage for the psyche through Ayahuasca's shadow lands. In the faint vibration and intermittent illumination of the cave, shuffling figures, shapes and statues are occasionally observable – placed for surprise and veneration as I pass them by.

Lo! There by the high-arcing entrance to the interior cave is the Mother of all matter. All who come this way must pass by her – through her… to her. She is full of accord and noble care. She is radiant peace acceptance to those who sit under, and gaze up into, her face. She holds in her hand a dancing candle of goodness and grace. The flickering of faint light casts further elongating shadows. Her gliding silhouette leads the way as though she is moving, but she is not. She is as still and impenetrable as a statue, yet ever watchful and guarding. My eyes do not adjust well to this manner of dark.

In one corner of the mountainous cave of shadows, I espy myself shuffling around in the form of an ancient cave-dwelling creature. From amongst the fallen rocks a Gollum comes to wrestle with me, comes to riddle me, comes to prise my precious from me. If I were to look for too long into his petrifying eyes I could turn to stone, frozen to the spot like a stalagmite. Or else I could dissolve into ash and just mysteriously disappear as freedom passes through a window into welcoming air. Like a sudden ghost vanishing.

If only I could let my prized pearl go, but I cannot. What is it that I still so desperately cling on to and treasure so dearly? Remnants of power? Past life or love or words of fear? What strange attraction does it still contain? I am enamoured by trinkets of former fascination. I know my pearl contains nothing but impurities, little more than popcorn to the initiate Mexican crystal skull with its devouring, chattering teeth. In consuming without thinking I have become consumed. I am lucky. It turns out to be a wonderful gift.

However, I am not free in this cave and door-locked chamber. The air grows thin, and I only vaguely remember how I got in. More importantly how do I get out? If I cannot escape I must surpass. There are difficult questions to ask. Who truly ushered me in here? Do I let myself out? Which way my mouse now? In this darkness I yearn to return to the ordinary world as someone different – as one re-born. Bright blue! At this moment I would follow you to anywhere, but for that I must climb to the top of the mountain through the cave. I yearn to survey the distant sunlit scene stretching before me. I long to resurface to find the buoyant sky of day. Must I go up to get down? In to get out? There seems no other way.

Yet there is no one else to follow here except my mouse, my Gollum and my stumbling f-f-fear – no sounds except for my scrabbling in the cave's profound silent shout. Will I have to dig my way out? Still my mind jabbers on, questioning. Somehow I have to reach the cave's quiet centre within the stillness of darkness. I have to go to the place where there are no birds or trains of thought or flapping words to disturb the silence. Travelling through the cavern, I feel alone, as though I have come to a solitary point. Like a snowy, dancing, ephemeral flake or a momentary blazing fleck of celestial light. Solitaire – to those who dare. I journey on to seek out the cave's inner sanctum.

In the broken stone's reaching shadow hands, up-rearing fortune, fight and fear are here. Right and might, flight and tear. Lachrymose, I am extinguished like the Mother's guiding candle. I am overwhelmed by a moment of pure darkness, yet still I struggle on. I must re-light. If I do not fight and find fire I might deny and die. Or worse! If I ignore, then I could collapse and crumble before these statues of gods and my Gollum – collapse and crumble to the cold stone floor. In denial of daemon, angel or sleeping hero I will lose myself. I do not wish that, so I must battle on.

Was this pursuing Gollum, this twisted shadow of former self, truly once like me? Am I so unrecognisable within this human heart of cave-like mystery? This is the story of one who did engage the dark and survived. Many an asylum is full of those who did not, but what am I doing here? Those primal screams I hear and fear. Are they ghosts? Are they the sounds of lost souls who did not successfully make the climb or are they accursed echo repeating whispers thus forever enshrined? What do these trapped souls avow? Which way out? Where am I now?

As I look around into the yawning chasm – what is there left, half-hidden, for me to detect? Upon what must I still ponder and deeply reflect? Poised somewhere between Heaven and Hell I am both above and beyond in a space of pure cosmic dark. Nearby, a gaping hole in the ground conceals the entrance to the cave's alchemical sacred heart. Protected by a thin layer of rising fiery dragon-breath, rose-flames hide the sacré-cœur and hold the defending realm of Masters. Within and without. Where do they reside if not right by our side? Shuffling in the shadows they meet and greet us all upon the way. Why are they so hard to find? Why do they not speak and stay?

In the cave's timeless hours, the Masters are eternal ever-guides, not mine, but ours. Yet I can wait no longer. The heroic efforts of my mouse are growing weaker, whilst conversely I am growing ever dragon-stronger. Within this cave and cosmic heart of dark I must continue on. Climbing over boulders and looking back down, I feel I am suspended nowhere. Am I beyond all space and time? Is it possible to be in such a place devoid of action and without a sense of sullying human crime? I wonder. How far does the swallowing gorge descend?

In the encroaching shadows void is here. Deep age and affliction too. Within this cave there is a spark of darkness and a hinted tale of doom. I am stone cold. I desire, but desire does not bring warmth of passion or fire, but storm and birth-curse. Out of night should come dream, and break of day, not thirst. There hides the cracking earth and beyond – abyss! There lies blame and retribution in the vapour's coiling serpent hiss.

As I travel away from such deep gazing into the ground's impenetrable mists, there is a sudden, overwhelming scent of kindness and sweet-perfume. I have stumbled into the cave's Moon-soaked Midnight Room. It is the smell of jasmine at night. Green-leafed, rain-wet, small white flowers all await the dawn of morrow's dancing light. They will wait patiently forever. In a nearby crevice of the cave there lies a child in a manger. In him there is a gift-of-light for every passing, dark-filled stranger. If this were a church I would kneel and pray. I would light a candle to celebrate his birth and take comfort in love's sweetest ray. Gladdened, I move on.

Further up, in the higher reaches of the cave, sits the Buddha-of-Our-Age – contemplating, waiting patiently for us to climb. I clamber up. In turning the prayer wheel, the Wheel-of-Life chimes. I feel a breeze upon my face. I am momentarily naught but a flag caught fluttering in the wind. My soul sails and burns in return. Here within the prayer wheel's churning, my two hearts yearn for Mother-Father God and cosmic dark's deeper understanding. Yet in my despair there is a small, gathering hope. If I can feel air then there is a possible way out.

Abruptly, I stumble upon a stable where three wise men, oriental and occidental, guide you to a bride and groom. Yet there should have been four. There were meant to be four. Do we know the tale of the one who did not arrive? What was his lost gift? Was it one of clemency? Was it the mercy of the erring you-and-me? I receive the cave's deepest midnight secret as wordless-gift. I perceive-believe the scent to be jasmine's all-pervading musk of mercy. Thus quickly raised up, I am all feeling. There is no cave floor or stony ceiling as I am suspended in a dark, affectionate space of grace. I reach out to touch an invisible face. It is one of love above all things. I am lowered to the floor as one in sleep by the aid of wings. It is the angel Temperance.

Inside the cave, the bride and groom salute the happy relationship in all its wise guises – a blessed branch with a diaphanous bloom. Like a sudden white church or a welcomed bright room. I spiral swiftly in amplified light, caught up within joy's sonic boom – momentarily heart-breaking, but further opening. Then darkness descends once more. Immersing. Fumbling along smooth surfaces of stone, I catch myself going around in circles here. I so long to see the Sun, yet there is nothing but my scrambling in encapsulating black. These well-worn walls and domed roof permit only the one traveller. You. Me. The I-alone. You. Me. Here – we are all undone.

Darkness swirls and curls about me like a black cat slipping around my homebound feet at midnight. Incantations mutter. Where is my bed? Is this my death? Who else is here beside me within this most mysterious cavernous grave? If only I could see. Be sure. But there is no certainty here. No ceiling or floor. Above. Beneath. All is cloaked in ancient mystery. I am enshrouded. Widow or bride, I cannot hide. Yet what strange body-of-light do I come to wear? As the Sun is my guide and groom – I do solemnly swear. But he is not here. Not yet. I hope he will not forget.

In my cave somnambulating, I espy a flickering light. I climb back down to the floor to explore. In one spacious curve of the cave stands a candelabrum – a single candle tree in celebration of the many revolving you-and-me's. Music is here. Not the language of the spheres, but singing. It is folk and fun. And light. And full of the magic of many meetings – past and bright. Voices fill the air. Sparkling. With so much singing and dancing comes friendship. This brief sweep of welcome human music fills my heart and ear – fills me with forgotten cheer, and includes all kinds of pre-arranged musical clattering. This moment is warm, friendly and oh so fascinating.

Here, in this particular chamber of stone, shadows and silhouettes dance in social embrace combining with joy, discomfort and grace. People meet and greet each other. Some people stay, some people leave, whilst some people are left alone to grieve. As I realise I am spinning, grinning within a fleeting memory, the dancing shadow players abruptly stop and turn to take a bow. They all have to leave now. Like smoke, skeletal and disappearing. As they go they blow the remaining candles out. Back to black. Was I briefly in a Viennese whirl, a sudden elated waltzing swirl? Am I now back lodged deep within a Vietnamese fighting hole? This tunnel, this vortex-funnel, is no Hell, but still I battle for crucial survival. Is this the cave's crux? Death within life and spirit-revival?

The filament running through the cave is activating again now. The finest lightening-streak rolls away into distant dark-cloud and rattling thunder. Briefly illuminated, this part of the cave reveals forgotten dragon treasure, gold hoard and Viking plunder. It is as though I am in some long-lost inner temple. What was once an arcade cave turns out to be my Aladdin's grave, for what use to me is this slope of cascading trinkets and gold that I scale now? I cannot claw anything back. Then blackout after the spark. I am going under into the ever-enveloping surge of cosmic dark. An indigo lagoon rapidly rises to fill the cave's many hidden nooks, crannies and silent surprises.

At my groping hands and slipping feet, desire treasures, both physical and spiritual, tremble on the verge of discovery. All of those things that lead to possession and satisfaction, yet I can grasp none of them now. My fingers reach helplessly in the rising dark; there is only one chance – soul recovery. I desperately scramble higher now, yet all the while I feel I am sinking low. Beneath. Underneath. I am slipping on the gold below. Suddenly, all the stumbling, crumbling winning-losing is given over to regaining. Yet what is it that I am re-claiming? Unconscious dream – unspoken life? A different memory before all is wiped?

Within the cave reaches of the higher dark, the sky-diamond night mind is filled with such sparkling light. The stone surfaces shimmer like faraway Stars glistening. Brilliant, iridescent gems of immensity, rich gifts from planetary seams and time immemorial, shine before me. The dark tide is high now, and I am compressed against the cave's hard rock. I find I am trapped, struggling next to a star sapphire, but I am becoming a Pearl Baroque – a blind, black jewel and an irregular inky dot. Here, the cave's facets are infinite numbers of doorways into the dark's unlimited dimensions and incomprehensible vastness. Slipping under the rising spell of darkness I can open none of them, but I find I no longer fear.

Upon a sudden etheric garment of white, an ink raiment of words gather to form this tapestry-of-truth wrapping about me, but still the black lagoon spirals up to engulf. Soon I shall run out of verse and words. As raven birds pressed upon swan-breasts of snow, I know I have to slip and sink to go below. I am swallowed by the cave's shadow. I am callow, yet still I seek. I am the mystery I could not keep. Humbled by such darkness, I am self-compelled to kneel and pray, to want and fill, to wait and weep. Thank Heaven! Thank Heaven! Thank Mother-Father God! I offer up all that is not understood. Unburdened, I am turned in the final gathering black. Darkness obliterates the everywhere and I can no longer hold all the harm at bay. I am here. God is there. Fortuitously, I am on a new heart's way.

Now come! Will you not take my hand? For I have fallen. Will you not lift me so I might stand or have we all truly forgotten? Come dance with me into the deeper dark. Come walk with me as we once did in a Summer's park – as lovers often do on a golden stolen afternoon. Come! Trance-swim with me. Come under. Surrender safeguarded identity. Recover night's tiger. Recover light's shark. Forever is here. Not fearful symmetry, but guardians of an ever-deepening, mysterious dark. Climb higher. Come climb. Reach out. Be touched by the welcoming rays of creation's new shine. Feel the fresh rise of Eternity's Springtime. Lift off! Rise up! Come hither. Come sup! Run! Come quickly. Come one. Come all. Stumble or fall, let us together discover Earth's centre and recover heart's spark. Let us all recover the indescribable truth. Come enter the dark. Come enter the cave that has no physical proof...

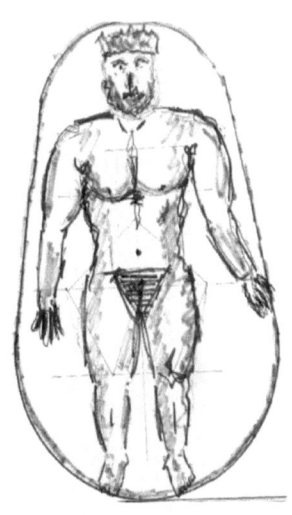

## ABOUT THE AUTHOR

Keith Brazil was born in Broadstairs, Kent, England. He trained in Dance Theatre at Laban Trinity Conservatoire, London, and was a founder member of 'Adventures In Motion Pictures' Dance Company. He has worked as a freelance professional dancer, choreographer, teacher, and dance lecturer. Keith has also trained as a Complementary Therapist in Spiritual Healing and Reflexology. He gained a degree in English Studies and is currently engaged in writing a collection of metaphysical, fictional and non-fictional stories, essays, poetry and novels. His revolutionary book 'The Wilderness Diary' was published in December 2012, with a second edition published in 2015. His observational notebook – 'In Consideration of Cats' – was published in November 2013. His metaphysical comedy 'Popcorn, Parasites, Precious and Pearls' was published in December 2013. His short story 'The Chameleon's Last Dance' was published in June 2014. 'An Alchemist's Wedding' – a wedding speech – was published in June 2015. 'The Land of Bliss' (a fairy story) is due for release in 2017 and completes the 'Anthology of Joy'. He lives and works in London.

www.ingramcontent.com/pod-product-compliance
Lightning Source LLC
Chambersburg PA
CBHW050014180626
46810CB00002B/407